EVOLUTION

Other books by Royo:
Dreams
Malefic
III Millennium
Secrets
Women

Each: $19.95

Add $3 1st item, $1 each addt'l for P&H

Ask for our complete color catalog:
NBM
555 8th ave., Ste. 1202
New York, NY 10018

See our website at
www.nbmpublishing.com

ISBN 1-56163-277-5

Translation by Robert Legault
Printed in Spain

5 4 3

EVOLUTION

LUIS ROYO

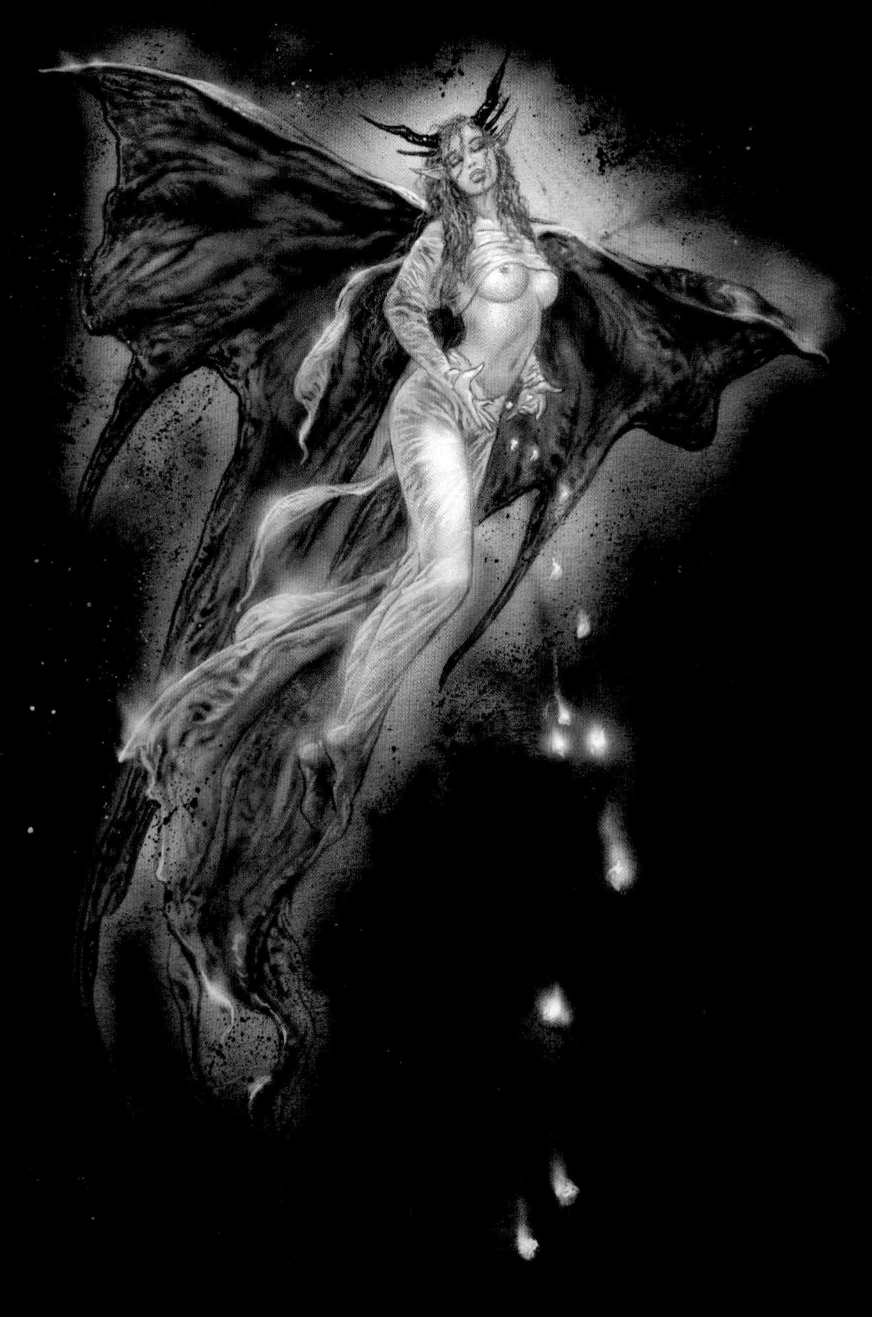

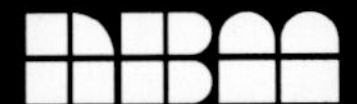

NANTIER • BEALL • MINOUSTCHINE
Publishing inc.
new york

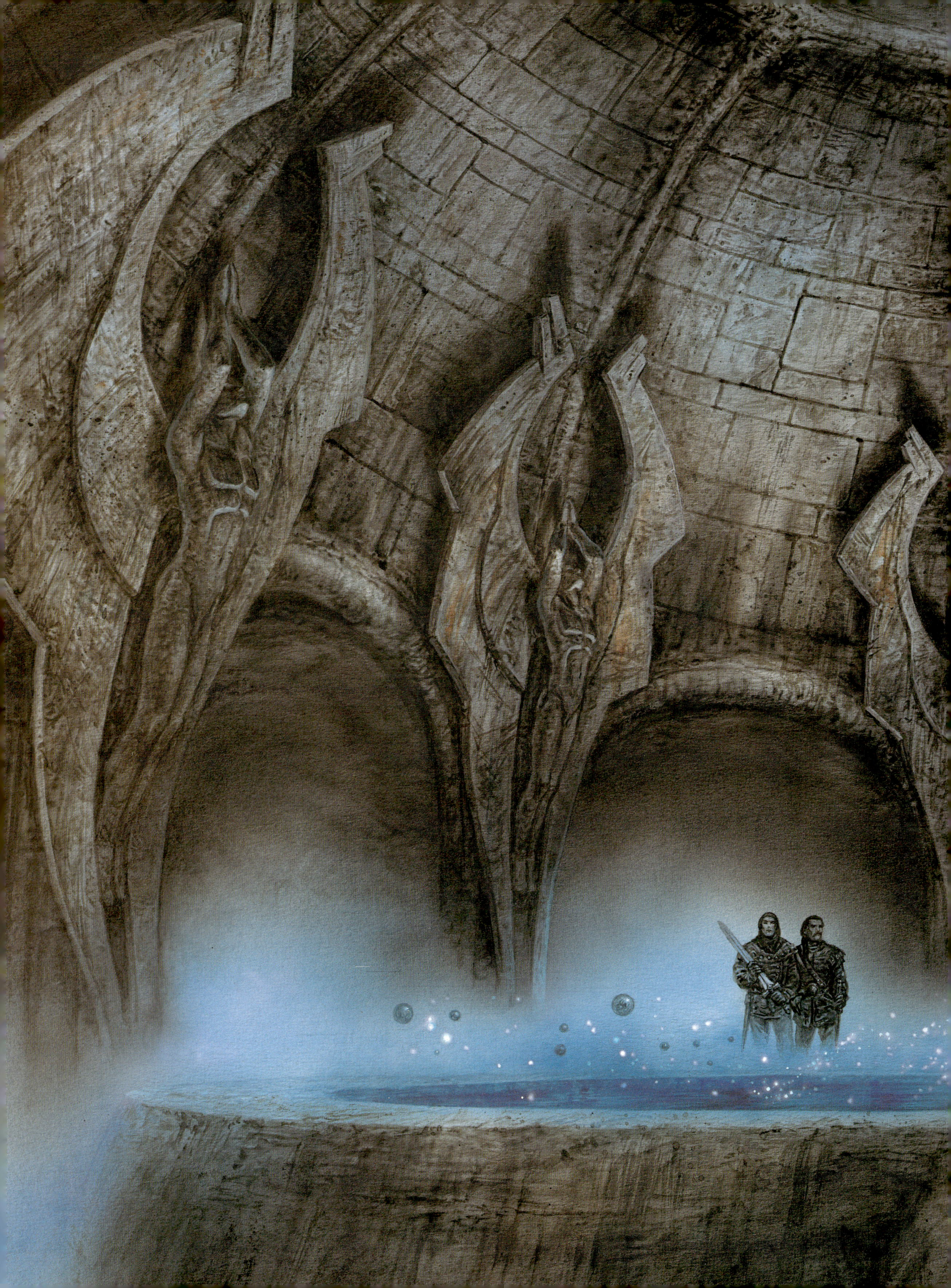

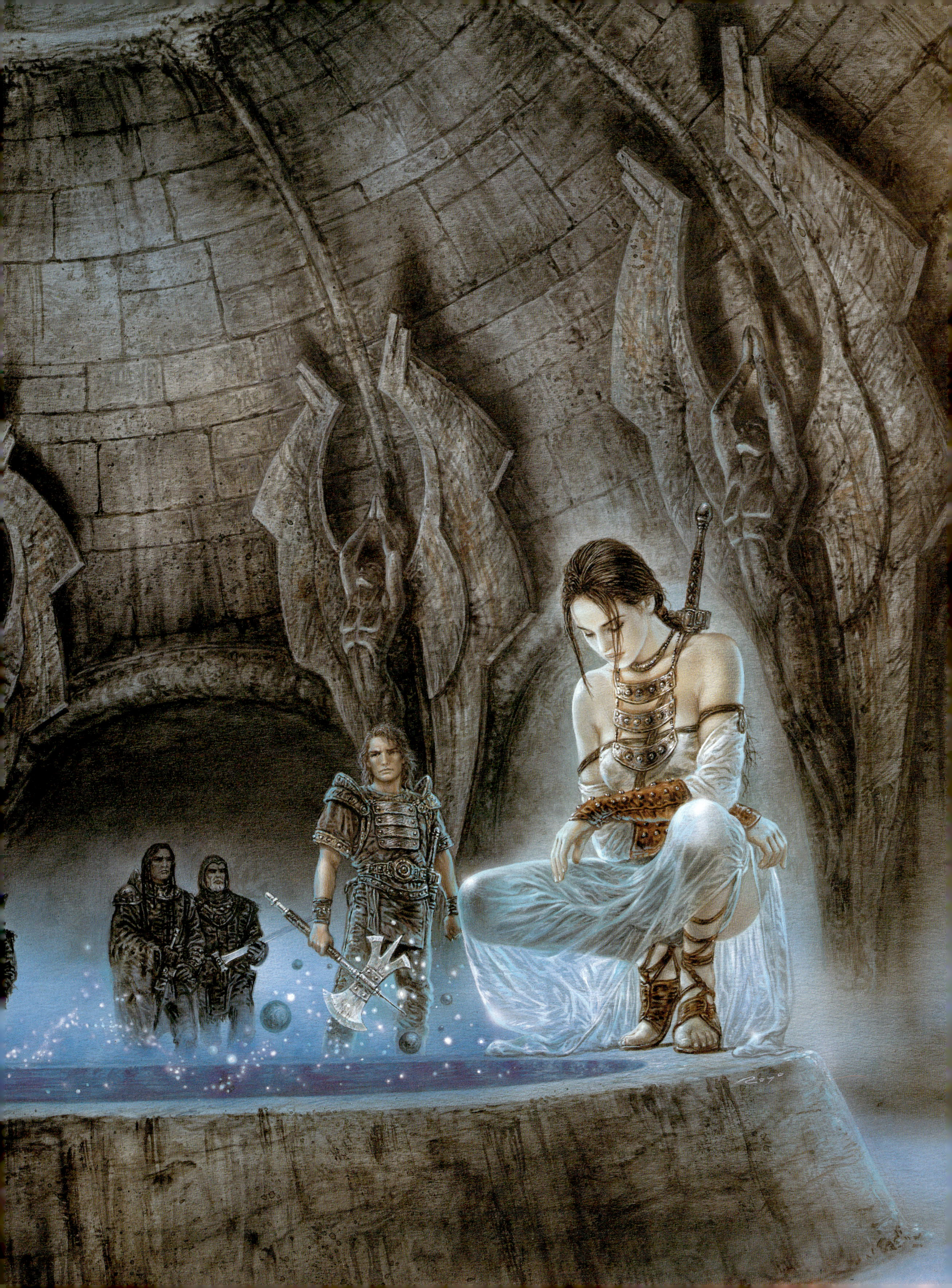

▲ **WAYFARERS REDEMPTION** (50 x 35 cm.) - TOR BOOKS, USA - 2000

This book is dedicated to the uncontrollable dance of the hands of the clock on my desk, hands that move forward or backward and come to rest at impossible times of day. It's also dedicated to certain images with a desire to embrace every medium they've encountered along the way.

It isn't that my clock has gone crazy; it's just that, one day, it got tired of carrying on that constant rhythm. The hands stopped that weary tread: one second, another, a minute, five, a quarter of an hour...They realized that, step by step, life was getting monotonous and boring, and they began to take great leaps, they paused in the remote past and advanced into the future. The papers and canvases on my drawing table were overjoyed—they could open up those invisible windows that every blank surface contains and let in the multicolored worlds that were hidden there.

Those playful clock hands have traveled to times where worlds, planets, and beings are different; they have become great friends to my eyes, which were also tired of contemplating the same old streets and the same old people every day.

But on this occasion, the hands, after many whispered discussions, have decided to show themselves to your eyes, so don't shut your lids—those images are coming out of the caves where they hide when they escape from the drawing table.

So, since those little hands have become our friends, let's transport ourselves to the ninth or tenth century and go back to using that magical word "illumination"—and let's hide that untrustworthy word "illustration" somewhere at the bottom of a trunk. In the present time, our images have illuminated books, as always, magazine covers, CD booklets, video games, calendars, trading cards, mouse pads, notebooks, and postcards; they've also illuminated the forms of three-dimensional figures, as well as playing card decks, T-shirts, and posters; and they've appeared as backgrounds and designs in the world of movies and animation. They've come alive painted on cars and motorcycle gas tanks, and even on human skin.

The images seem crazy the way they jump from one medium to the next.

They want to illuminate; they're obsessed with raising eyelids.

Evolution is a tour of images in different media and how they came to be

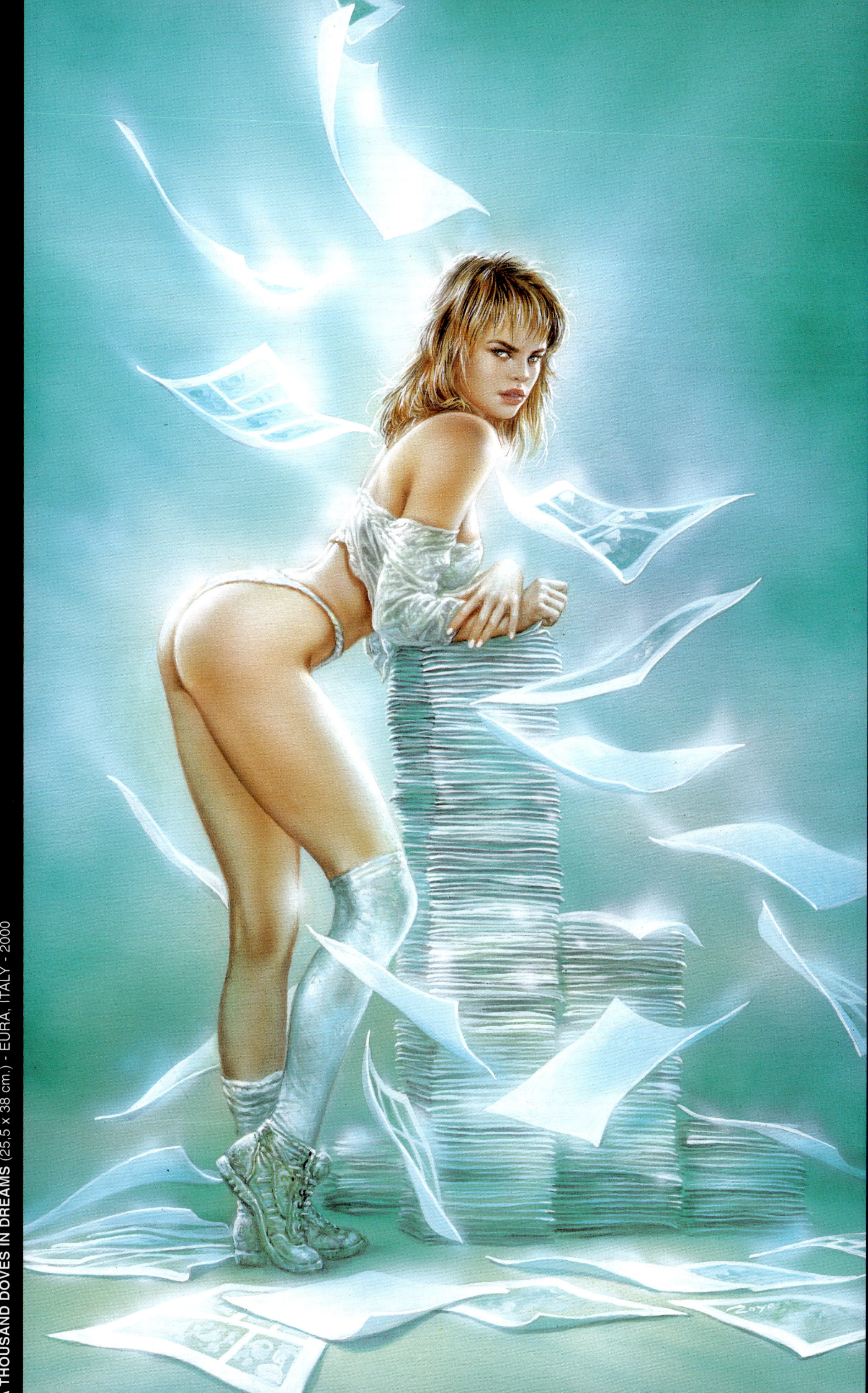

A THOUSAND DOVES IN DREAMS (25,5 x 38 cm.) - EURA, ITALY - 2000

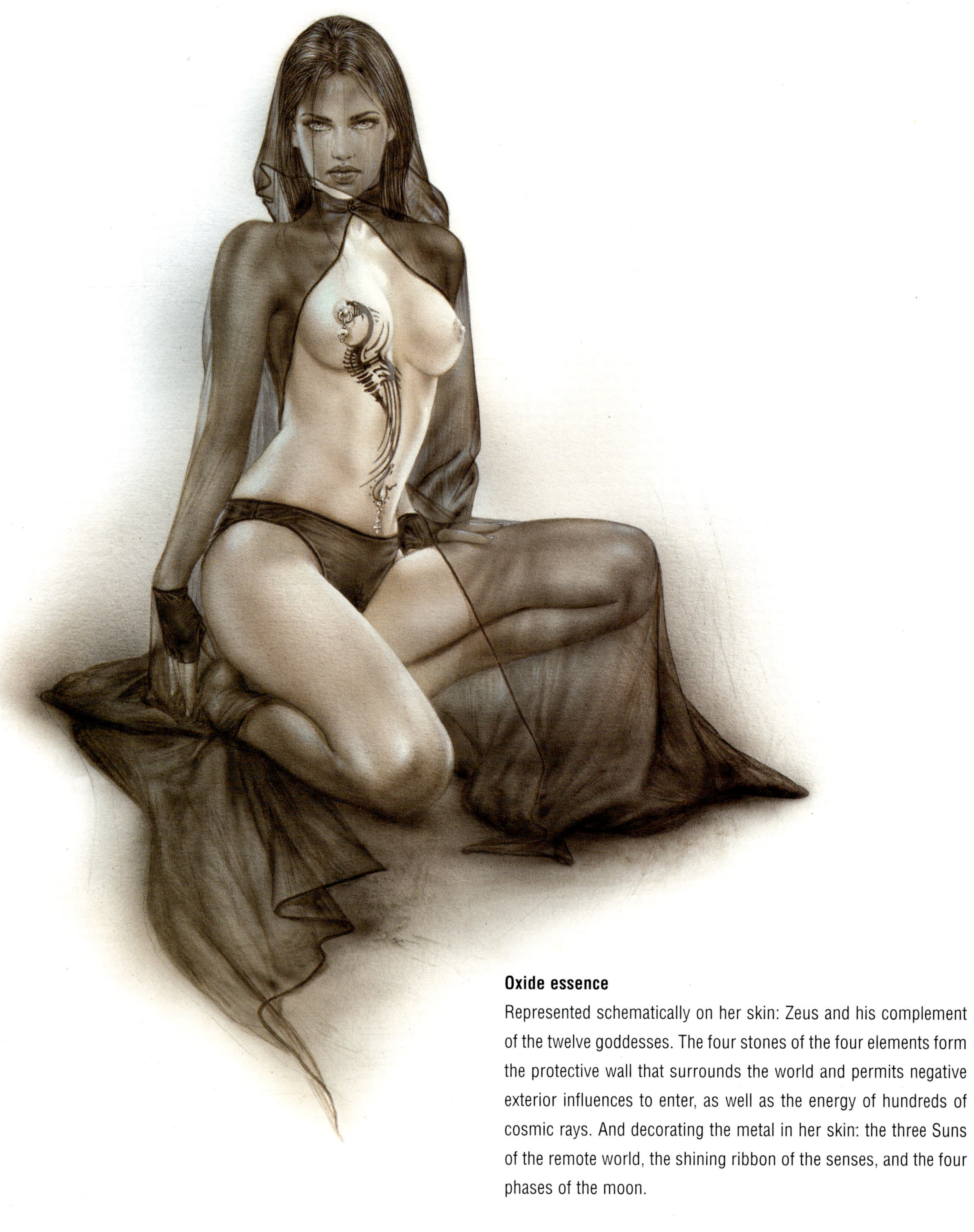

Oxide essence

Represented schematically on her skin: Zeus and his complement of the twelve goddesses. The four stones of the four elements form the protective wall that surrounds the world and permits negative exterior influences to enter, as well as the energy of hundreds of cosmic rays. And decorating the metal in her skin: the three Suns of the remote world, the shining ribbon of the senses, and the four phases of the moon.

DRAGON 1 (35 x 48 cm.) - 1999

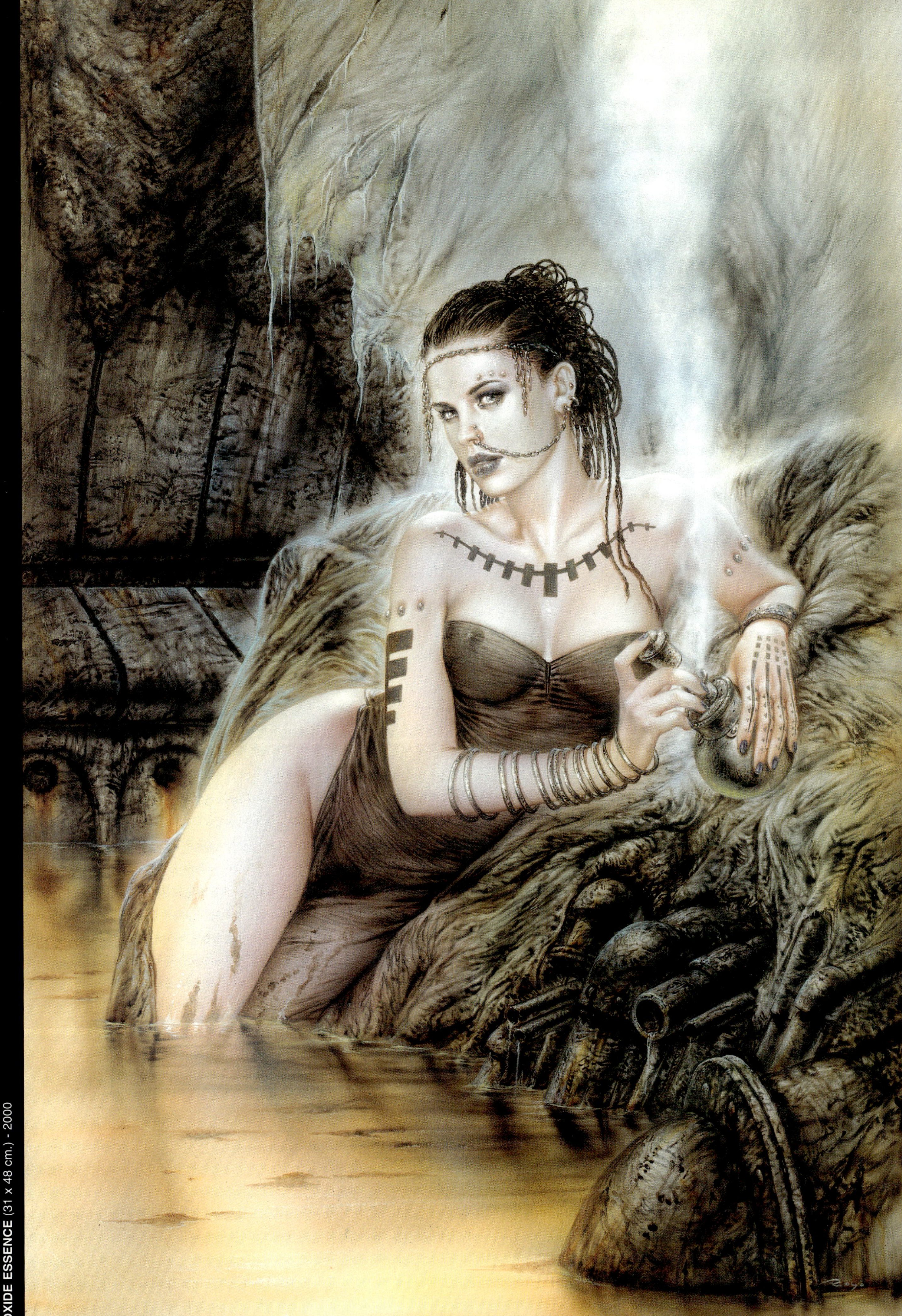

OXIDE ESSENCE (31 x 48 cm.) - 2000

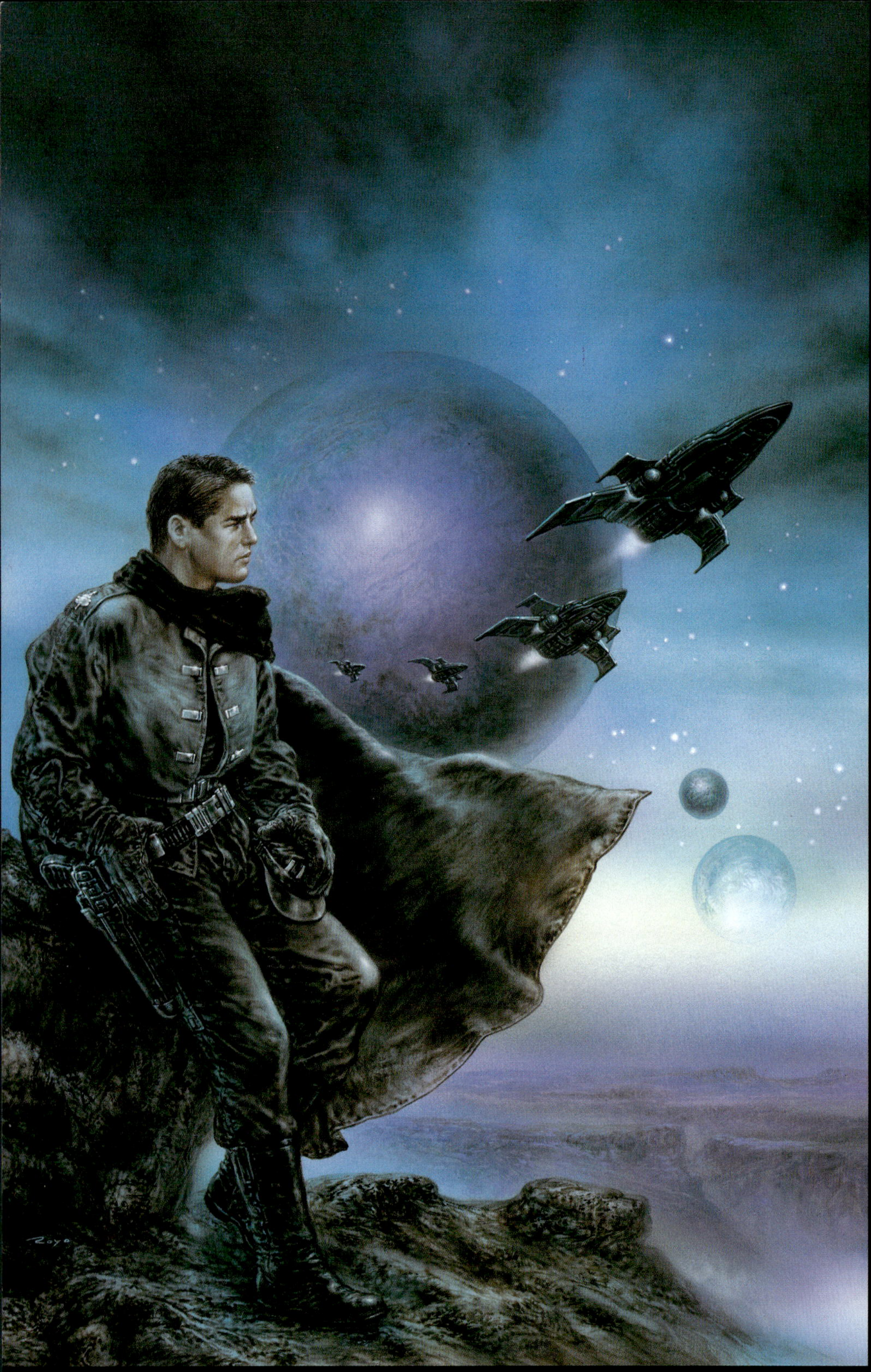

ENSIGN FLANDRY (28 x 42 cm.) - DOUBLEDAY, USA - 2000

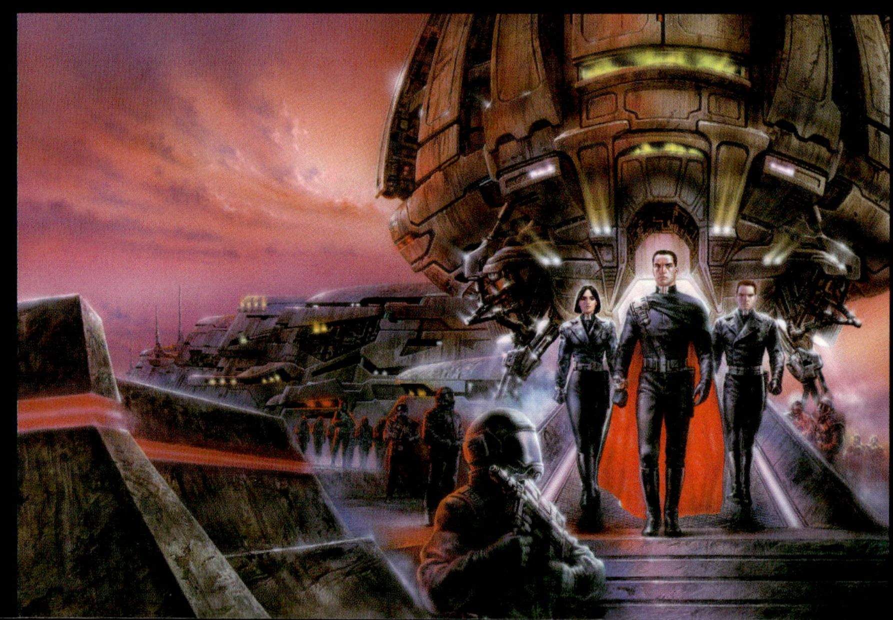

OTHER (52 x 36 cm.) - TOR BOOKS, USA - 1994

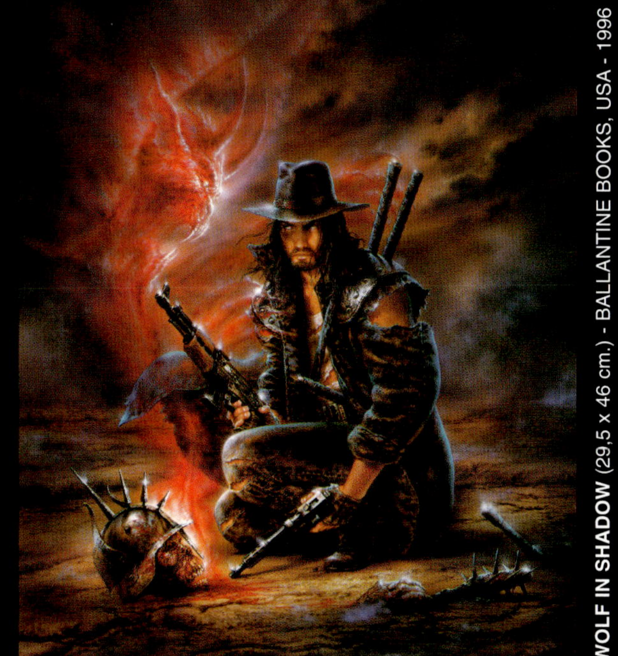

WOLF IN SHADOW (29,5 x 46 cm.) - BALLANTINE BOOKS, USA - 1996

BIODERM & DIAMOND SWORD (37 x 25 cm.) - DINAMIX, USA - 1999

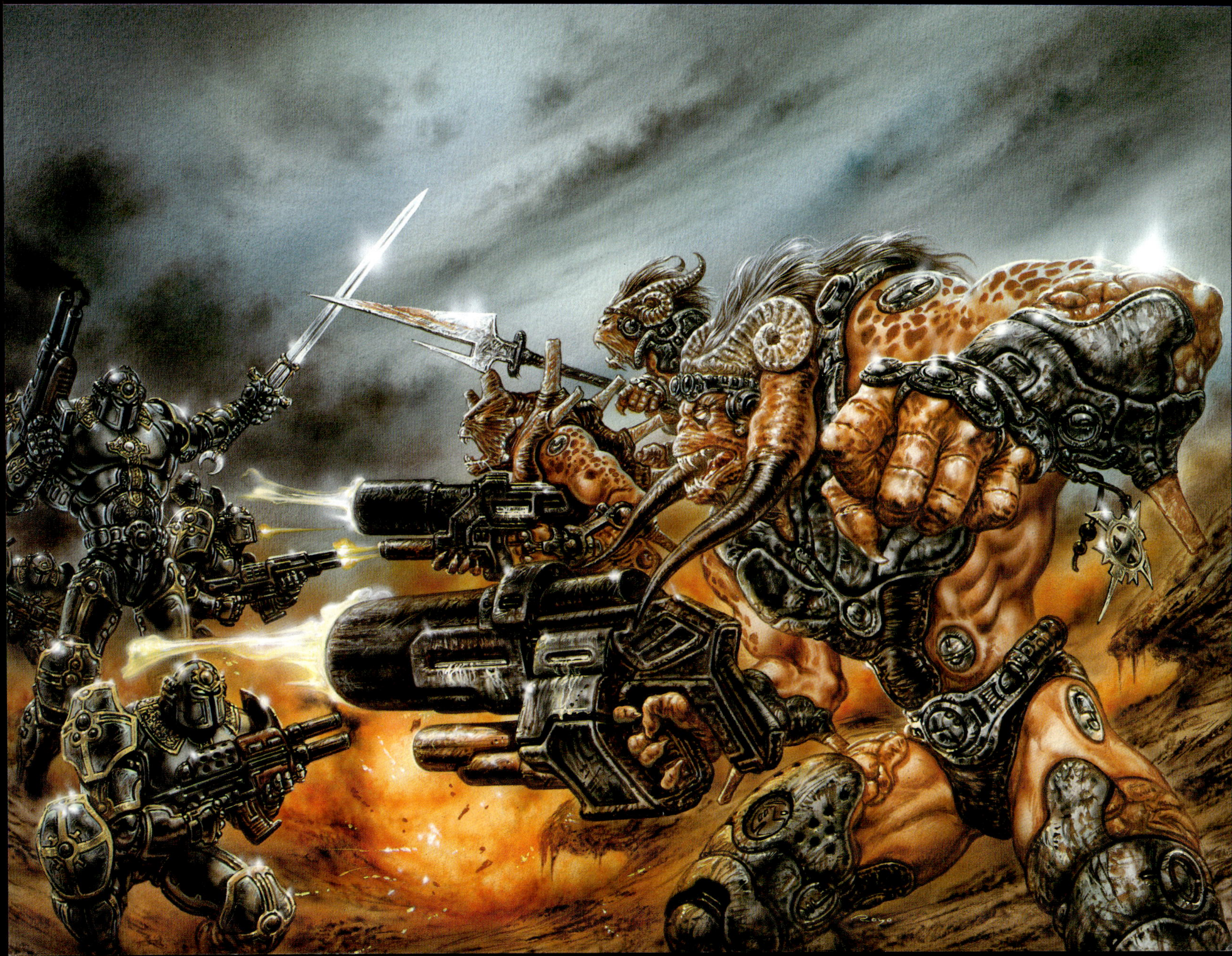

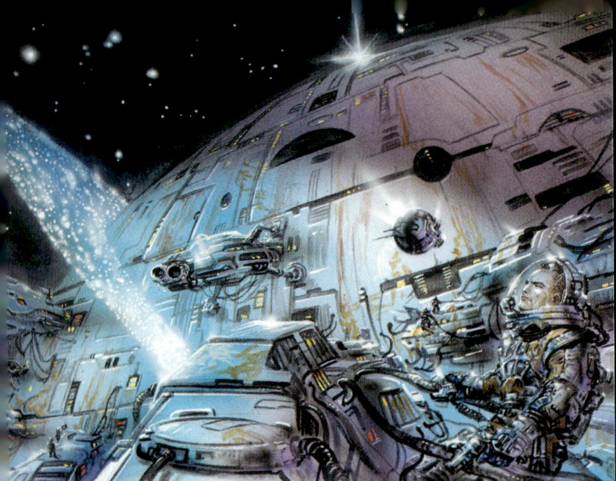

SKETCH 1

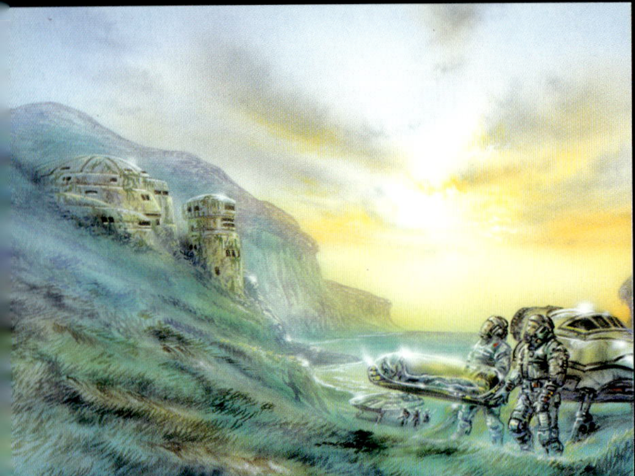

SKETCH 3

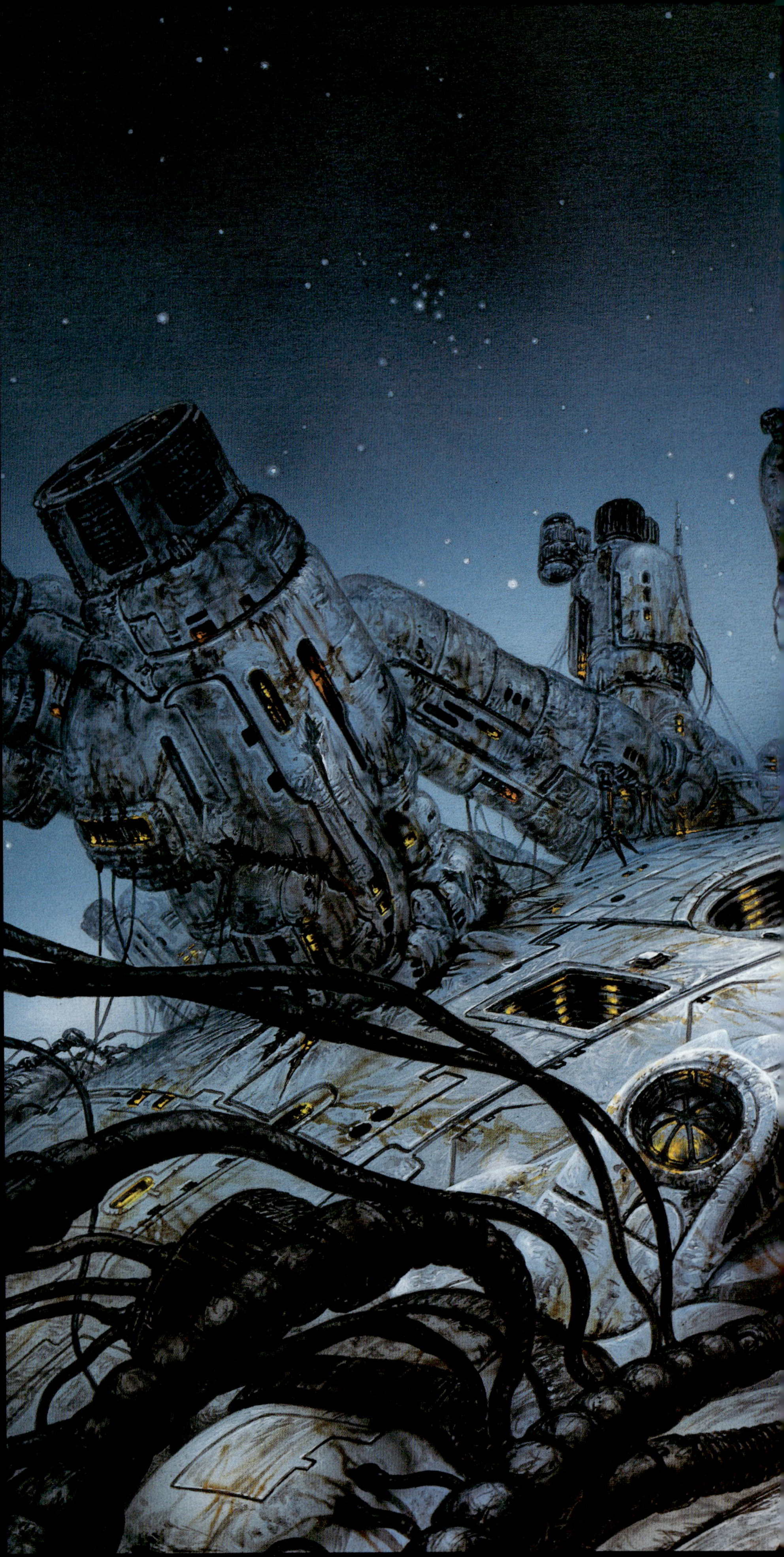

IN THE COMPANY OF OTHERS (51,5 x 36 cm.)
DAW BOOKS, USA - 2000

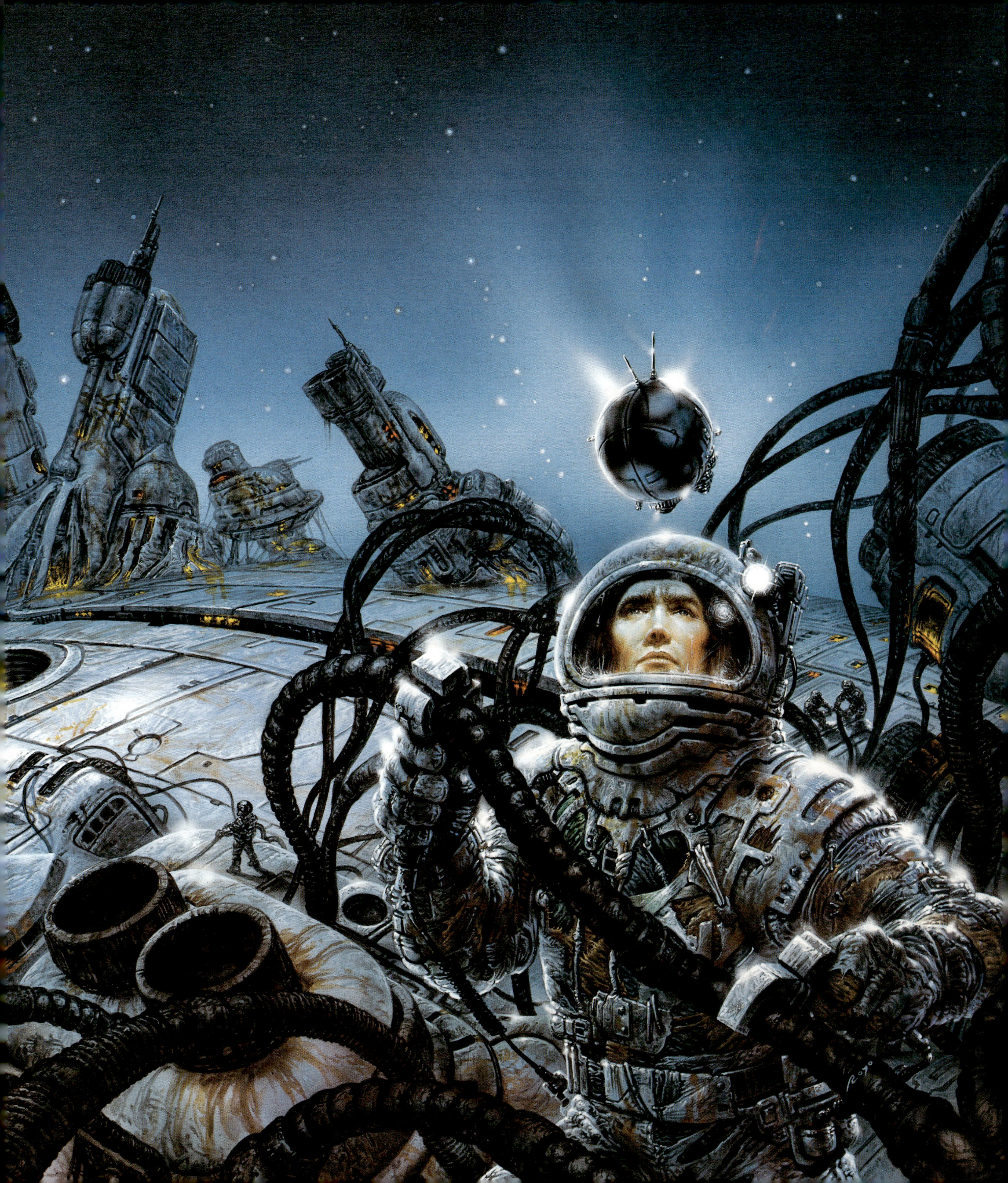

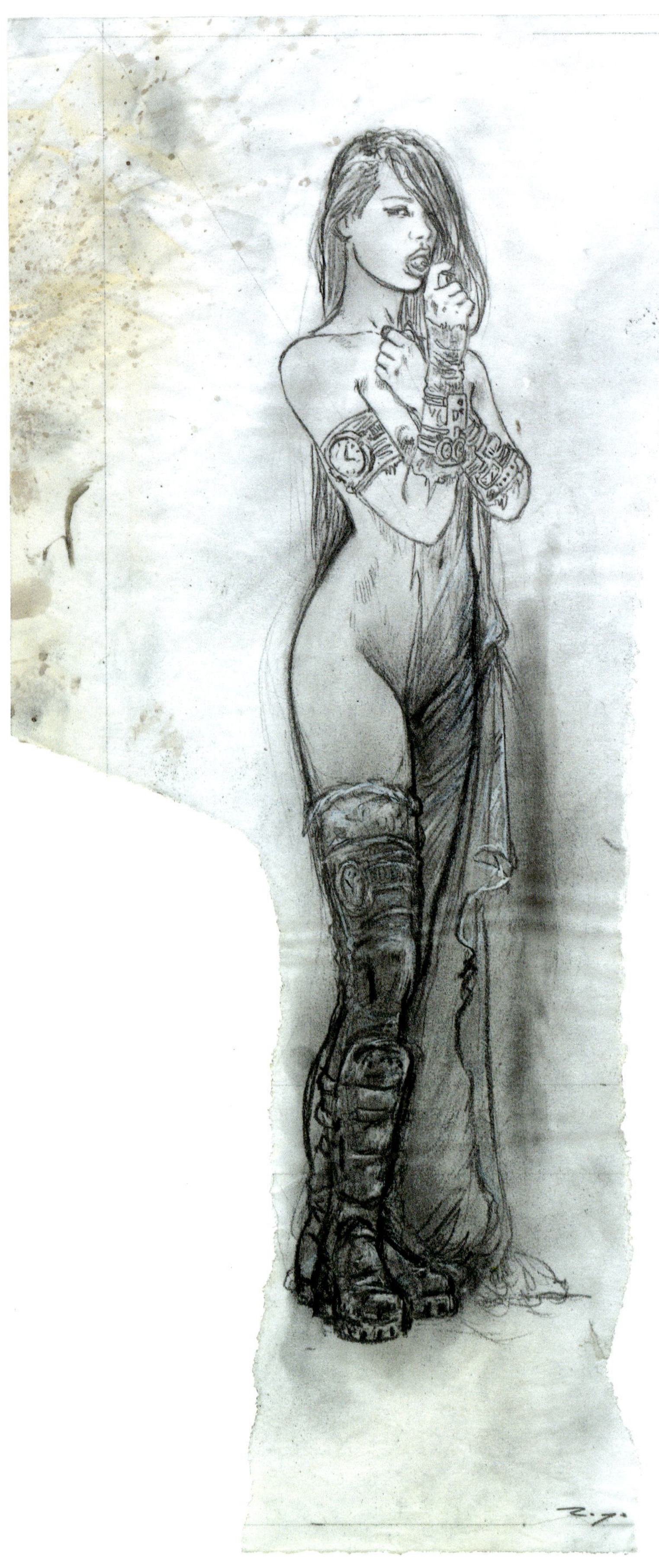

Preliminary

The Sun with its light, heat, and life. With the eighth letter of the Hebrew alphabet, symbol of existence and foundation.

The labyrinth where all bad intentions remain locked up and lost. And the regenerating fire of all the senses.

Everything is written on her skin and, captured by her, the four properties: hot, cold, wet, dry.

To sum it all up: the precision of shiny metal.

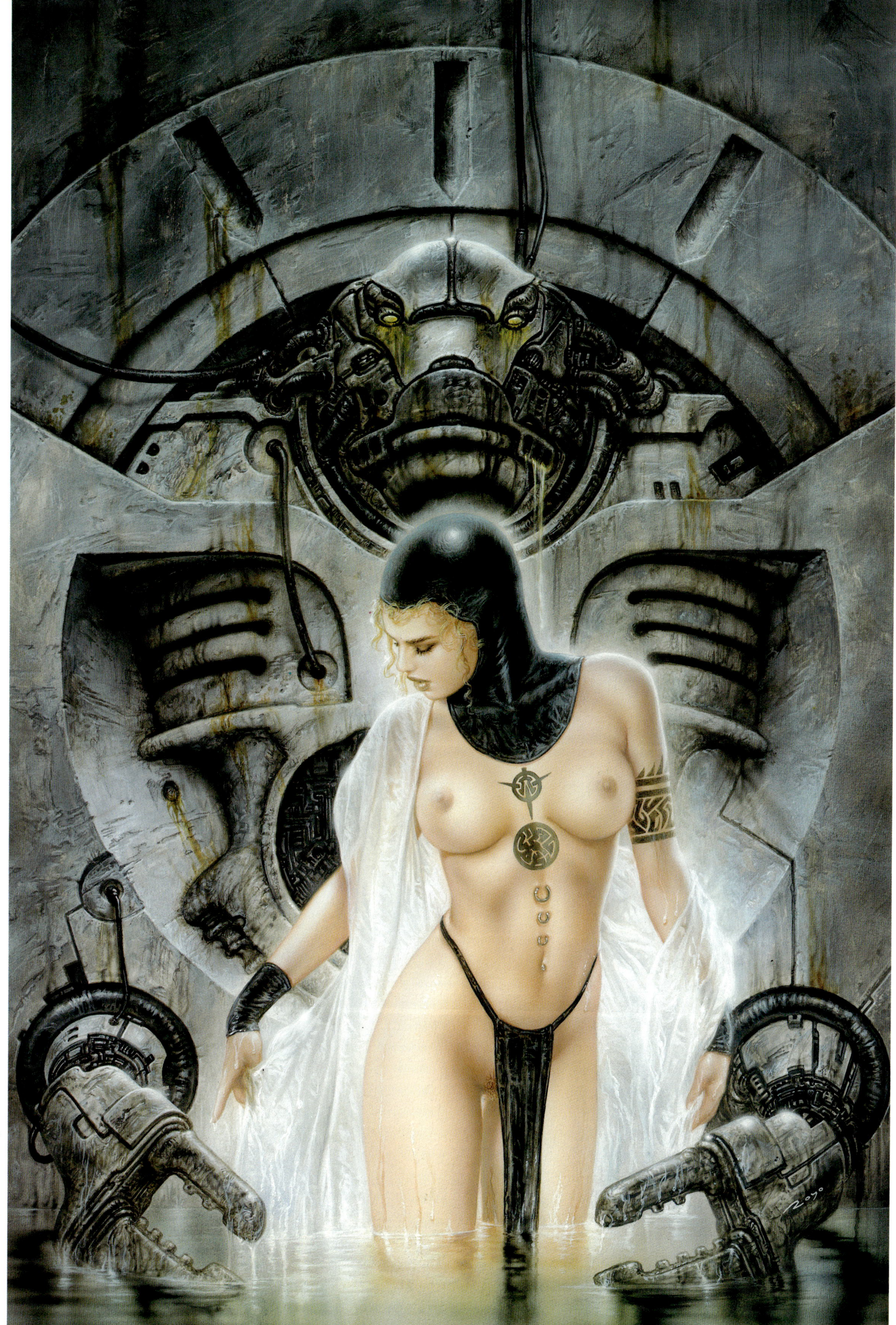

PRELIMINARY (28 x 42 cm.) - 2000

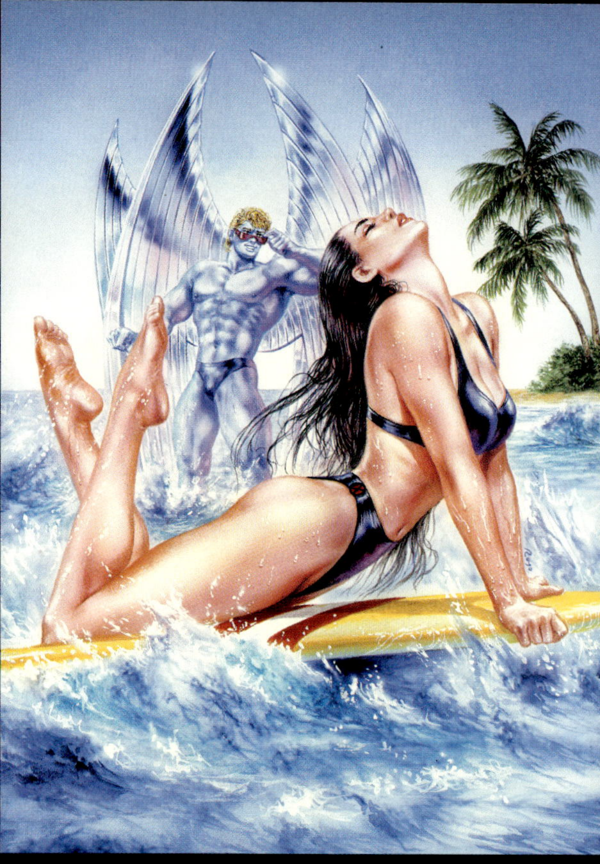

PSYLOCKE & ARCHANGEL
(19 x 26 cm.) - MARVEL, USA - 1994

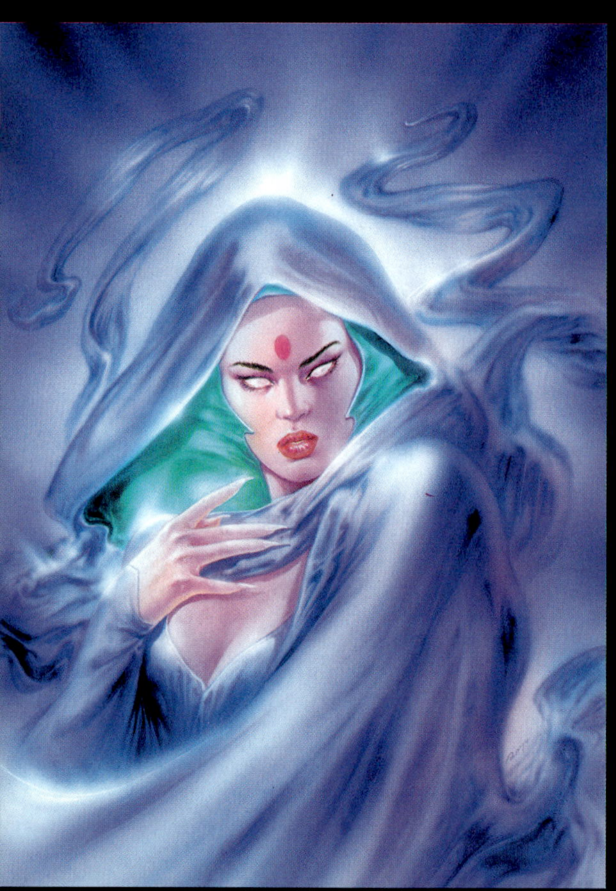

CHAKRA (17 x 23,4 cm.)
MARVEL, USA - 1994

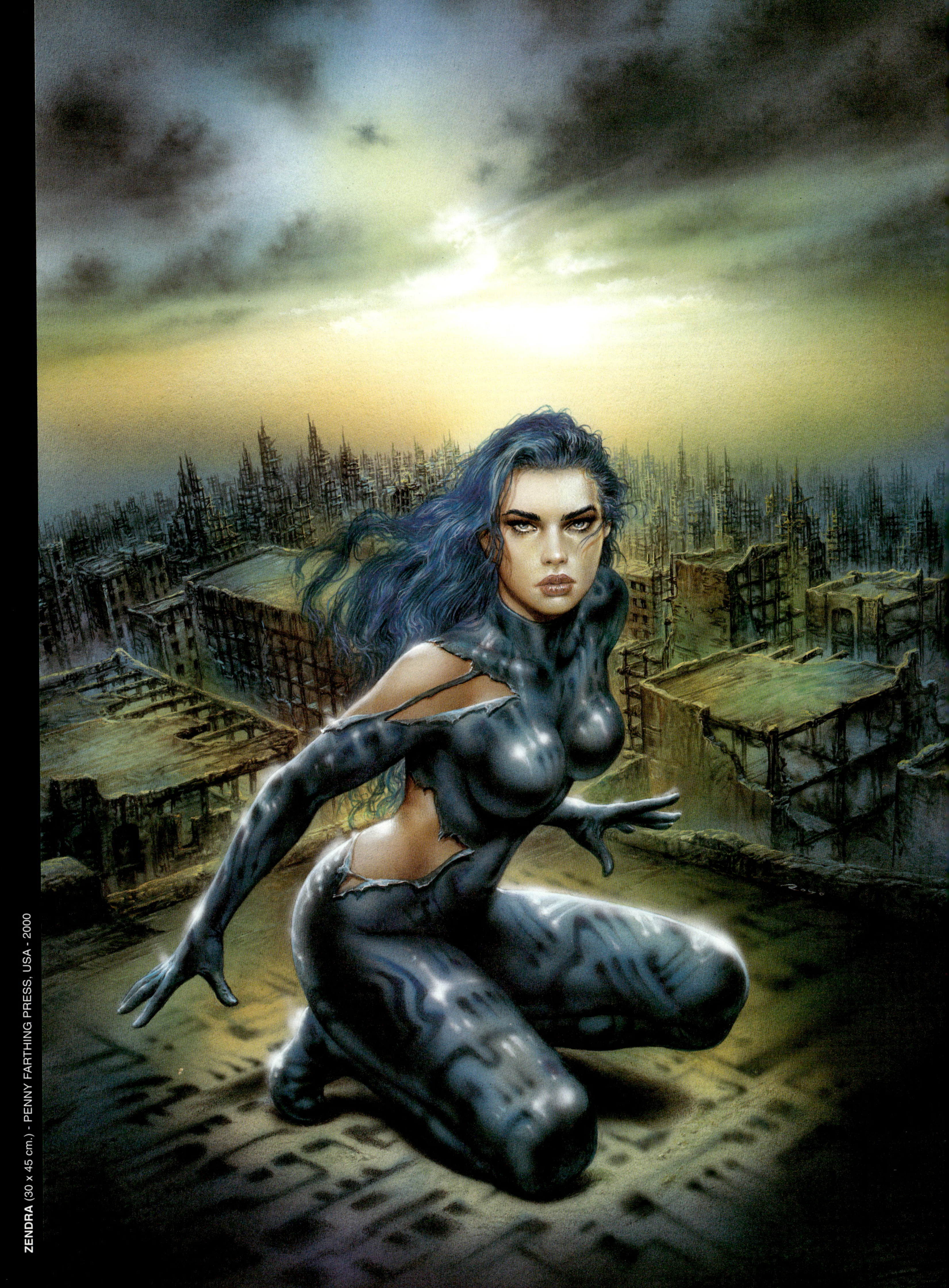

ZENDRA (30 x 45 cm.) - PENNY FARTHING PRESS, USA - 2000

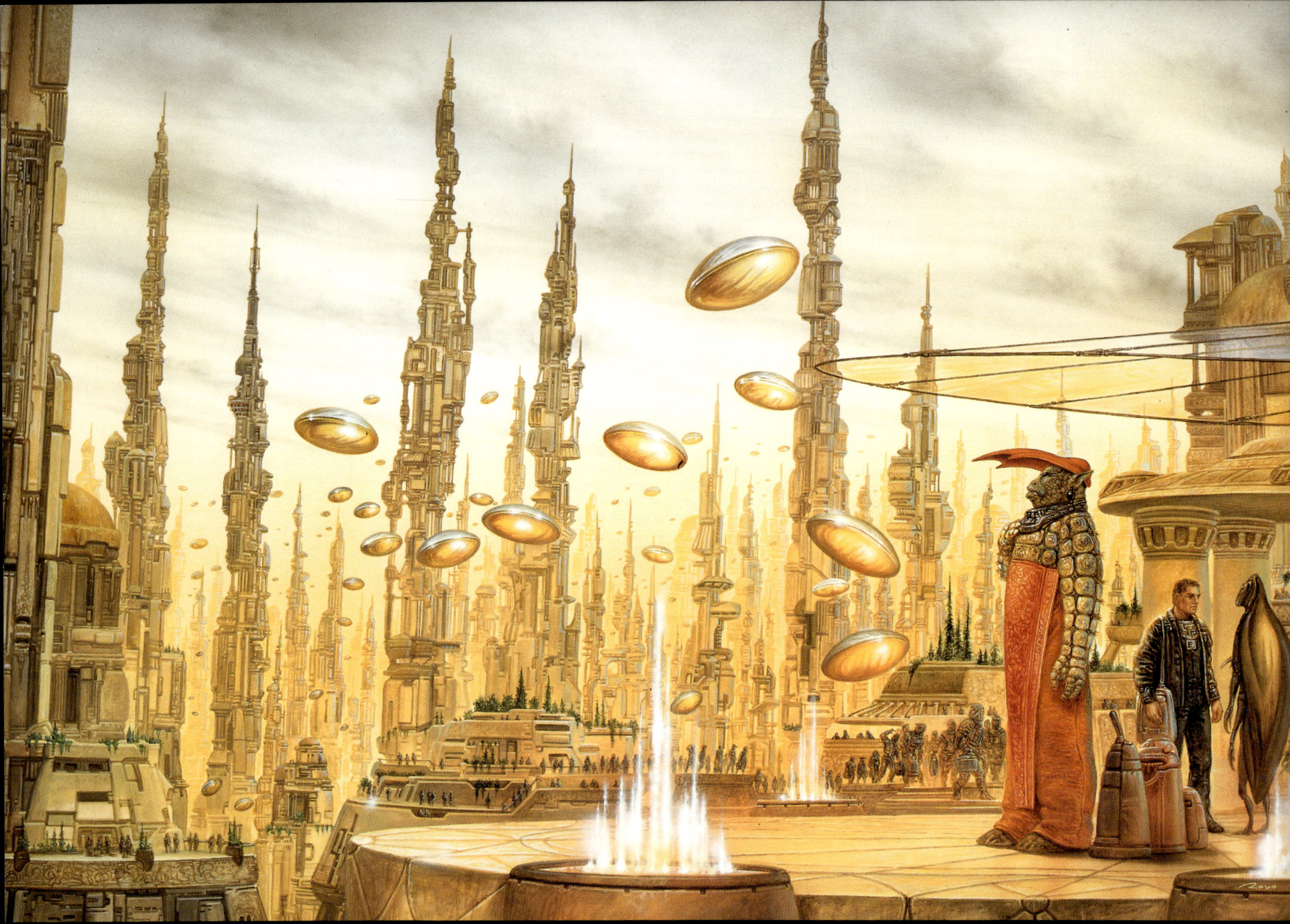

CHANGING VISION (41 x 28 cm.) - DAW BOOKS, USA - 2000

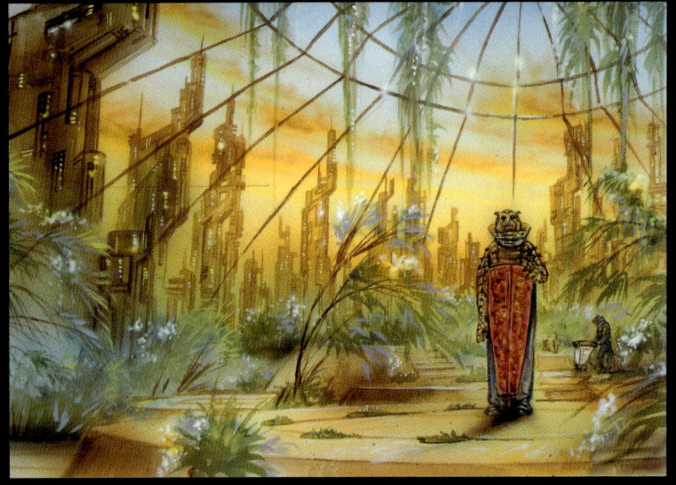

SKETCH 5

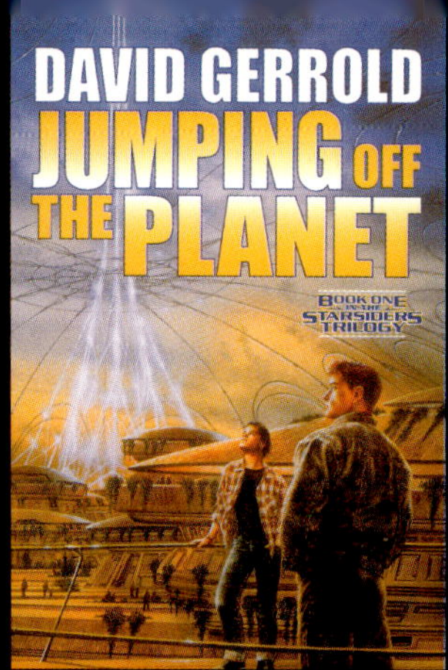

Jumping Off the Planet - Tor Books - *David Gerrold*

When you get close enough, the bottom of the Line starts rising up over the horizon like a big white mountain. It spreads down and out and out and just keeps getting bigger and bigger the closer you get...The top of the cone part is over two kilometers high. At the apex there's a ring around the Line, an observation tower where you can view the surrounding countryside or just watch the Line-cars go sliding up into the sky.

Closer still, you can see that there are wide gaps along the bottom of the cone- like a tent just a little too short for its ropes....

Terminus is more than just a launching station, it's a domed city- bigger than enormous, twenty klicks across. Think of a gigantic tent that uses the three cables of the beanstalk as the central mast, the tent fabric is made out of the same monofilament stuff as the Line, and all of the supporting cables are actual beanstalk filaments anchored off axis for additional stability... Distances don't look the same. You can't tell how near or how far anything is. And everywhere, the filaments of the beanstalk spread out like rays of the sun, stabbing into the ground and anchoring themselves deep in the bedrock.

The top of the Terminus dome goes up so high it fades away in the distance... But the outer surface of the tent is painted with solar crystals to generate power for the air-conditioning inside...

JUMPING OFF THE PLANET (53 x 36 cm.) - TOR BOOKS, USA - 1999

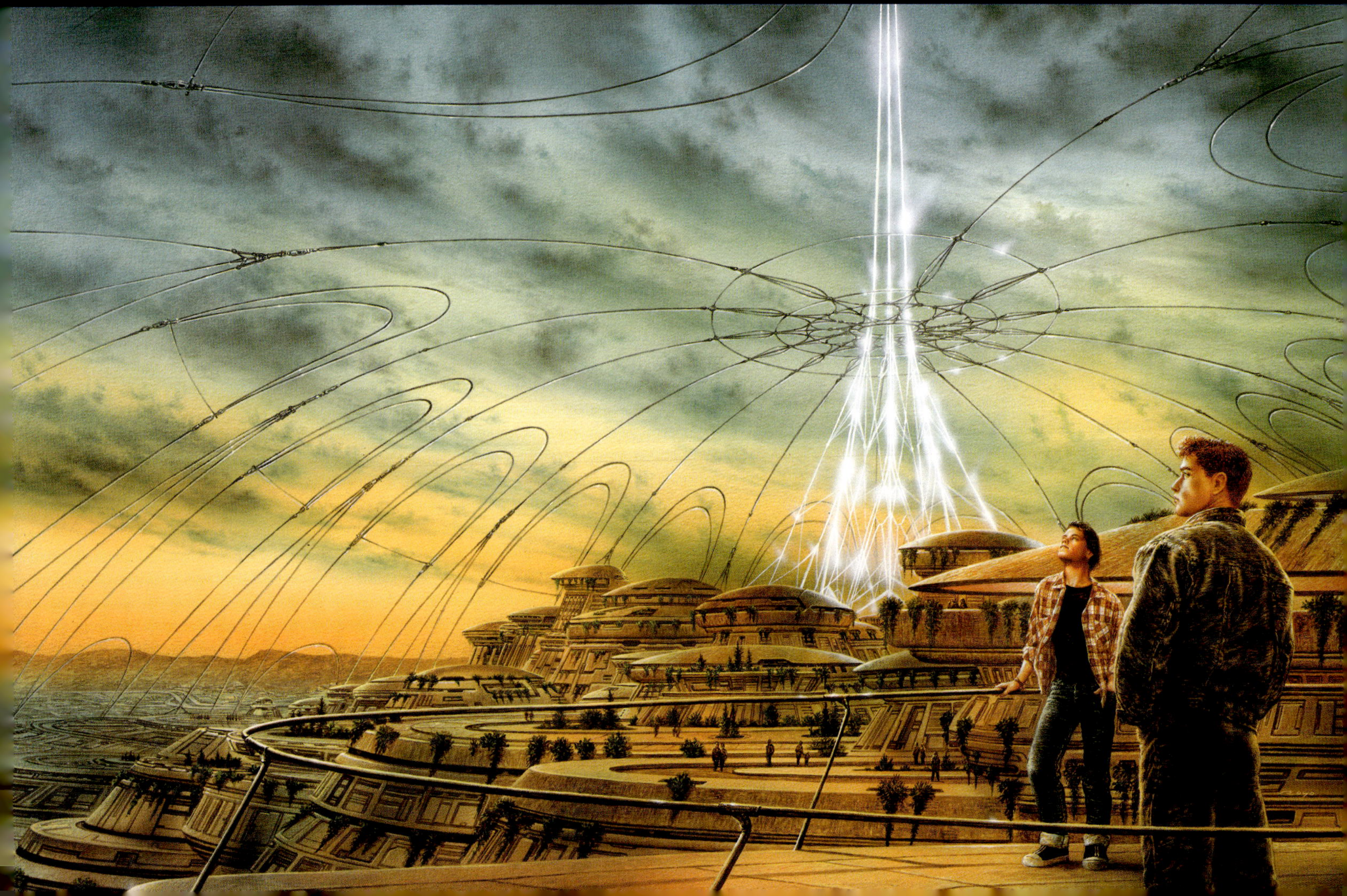

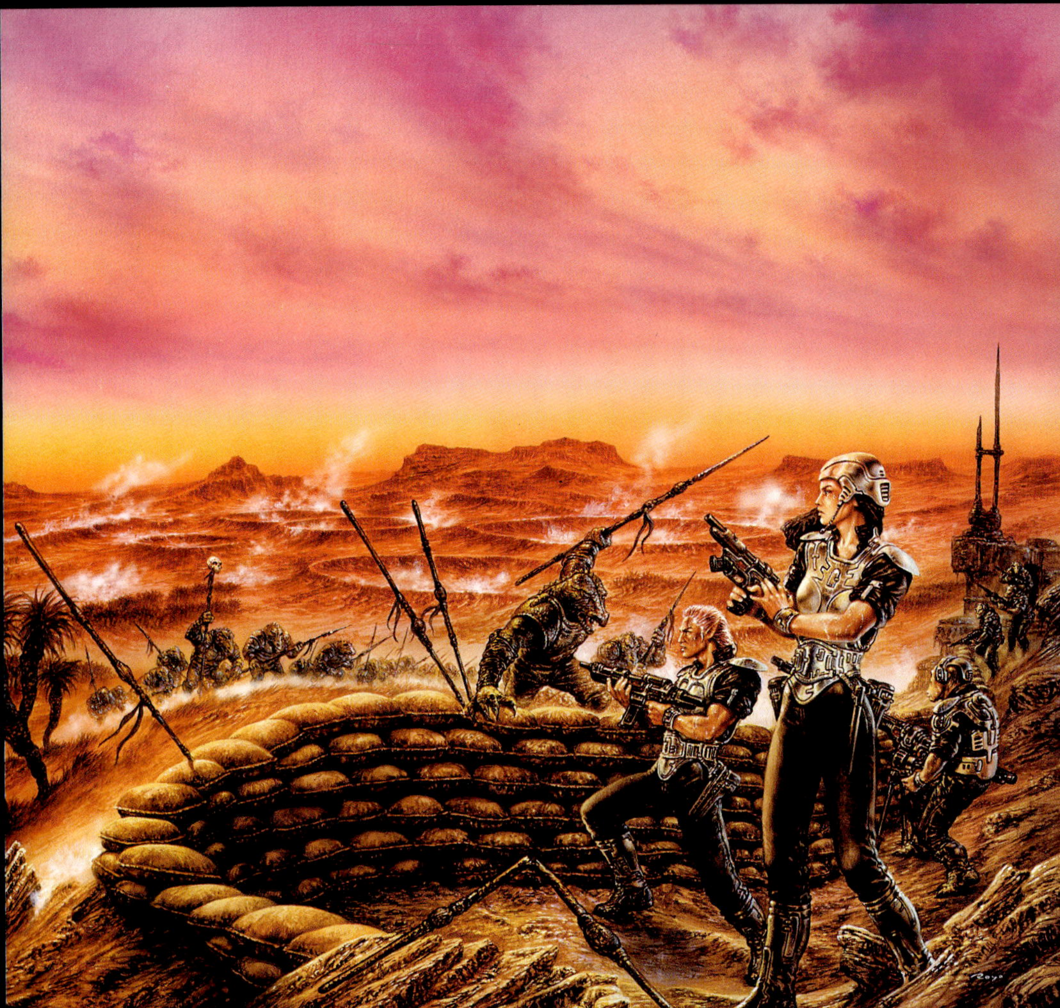

VALOR´S CHOICE (48,5 x 35 cm.)
DAW BOOKS, USA - 1999

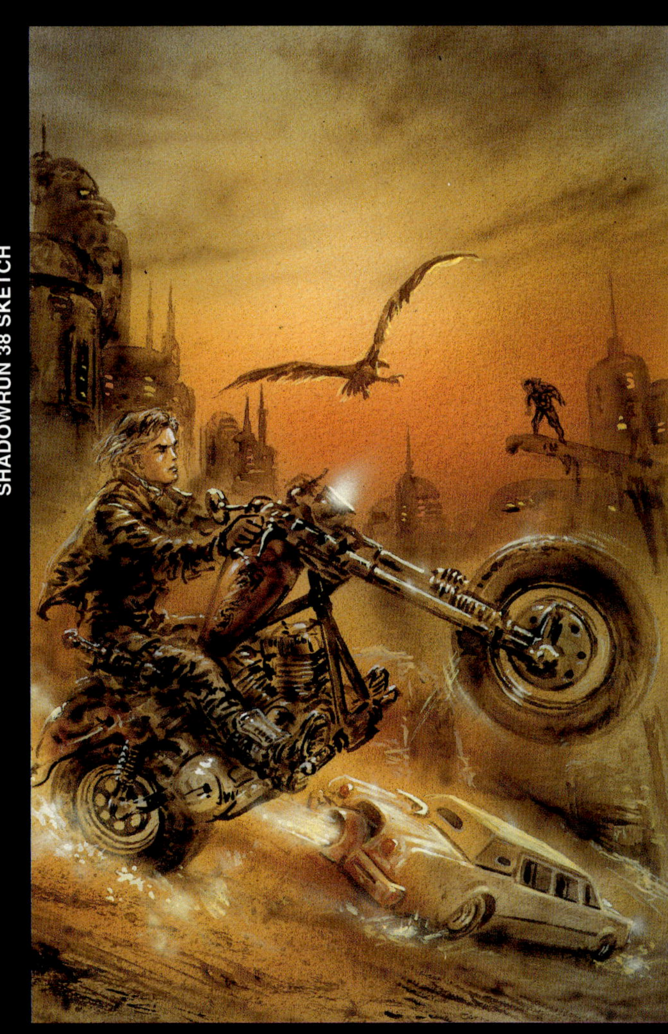

SHADOWRUN 38 SKETCH

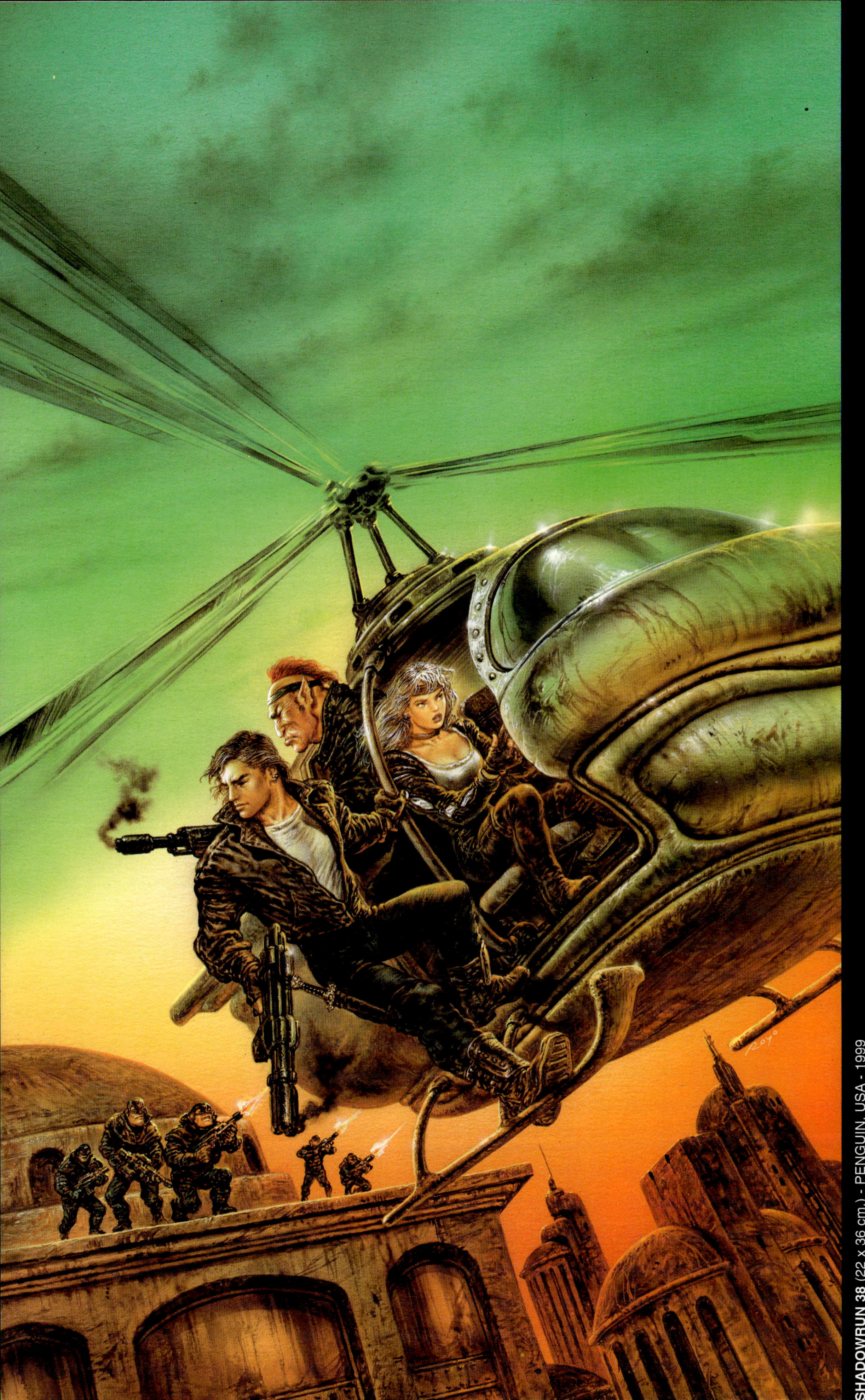

SHADOWRUN 38 (22 x 36 cm.) - PENGUIN, USA - 1999

Sodom's Princess

The pigments on the skin form the horned image of the goat. Since the festivals of Dionysus, it's been the emblem of tragedy, lust, and perversion. The king of the underworld in the West, the god of fire in India, the symbol of virility in Africa. The skull is to remind us of the ephemerality of our existence. The abstract skeleton of a great primitive monster.
Metals to represent the star-spangled sky, the rainbow sign of Jonah's whale, and the eclipse of the Moon.

ACT I - THE LIGHT CORNER 4 (40,5 x 29 cm.) - 1999

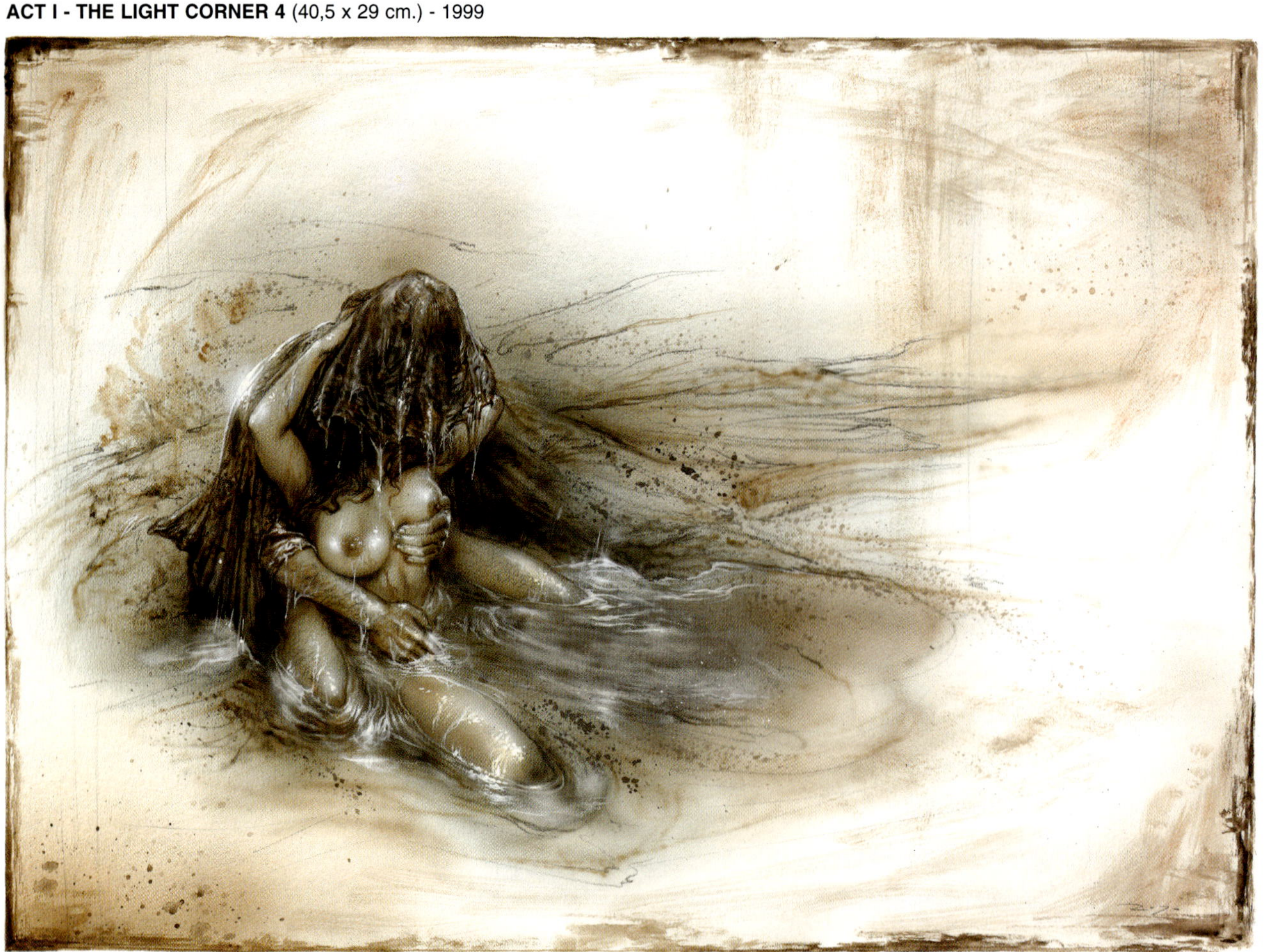

SODOM'S PRINCESS (32 x 49 cm.) - 1999 ▶

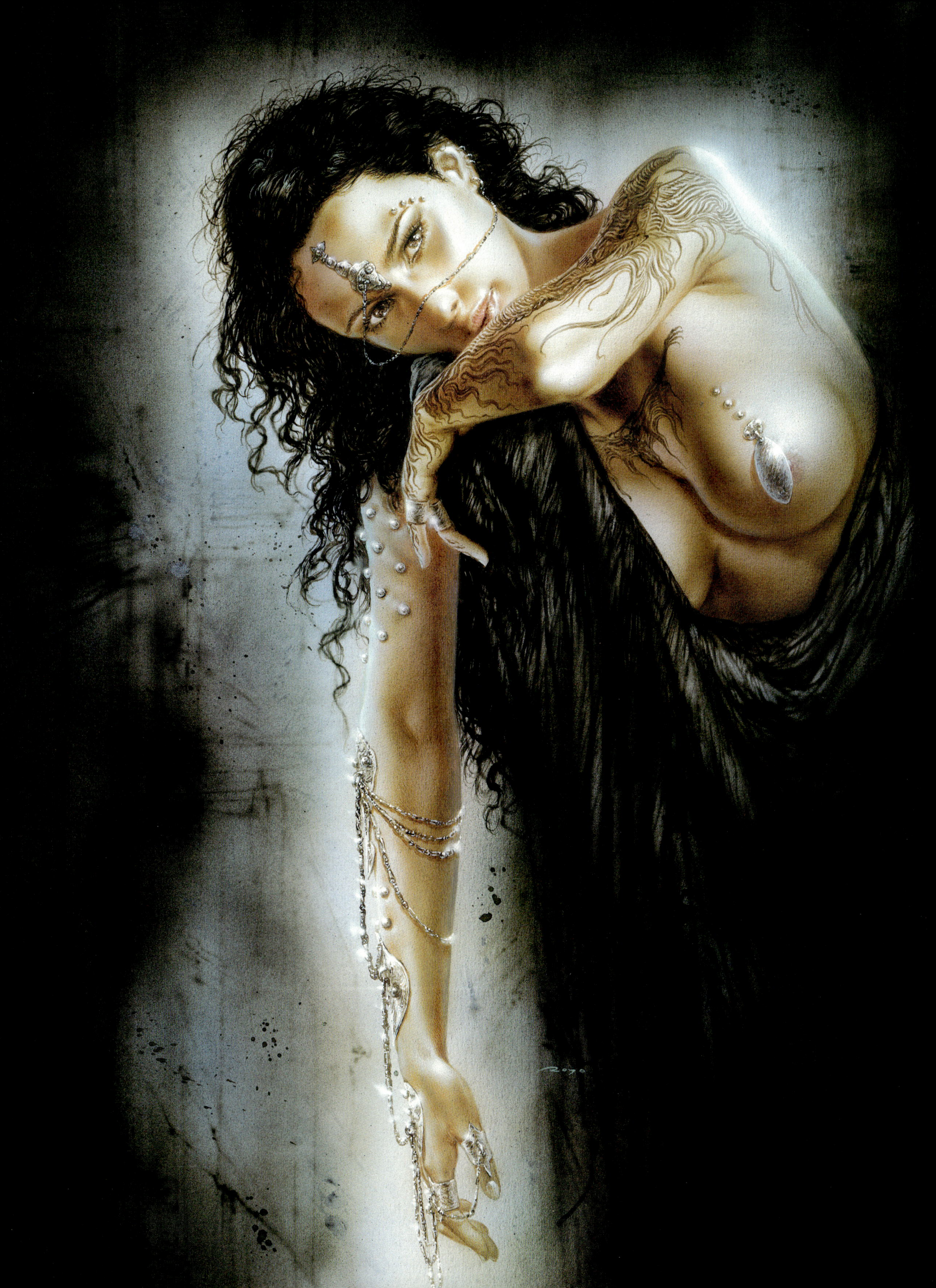

Julie Smith's Temptation

The circle of perfection, of results we've created, of projection and expansion. The badge of excellence of the different eras that the arrow of destiny has flown across. Everything is based on three, the fundamental number that expresses the order of the cosmos. The three inverted triangles form nine angles, the sum of the three tertiaries, the sum of the three worlds identified with the triangle: Heaven, Earth, and Hell.

At the end, I begin all over again on a new plane.

The tower of a hundred eyes to observe life and a thousand wings to taste it, presided over by the Sun and the labyrinth.

And the dazzling ribbons that communicate one thing only: sex.

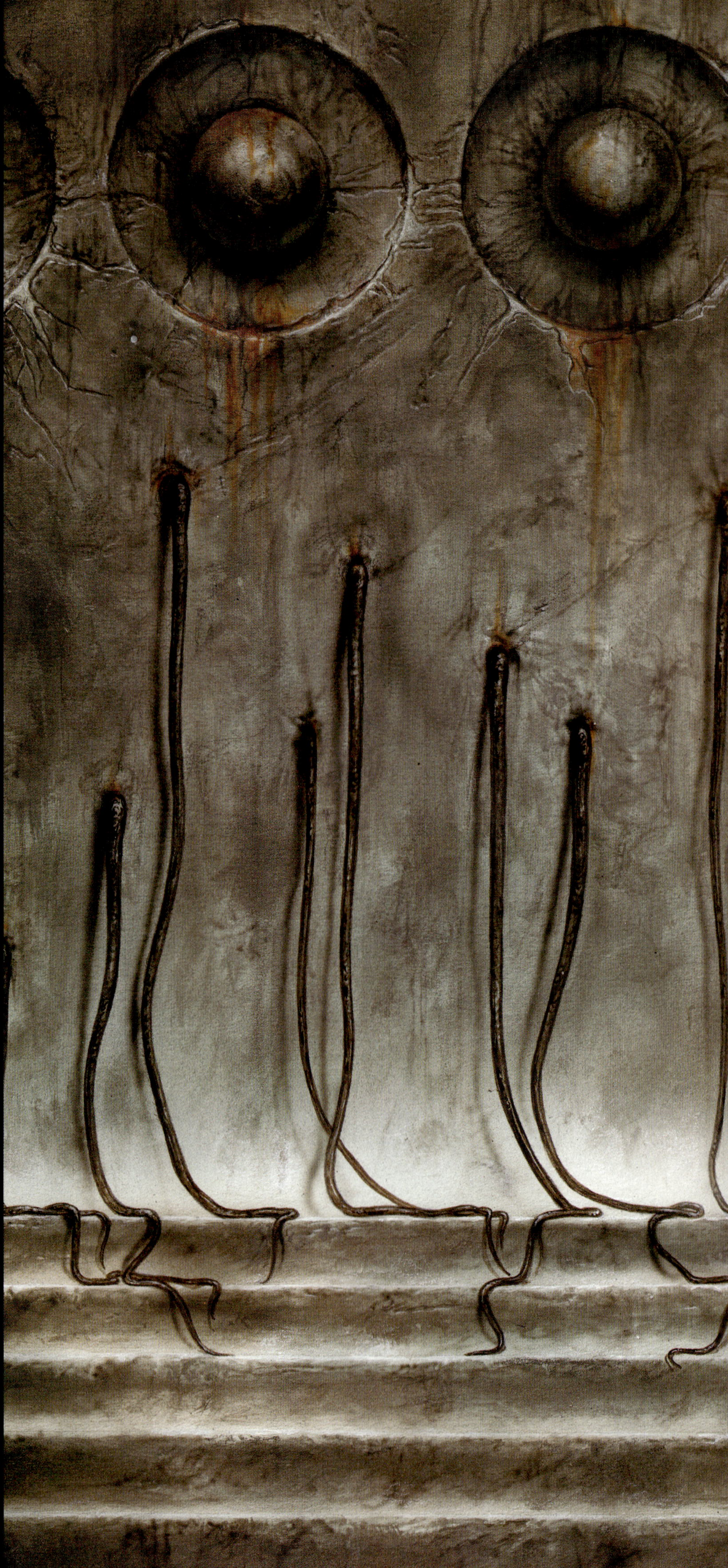

JULIE SMITH'S TEMPTATION (48 x 36 cm.) - 2000

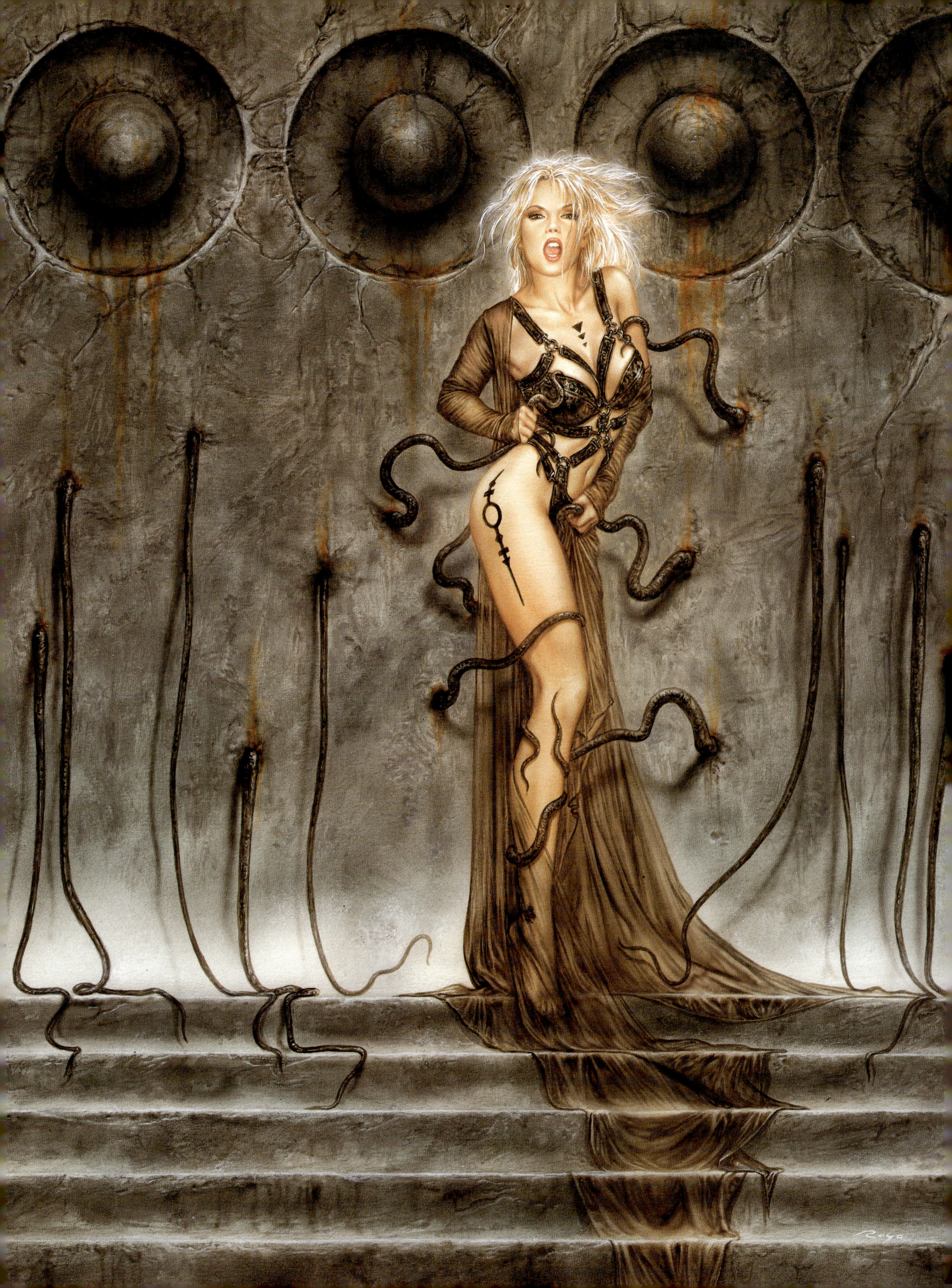

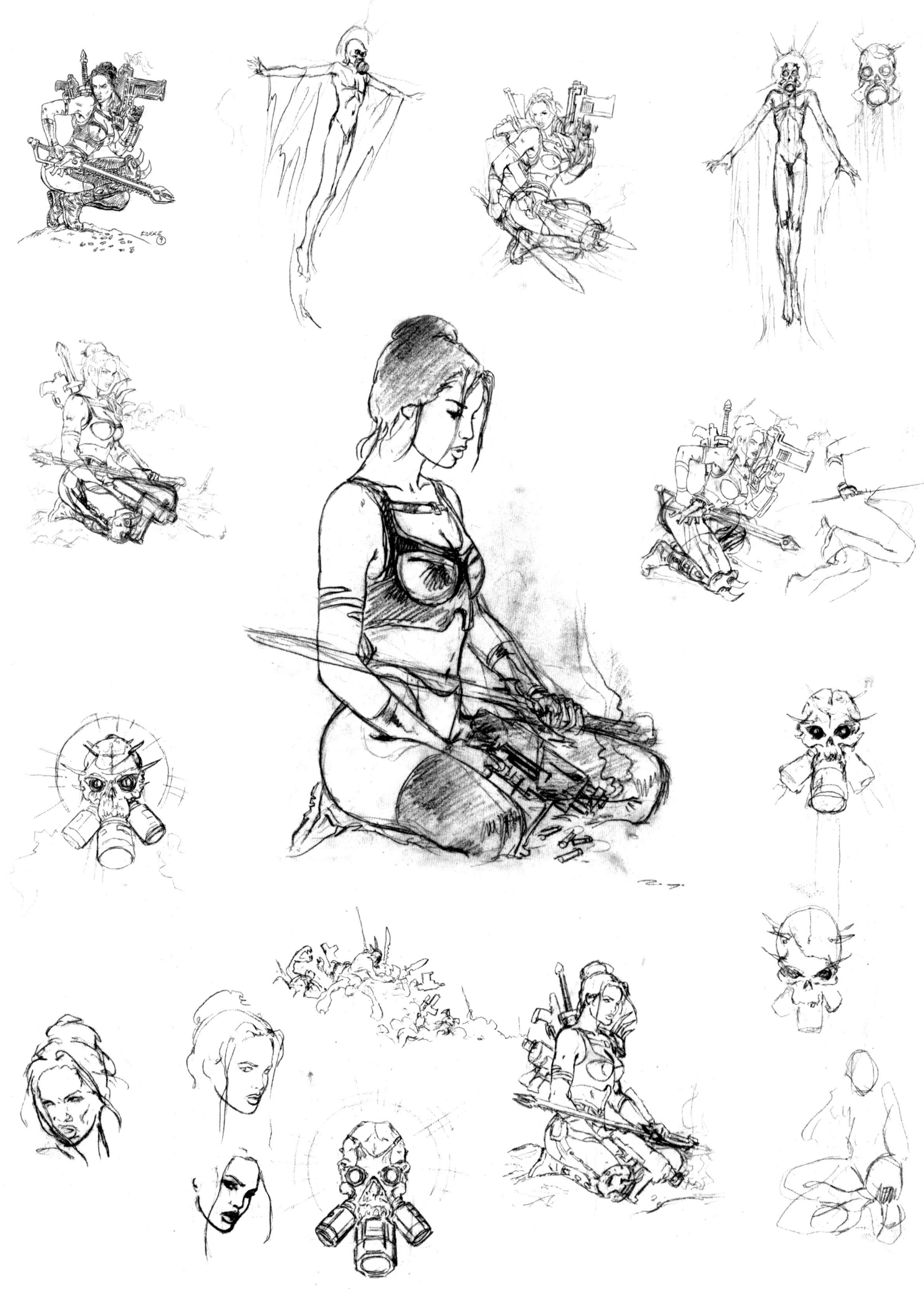

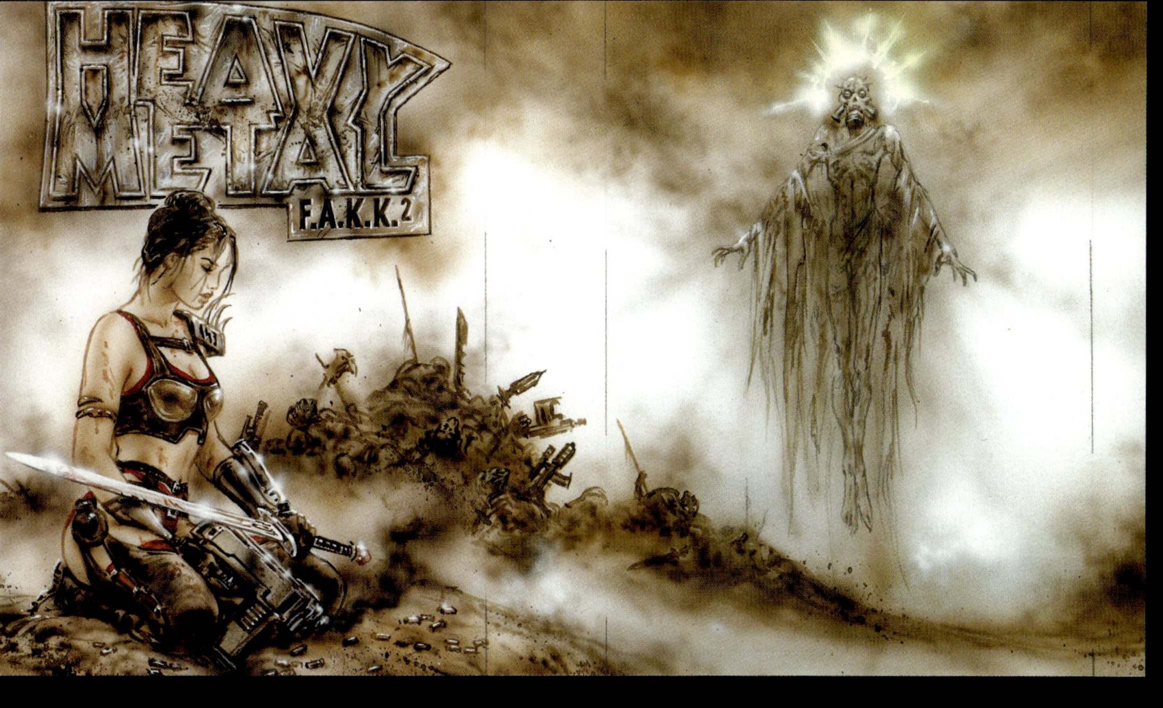

SKETCH 1

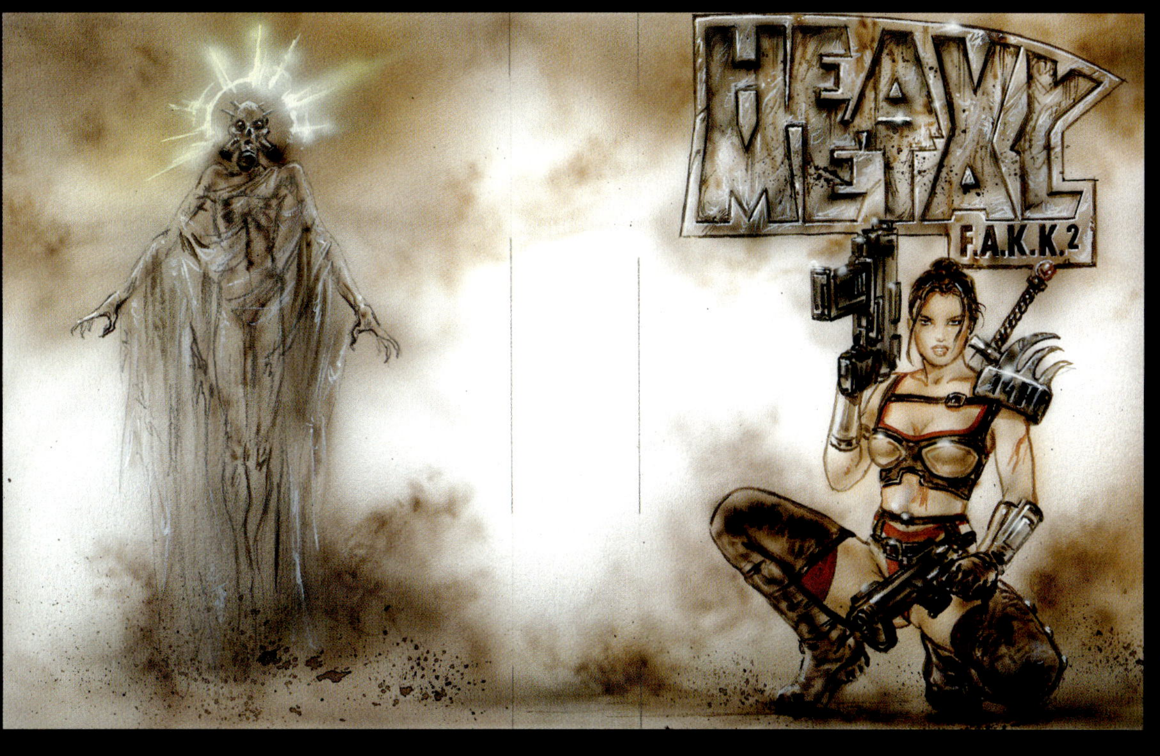

SKETCH 2

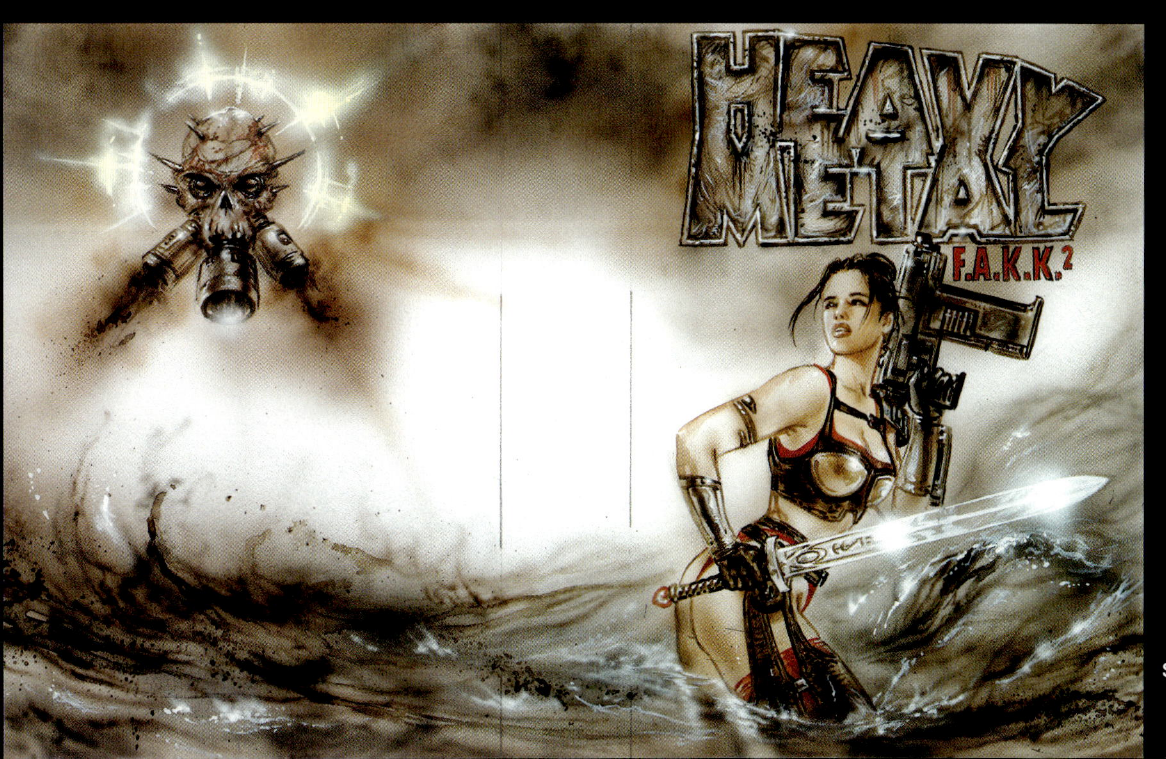

SKETCH 3

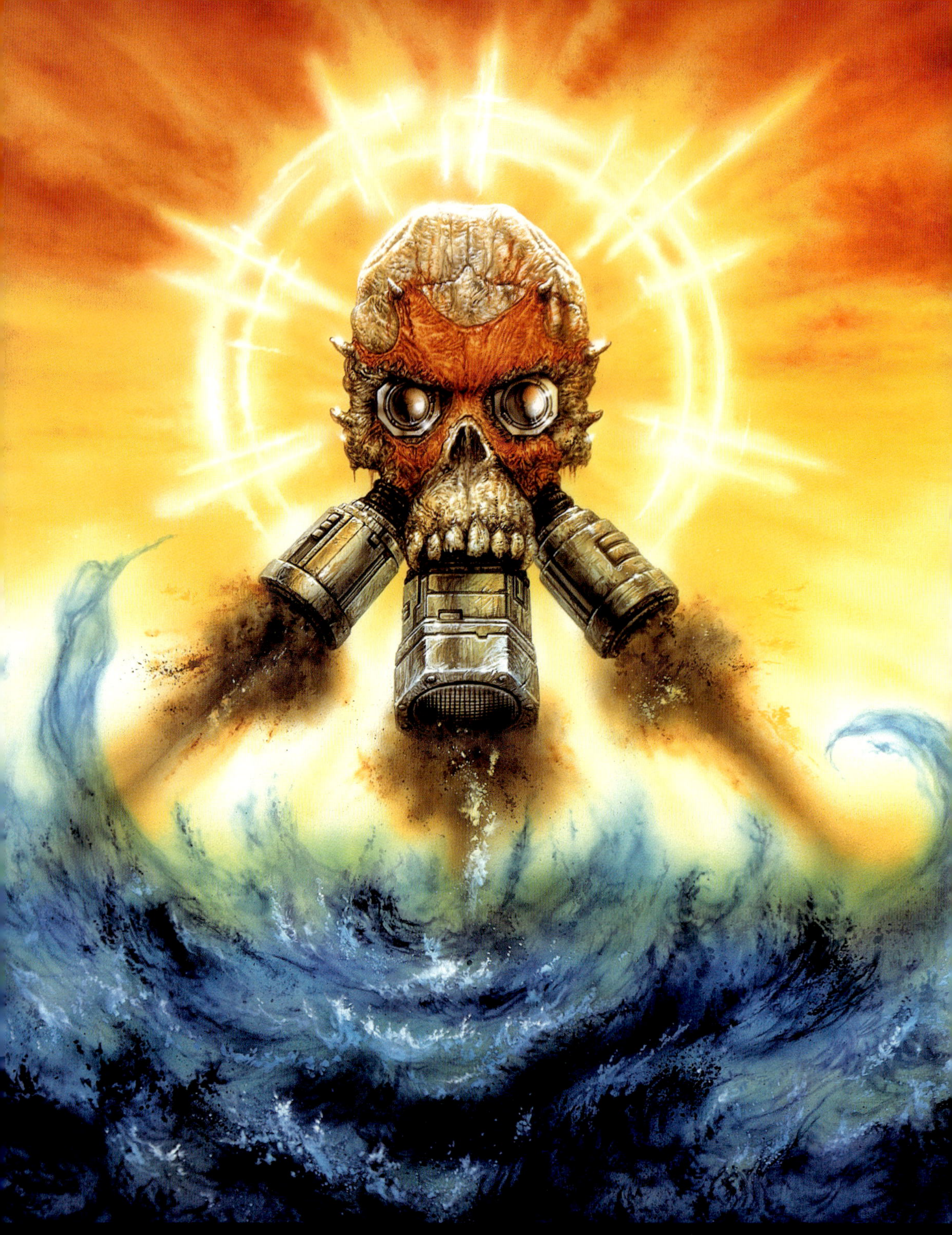

F.A.K.K. 2

Work done for Heavy Metal's video game character F.A.K.K. 2

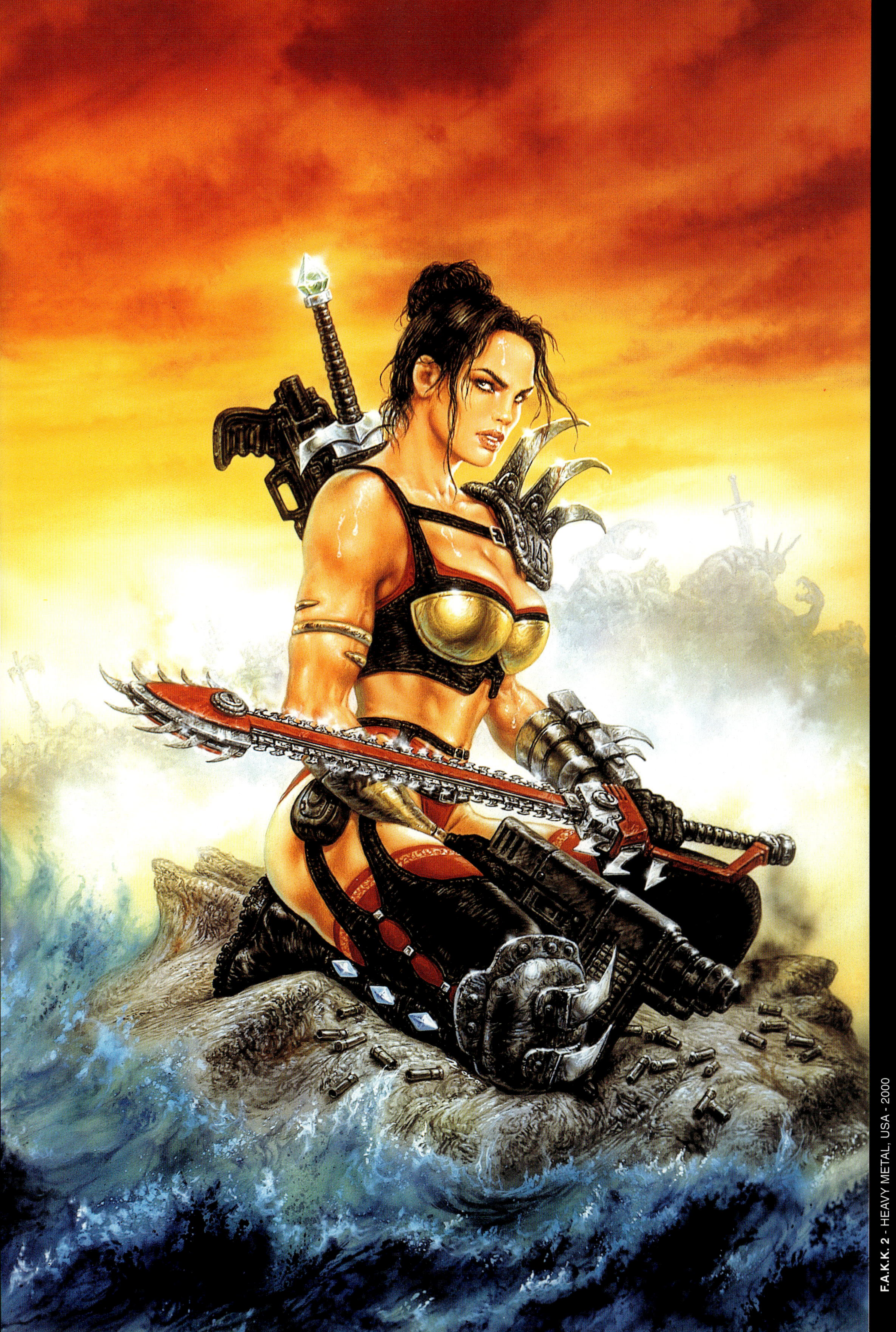

F.A.K.K. 2 - HEAVY METAL, USA - 2000

The Last Prince of Ireland - Tor Books - *Morgan Llywelyn*

Donal thought quickly. To the left there was a deep marsh covered with trees. He turned and rode toward it, followed by his army of ghosts. The English began to follow them. When they reached the marsh, Donal's men about-faced and formed a defensive line, with which they surprised the English cavalry. The musketeers opened fire. Then the real carnage began, a tangled and savage battle. All were overcome by a blind fury.

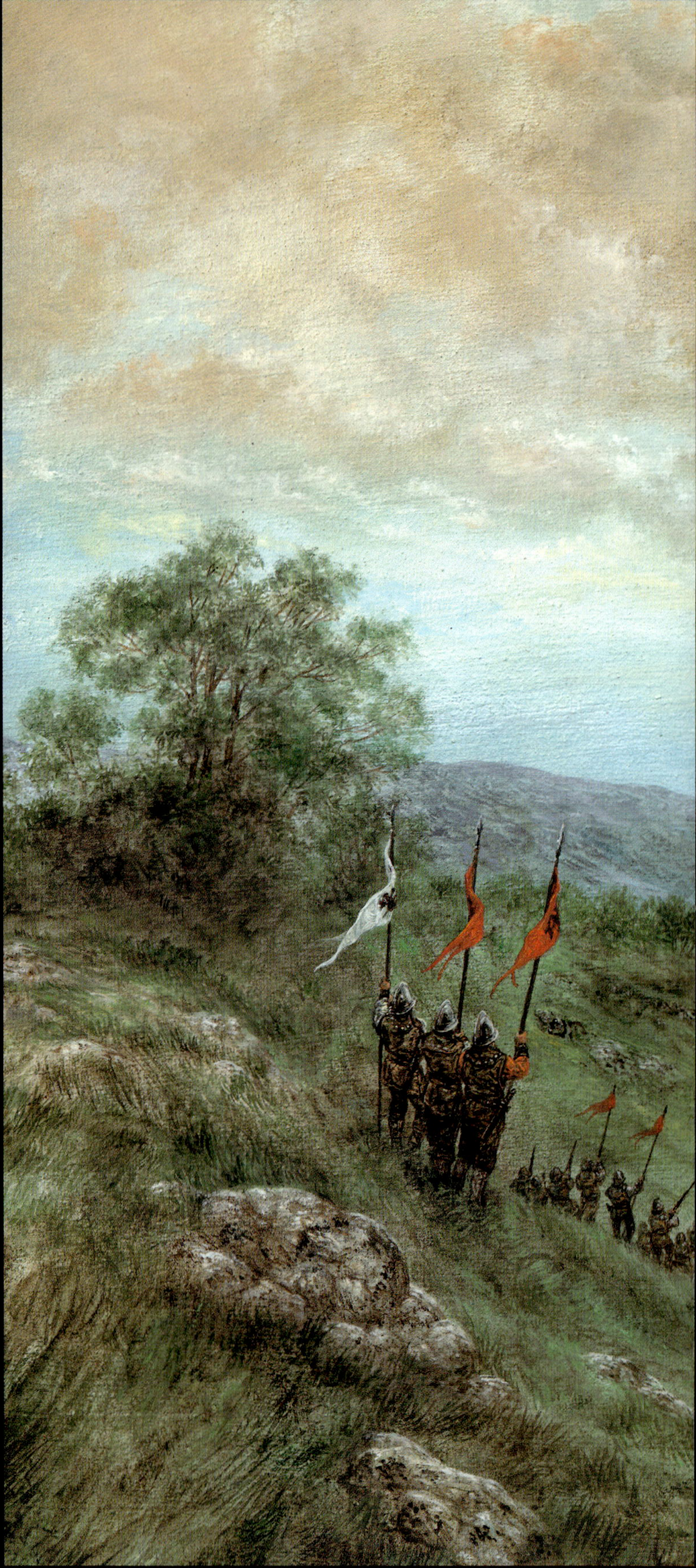

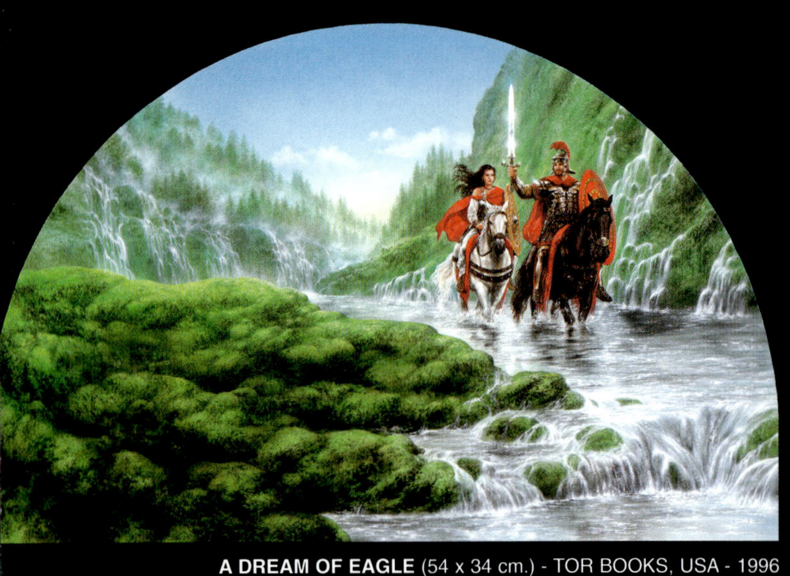

A DREAM OF EAGLE (54 x 34 cm.) - TOR BOOKS, USA - 1996

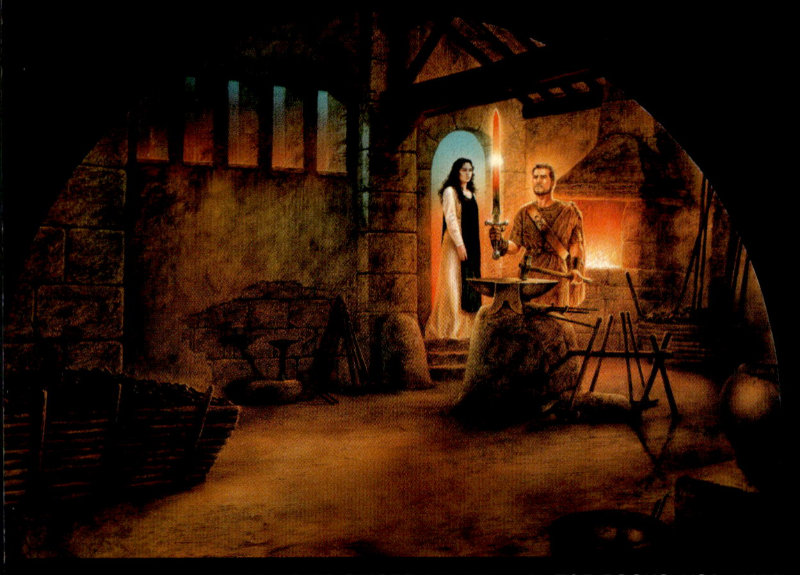

THE SINGING SWORD (57 x 38 cm.) - TOR BOOKS, USA - 1996

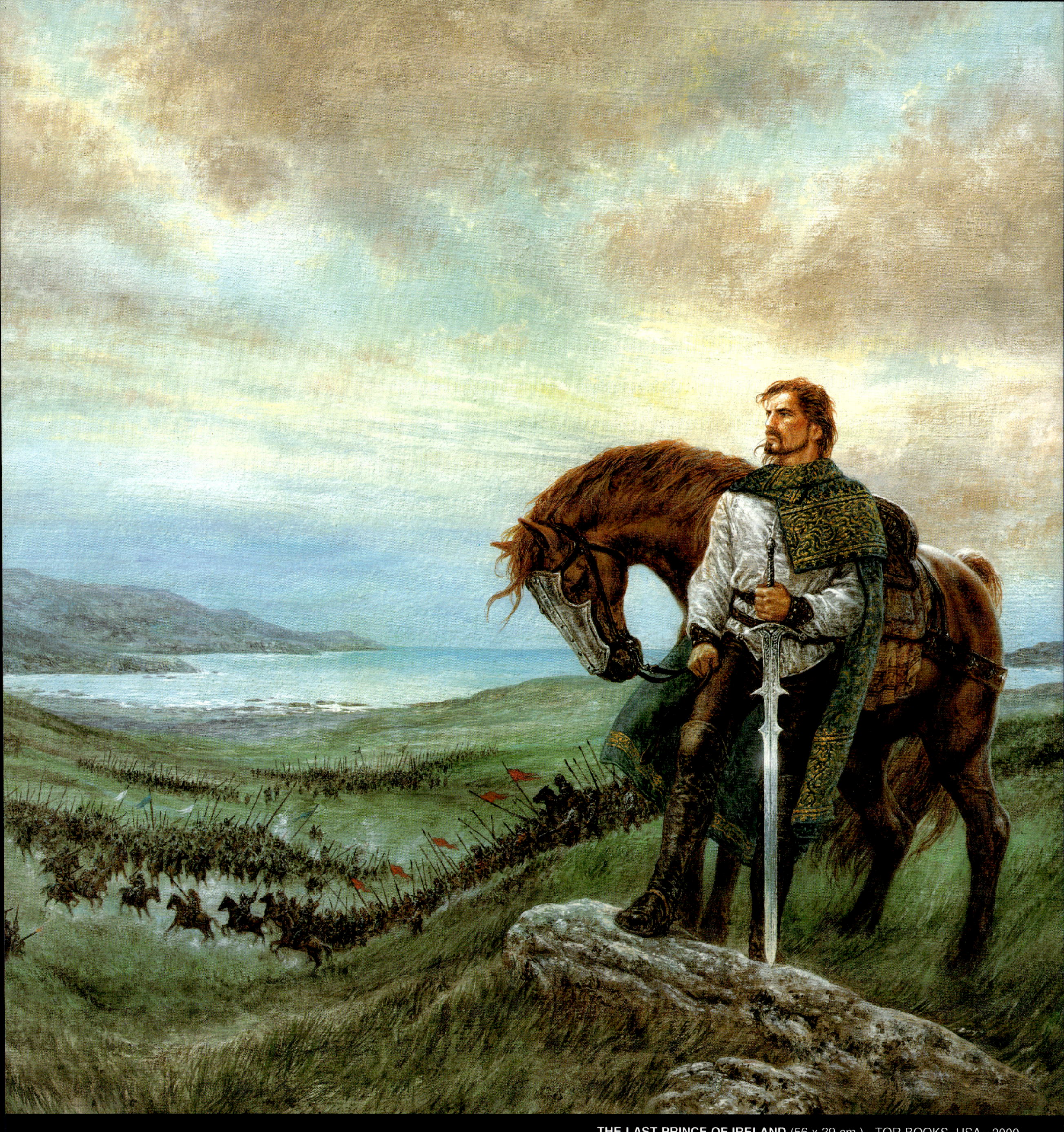

THE LAST PRINCE OF IRELAND (56 x 39 cm.) - TOR BOOKS, USA - 2000

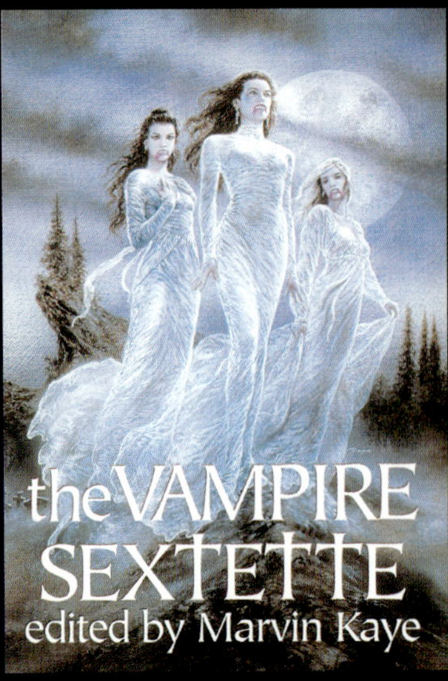
the VAMPIRE
SEXTETTE
edited by Marvin Kaye

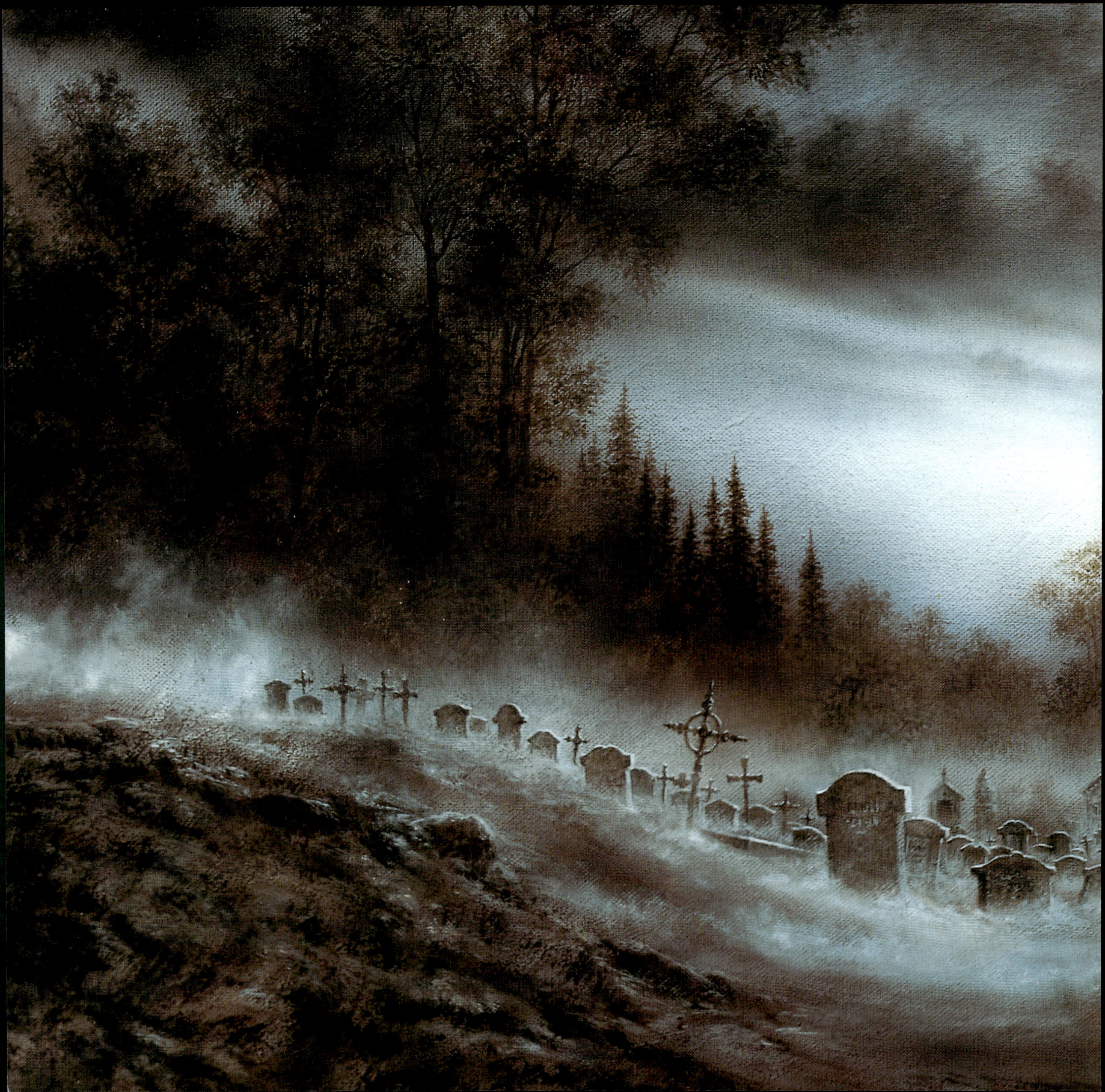

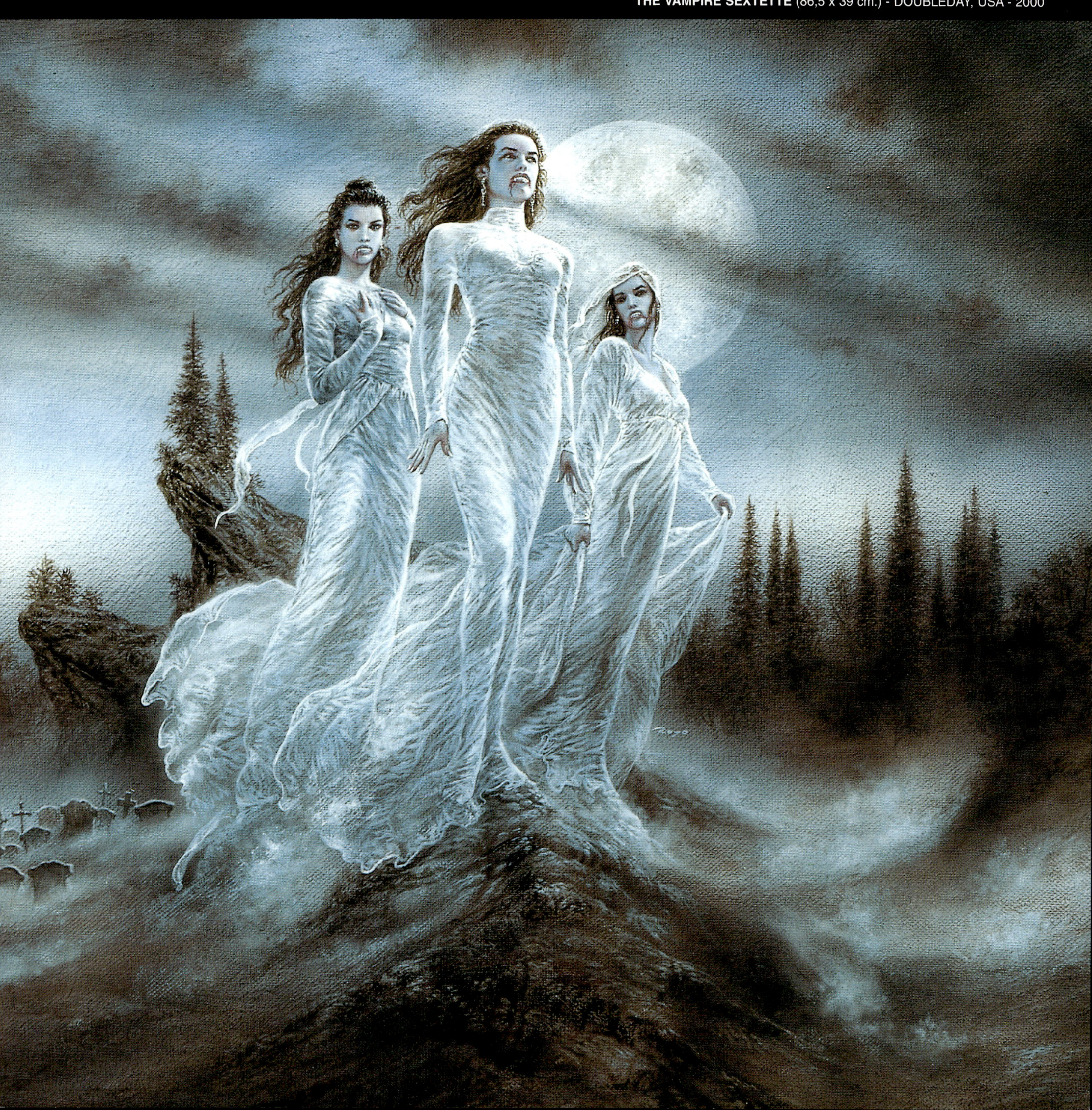

THE VAMPIRE SEXTETTE (86,5 x 39 cm.) - DOUBLEDAY, USA - 2000

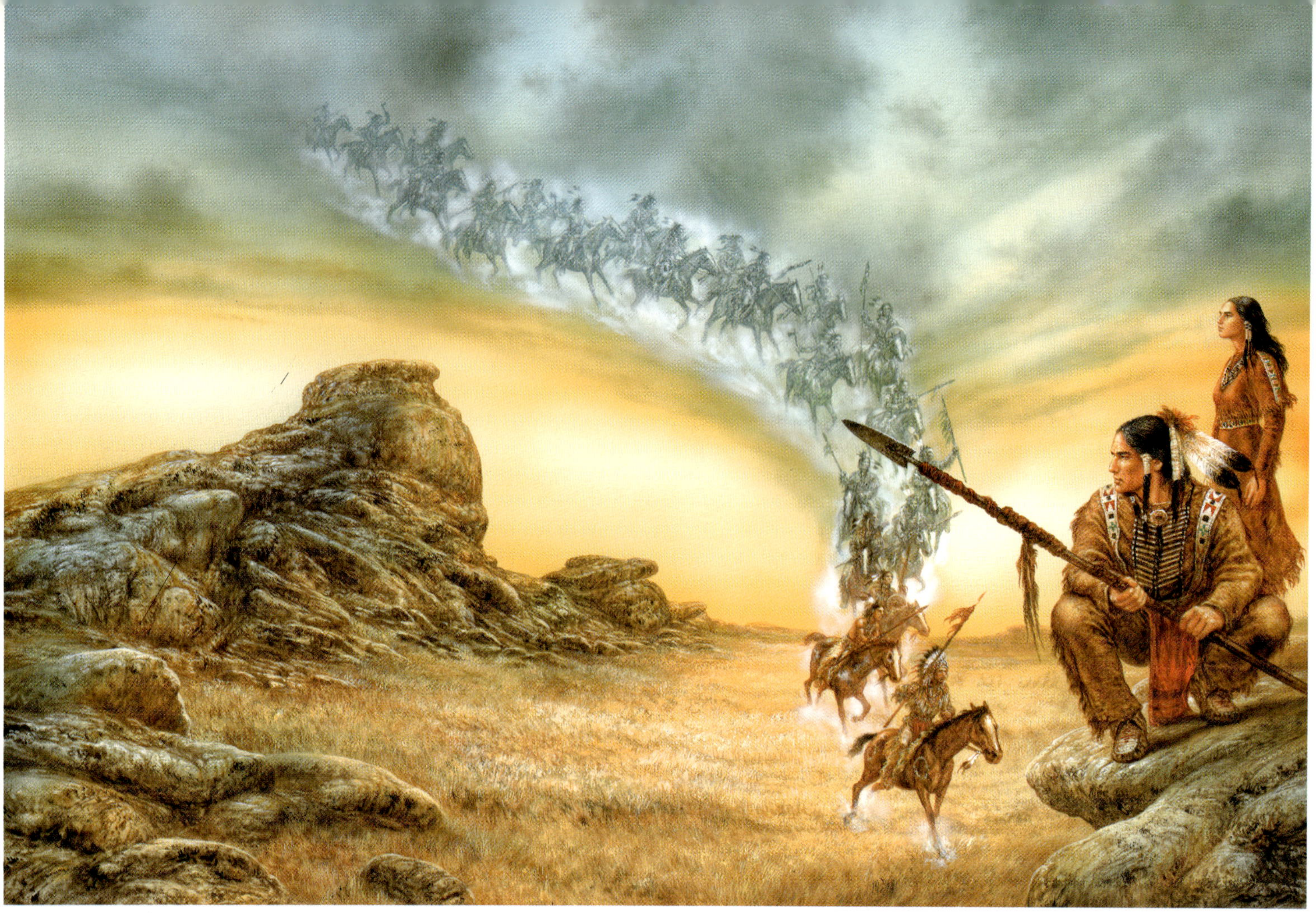

MYSTIC WARRIORS (51 x 36 cm.) - TOR BOOKS, USA - 2000

These pages, like those preceding, are cover images for collections of period stories with distinctive themes or settings.

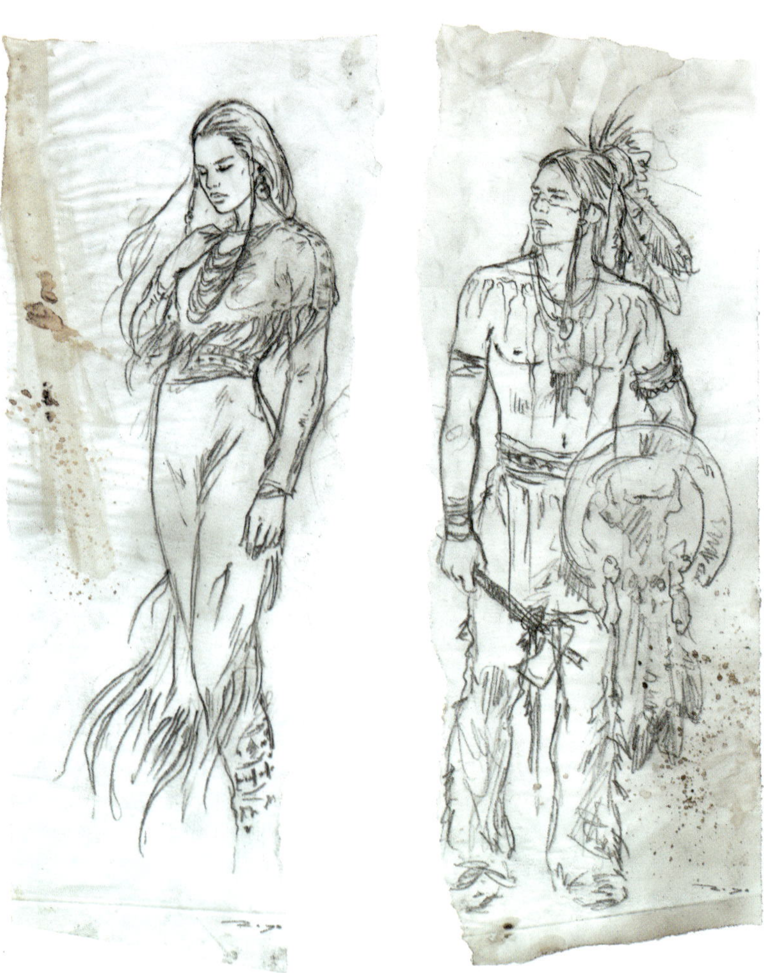

MYSTIC VISIONS (22 x 36 cm.) - TOR BOOKS, USA - 1999 ▶

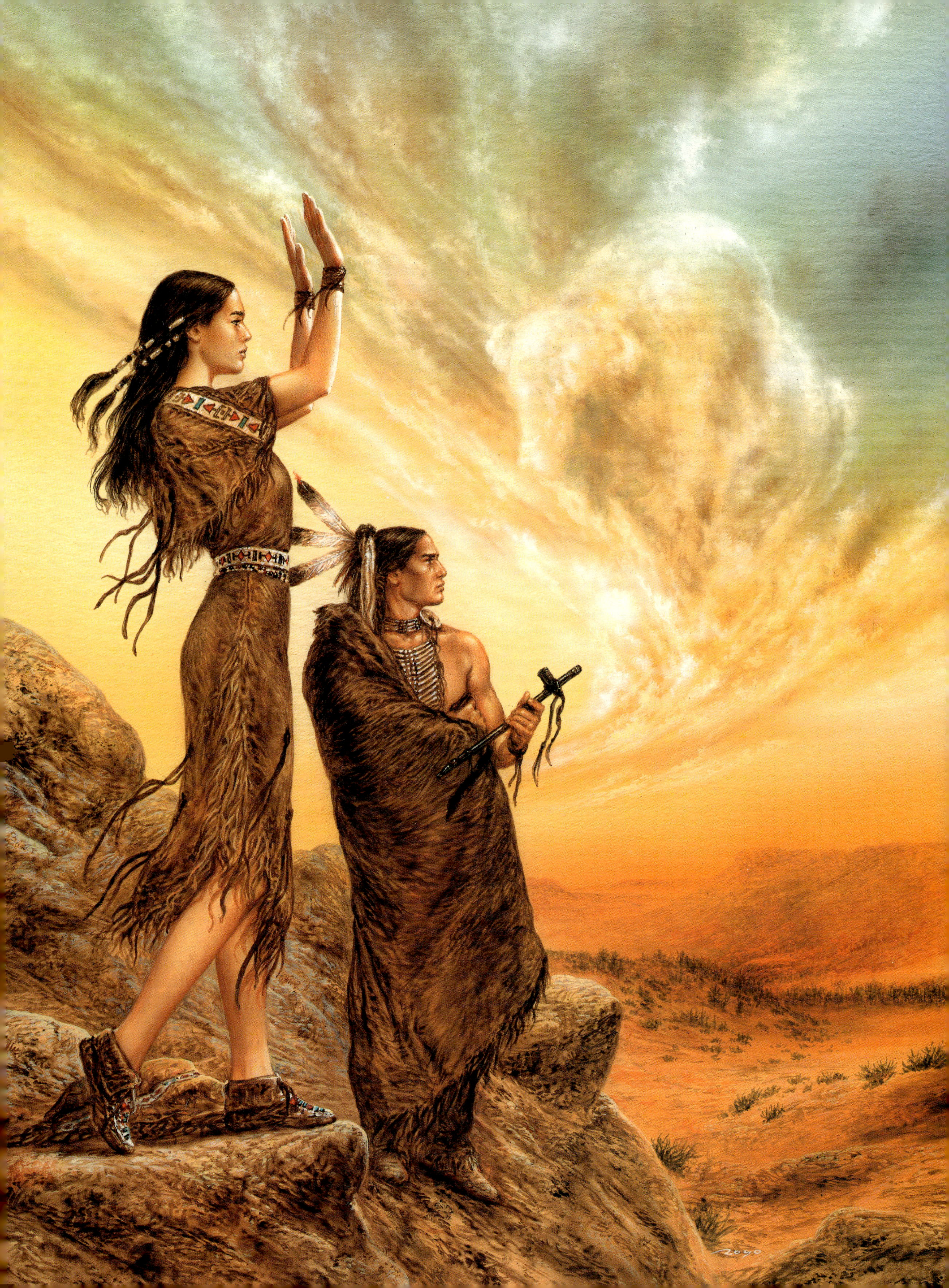

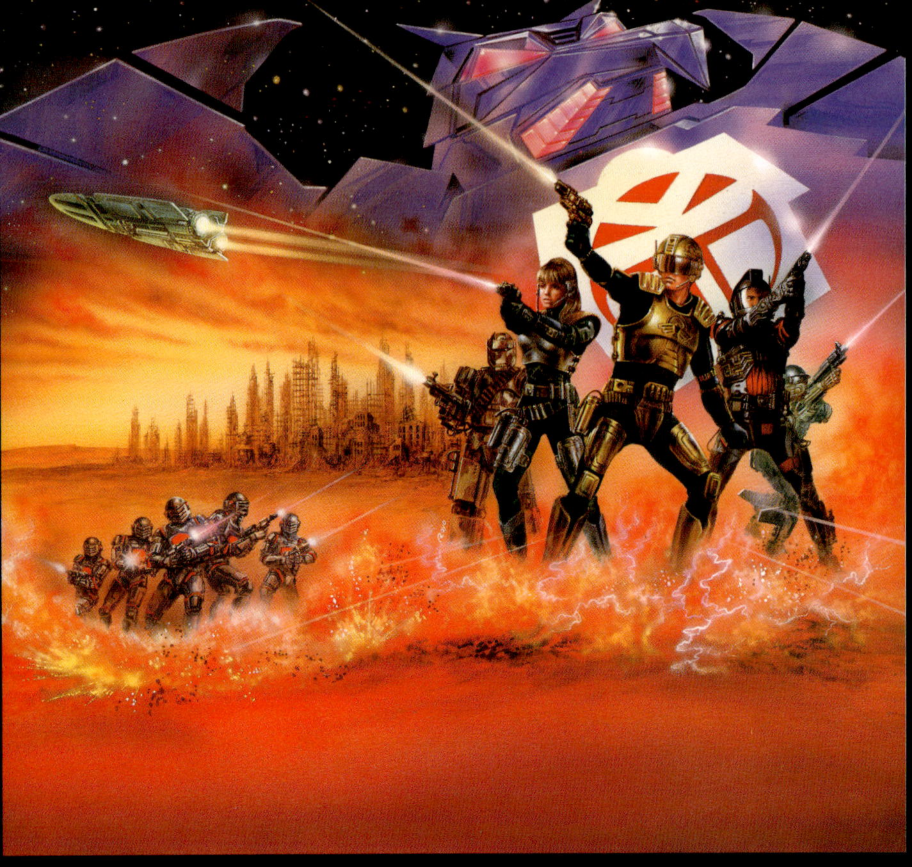

CAPTAIN POWER 2 (46,5 x 33,5 cm.) - 1988

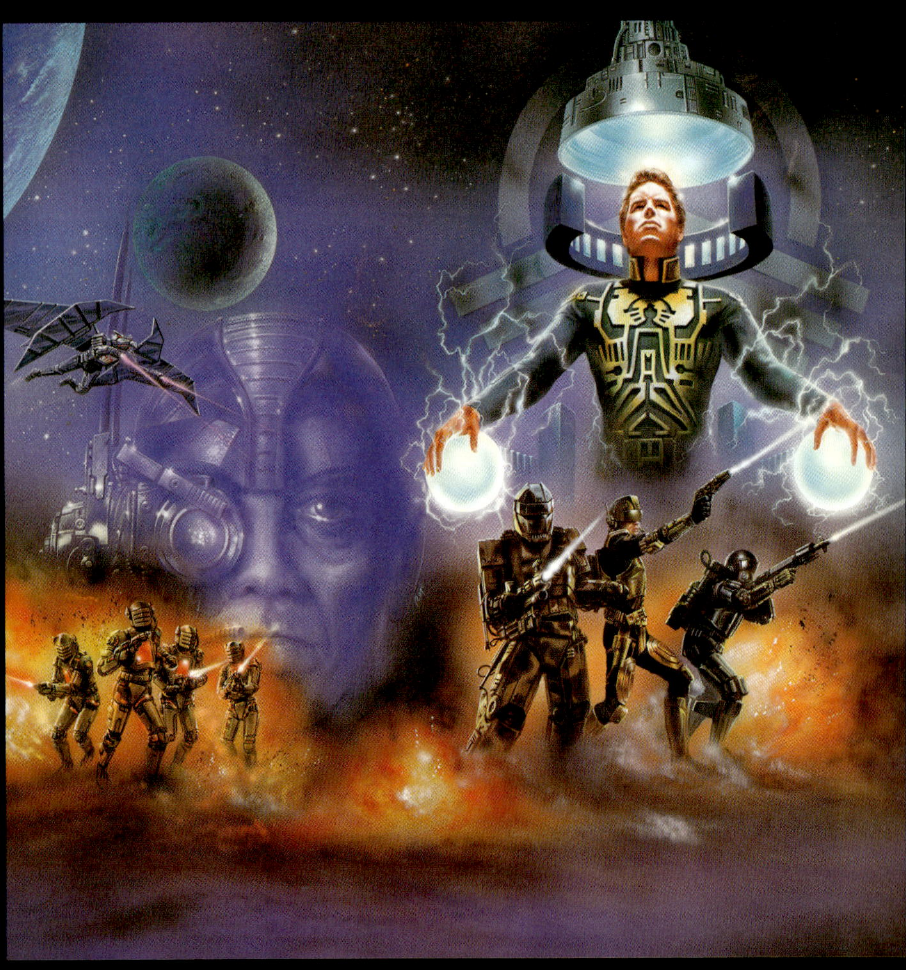

CAPTAIN POWER 1 (58 x 42 cm.) - 1988

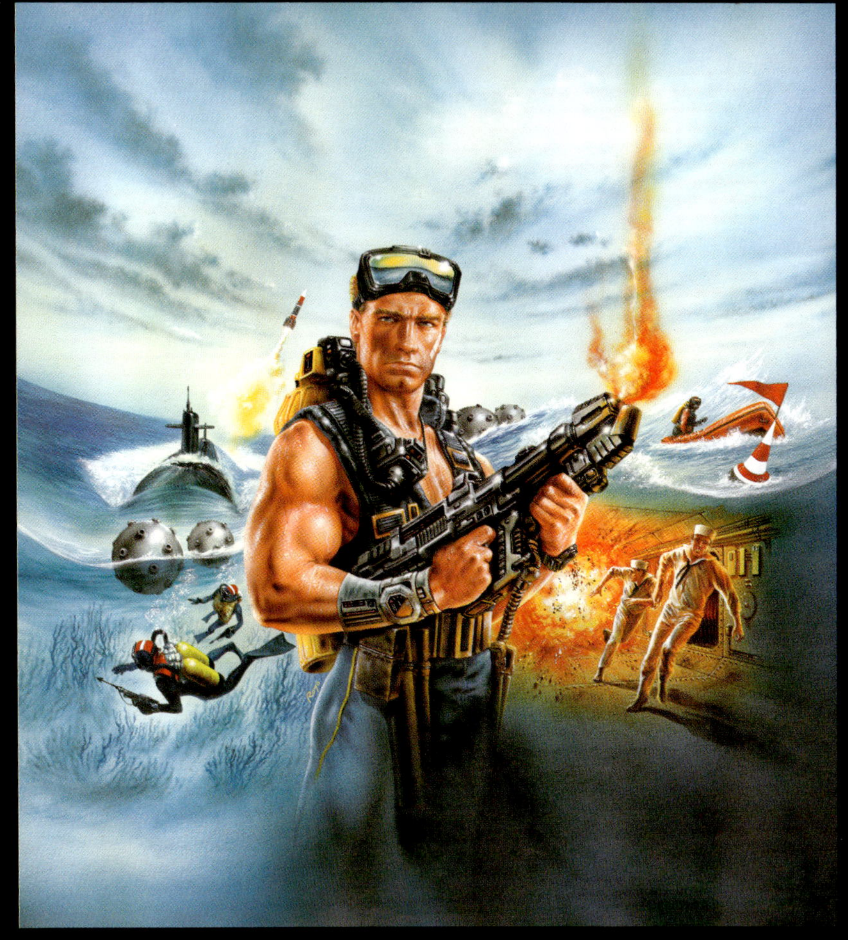

NAVY MOVES (54,5 x 45 cm.) - 1988

SUB WARS (57 x 31,5 cm.) - NEW AMERICAN LIBRARY, USA - 1992

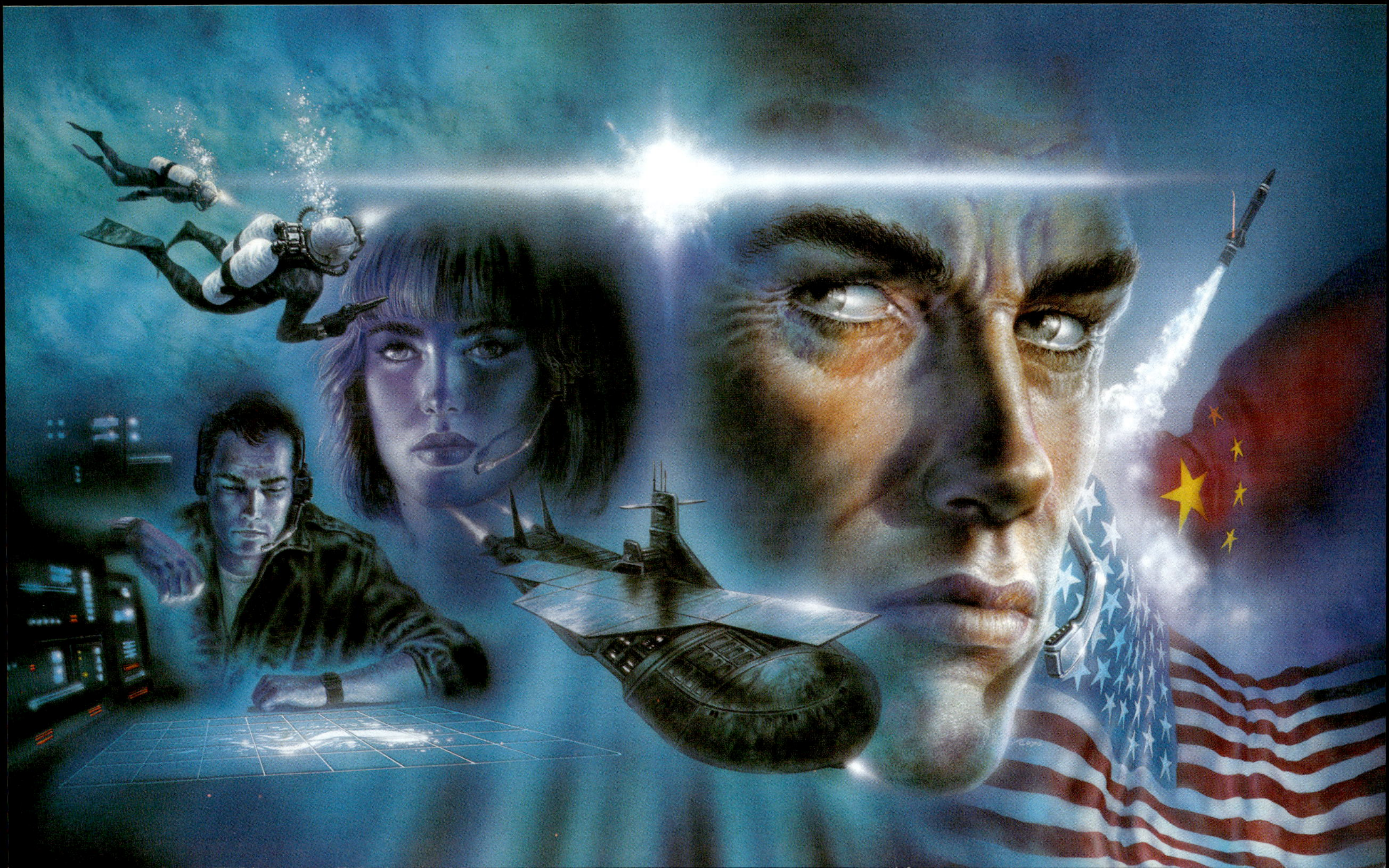

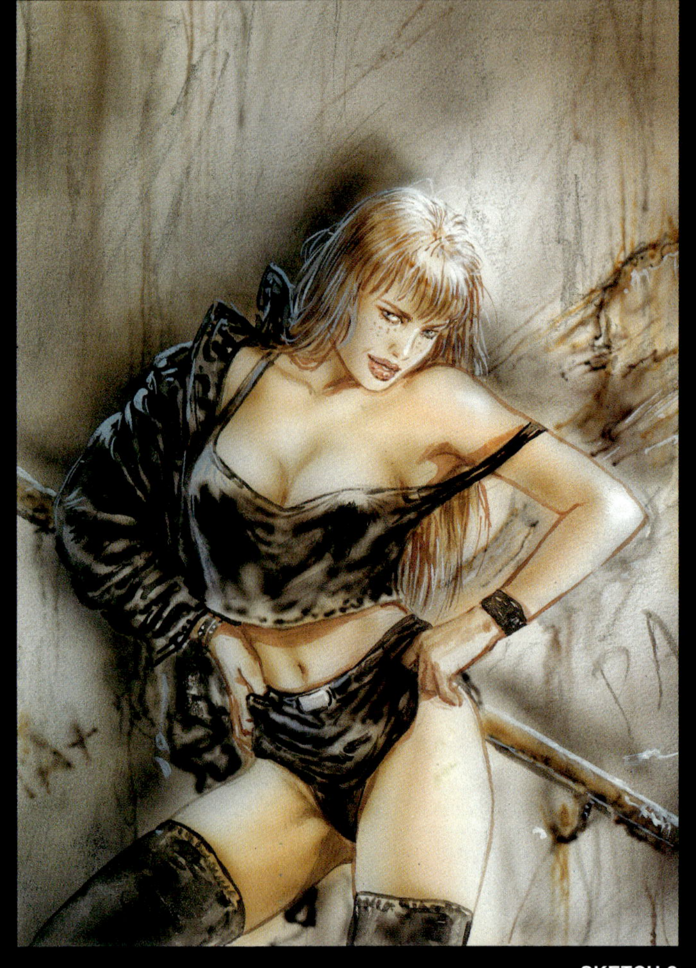

SKETCH 2

Cover of a character created by Horacio Altuna for a special issue of Heavy Metal devoted to his erotic comics

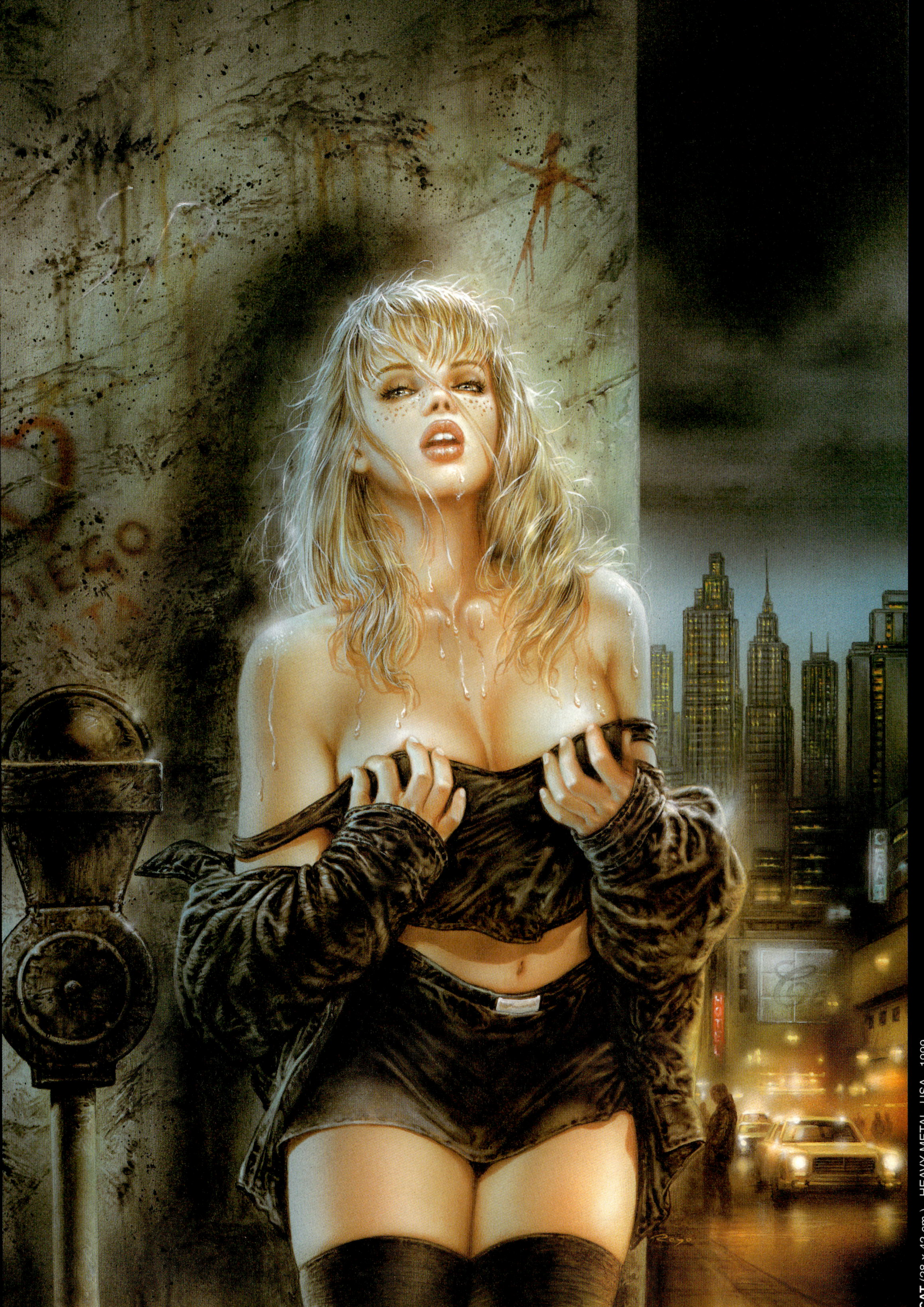

CAT (28 x 42 cm.) - HEAVY METAL, USA - 1999

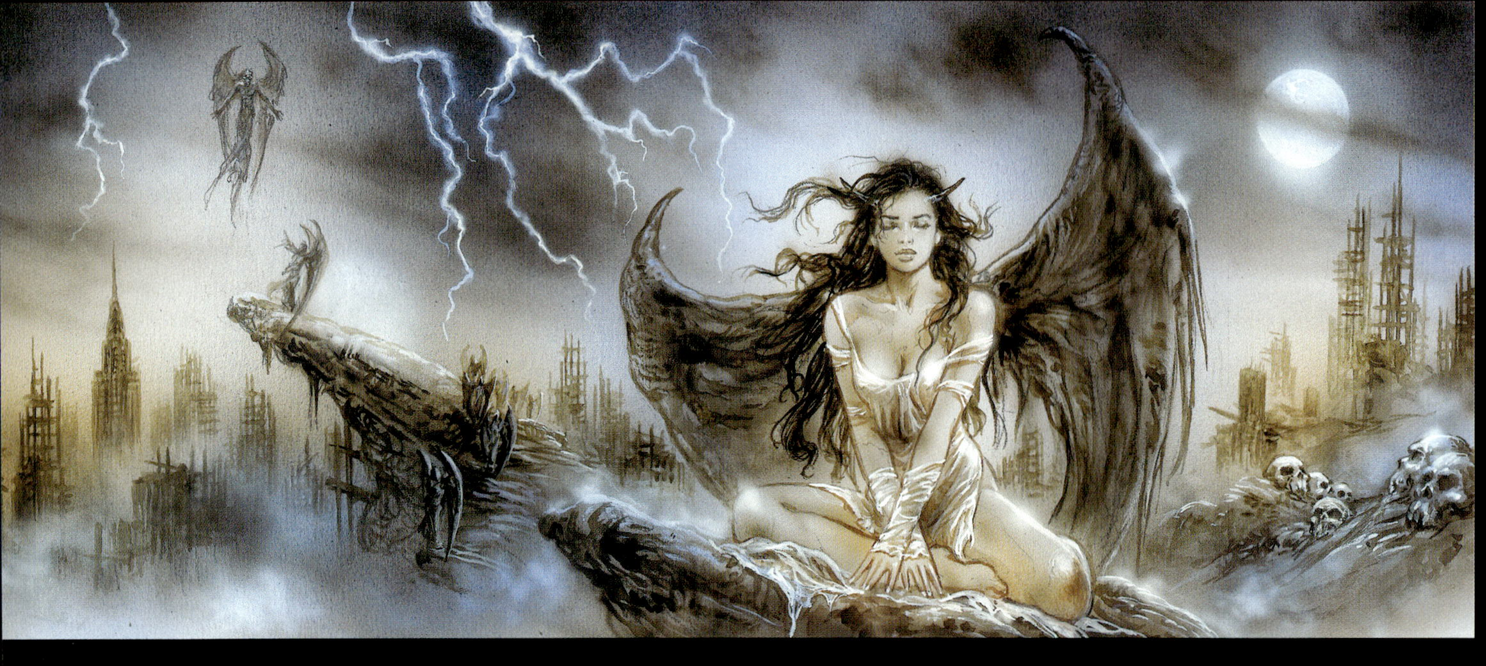

SKETCH 1

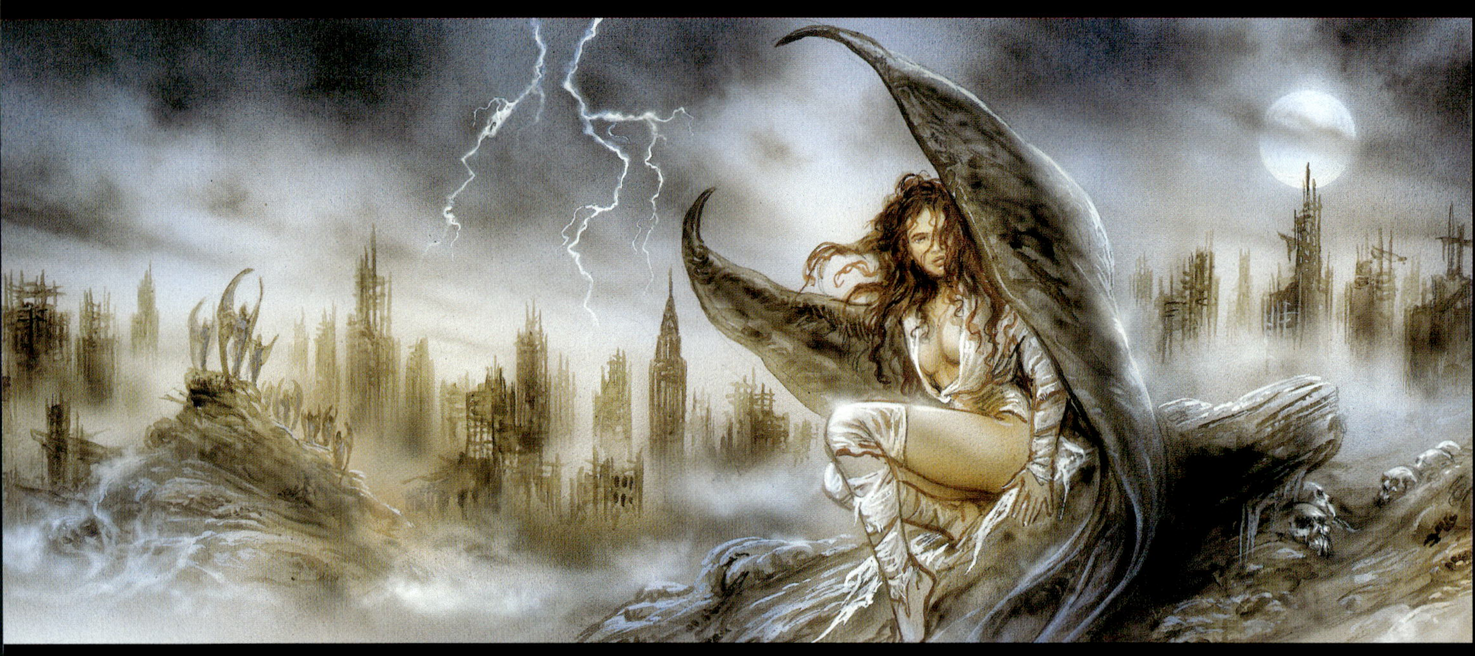

SKETCH 2

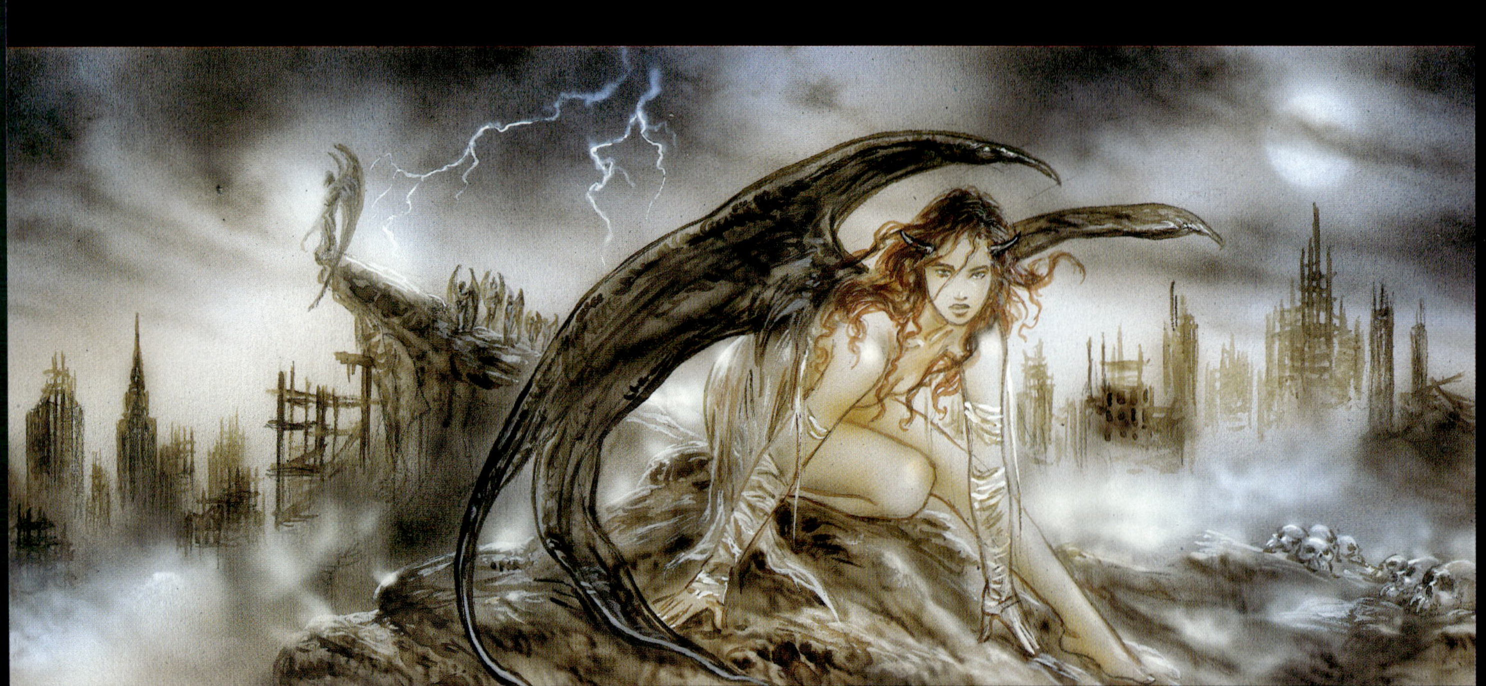

SKETCH 3

BLUE 1084 (36,5 x 51 cm.) - 2000

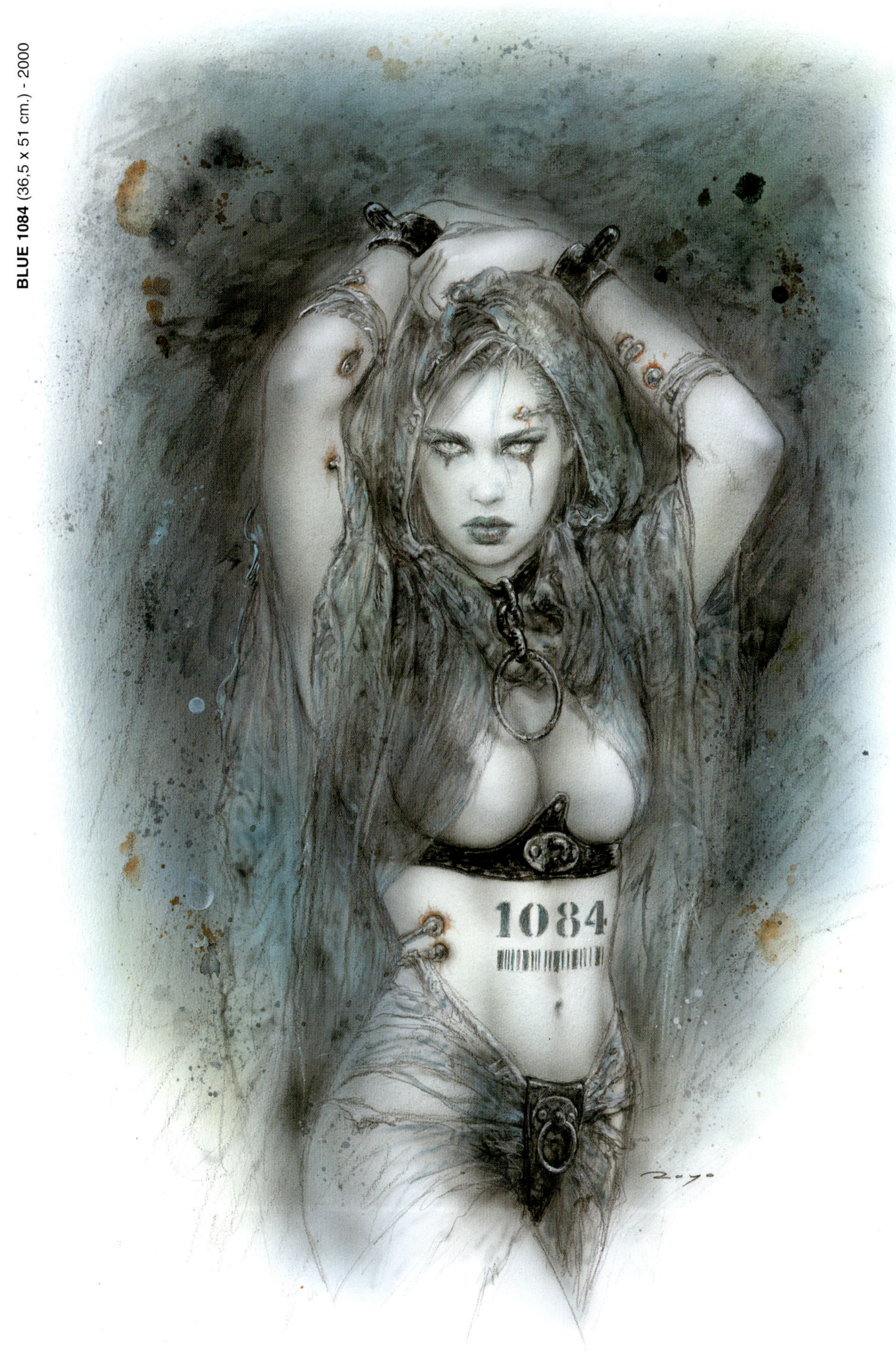

Previous page: sketches for the CD *Fallen Angel* by the heavy metal group Avalanch.

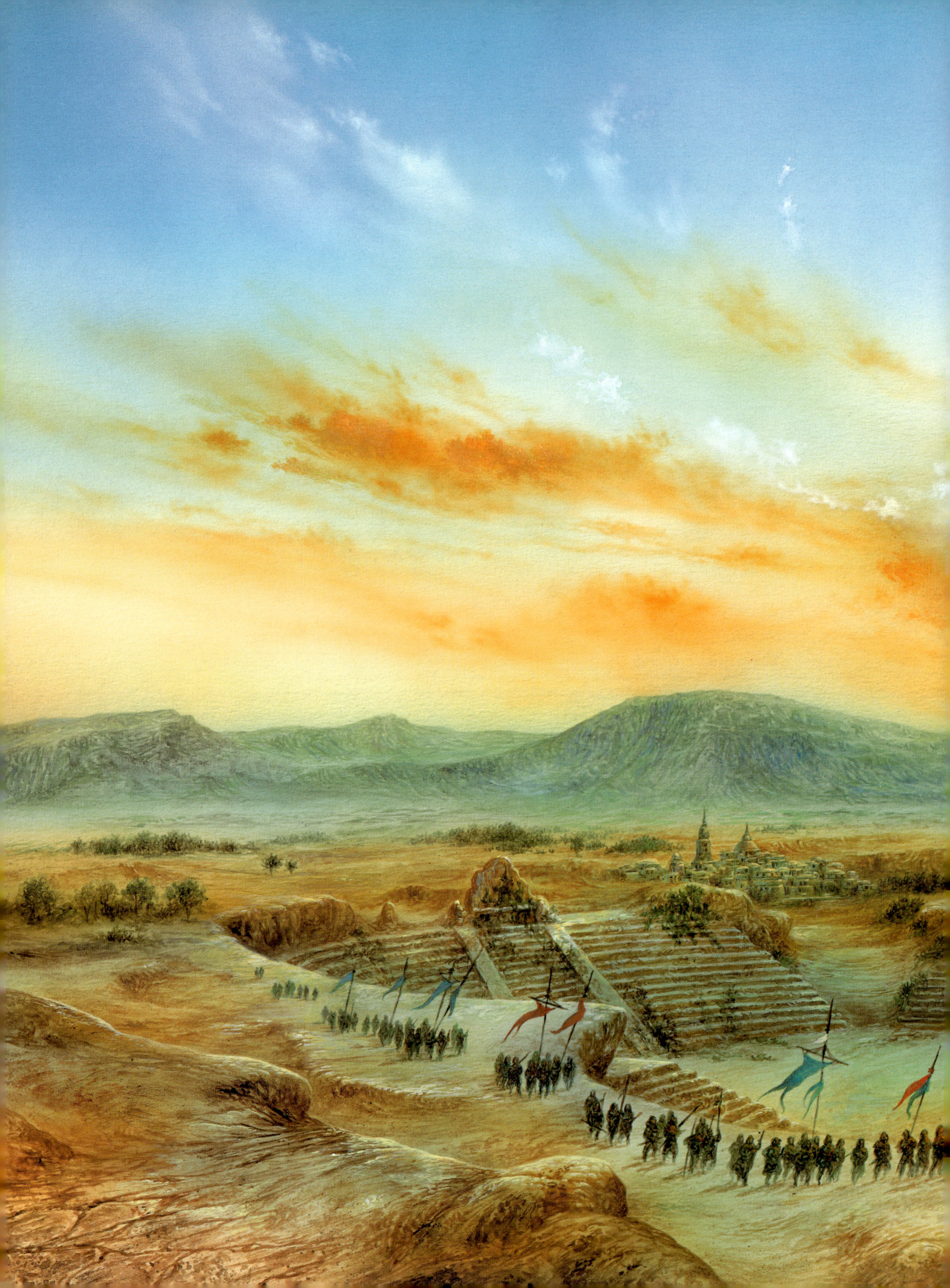

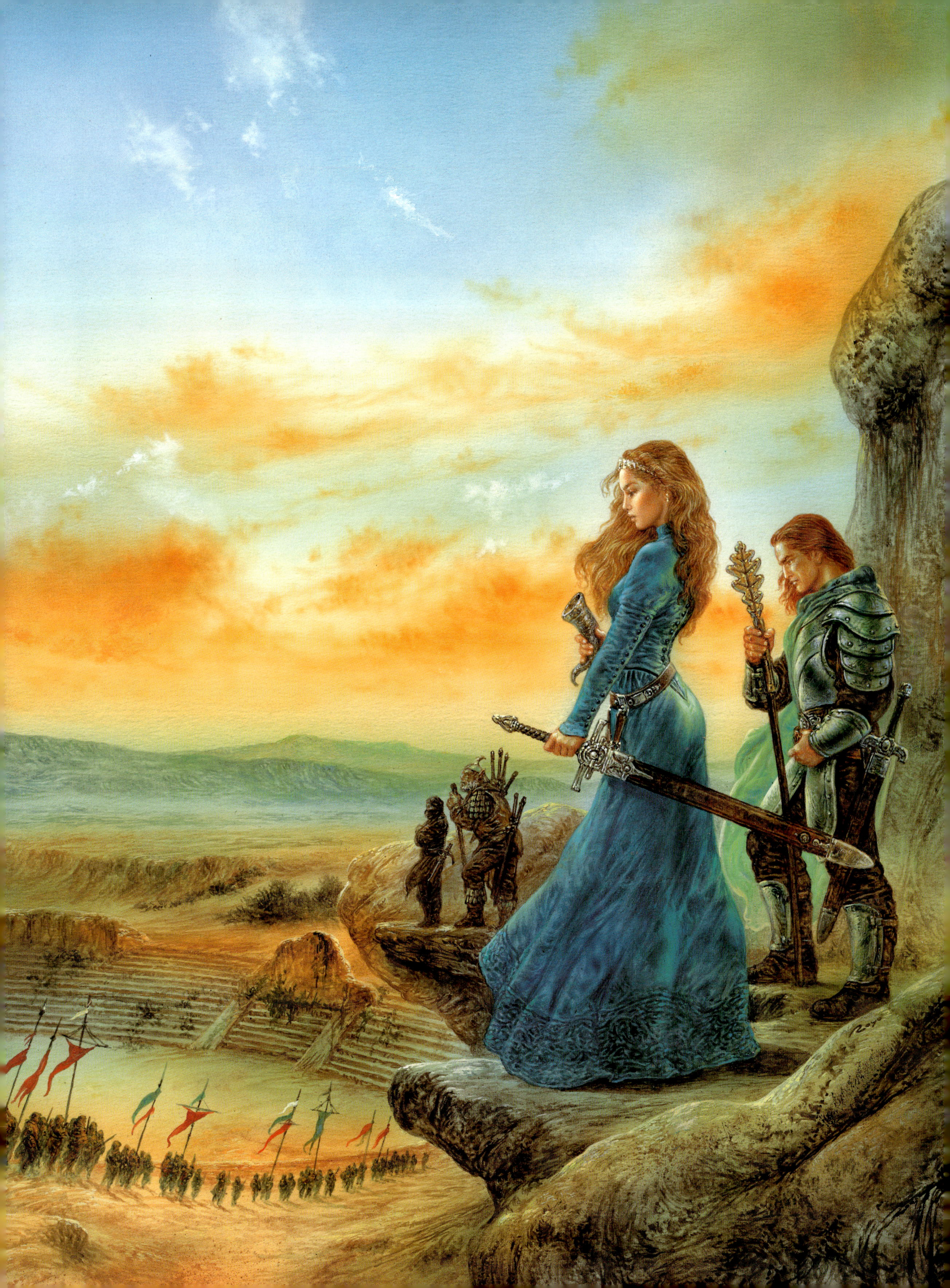

Destiny: Child of the Sky - Tor Books - *Elizabeth Haydon*

The Bowl itself was immense, larger than the gambling complex in Sorbold. What nature had not sculpted into the geologic bowl, the Cymrians had, although so many centuries had passed since it had been used as a gathering place that it was difficult to discern what was the work of natural forces and what was the work of man. A series of rising ledges had been hewn into the earth around the circumference of the Bowl, following the glacier's lines, to allow seating for tens of thousands. Enormous wedges had been cut from some areas of the Bowl's side to allow access and egress from the arena. Though overgrown and forgotten by all but Time, it was the perfect place for a convocation.

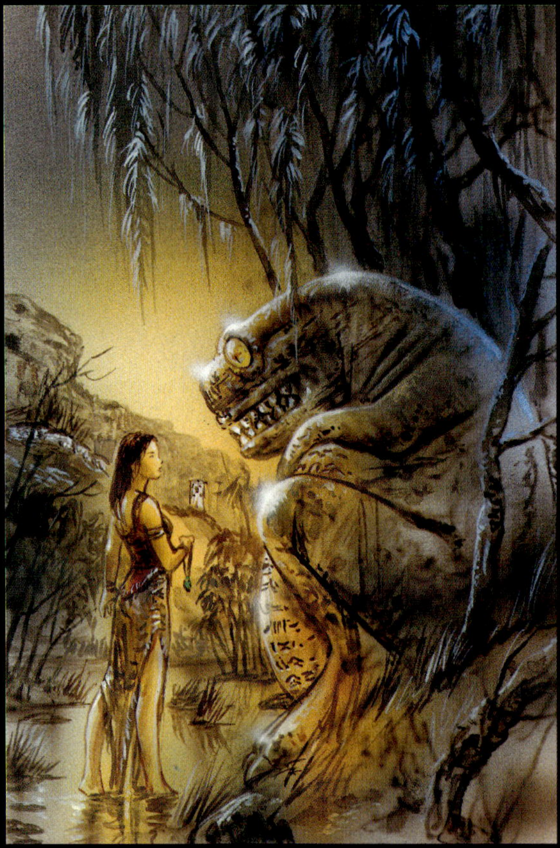

SKETCH 2

To the King, a Daughter - Tor Books - *Andre Norton and Sasha Miller*

The statue is large. It looks like a toad, but without such a wide neck. It's made of a reddish-gray stone, and rests on its powerful hindquarters, supported above a bed of green rushes. Its foreparts rest more or less above its big round belly, the way a pregnant woman would rest her hands on her tummy. On the top of its head, a pair of brilliant eyes, yellow with read pupils, bulge out; they seem to be made of some polished gemstone, but not carved. Beneath its forefeet, its belly is marked with some sort of writing carved in the stone. The marks are mostly lines and dots.

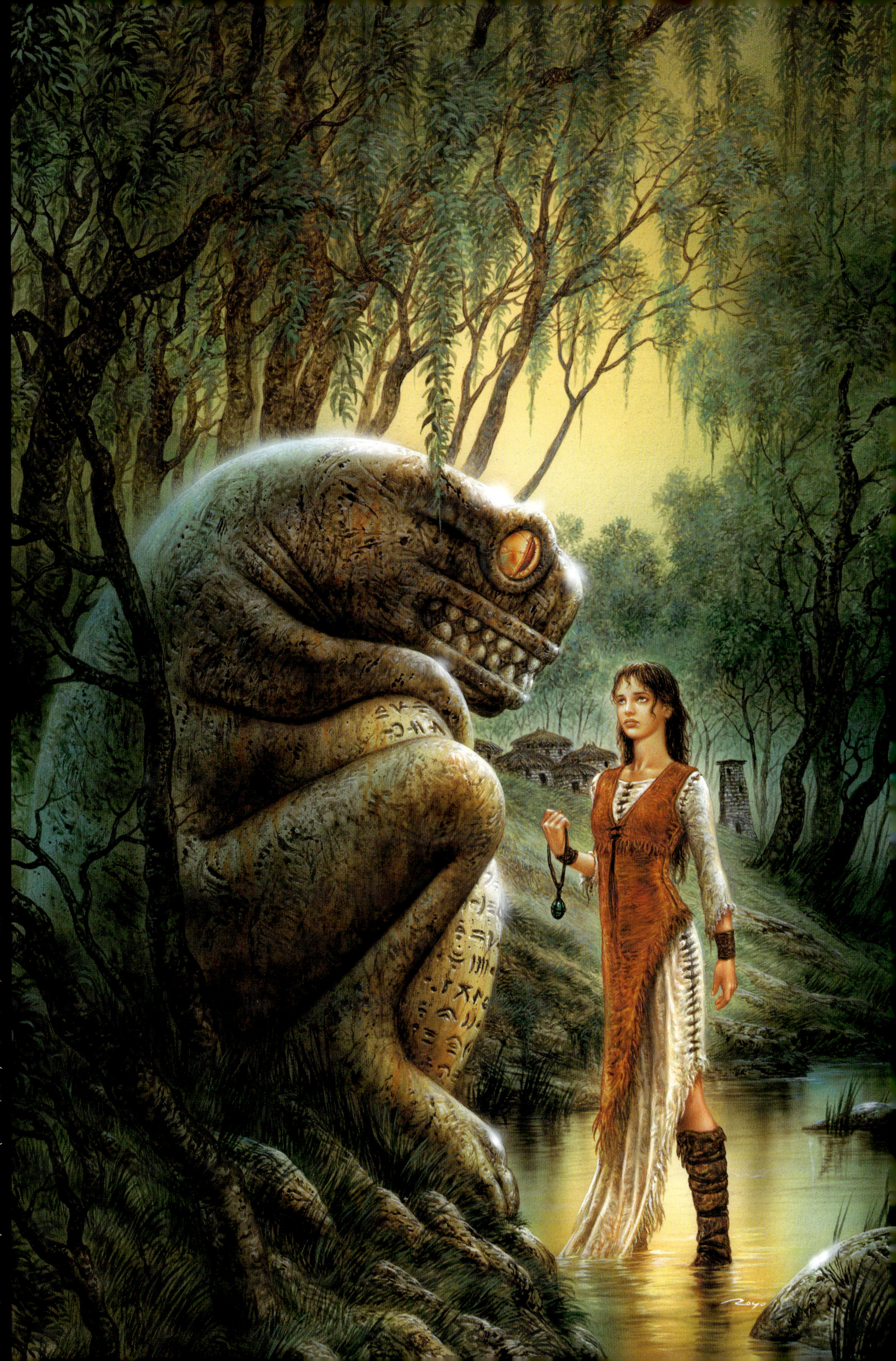
Royo

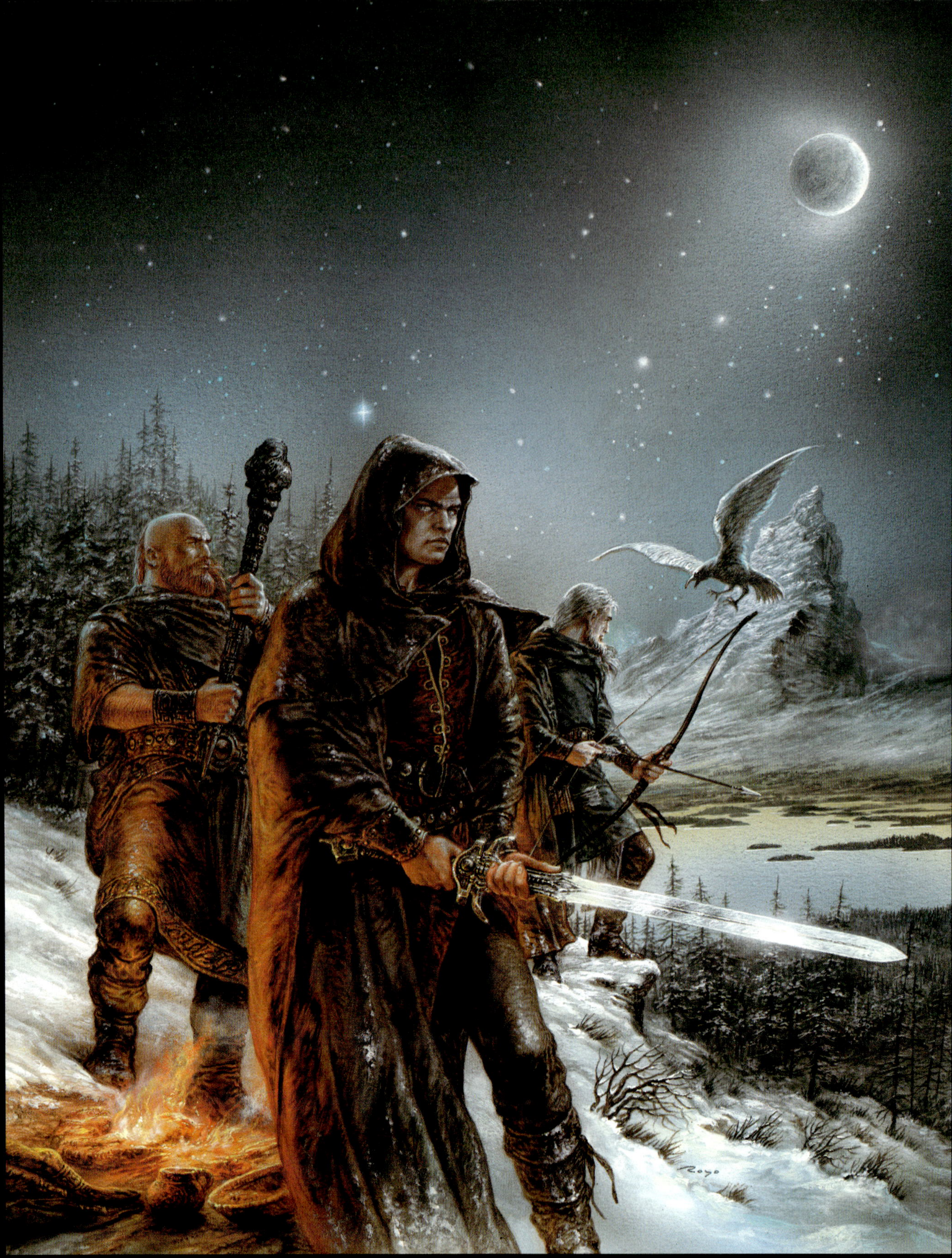

WINTER WARRIORS (30 x 38 cm.) - BALLANTINE BOOKS, USA - 1999

Winter Warriors - Ballantine Books - ***David Gemmell***

The night sky above the mountains was clear and bright, the stars shone like diamonds above a sable skin. It was a cold winter night of terrible beauty, and the snow was accumulating on the branches of pines and cedars. There was no color nor any sensation of life. The earth remained in silence, except for the occasional sound of falling snow, pushed by the north wind.

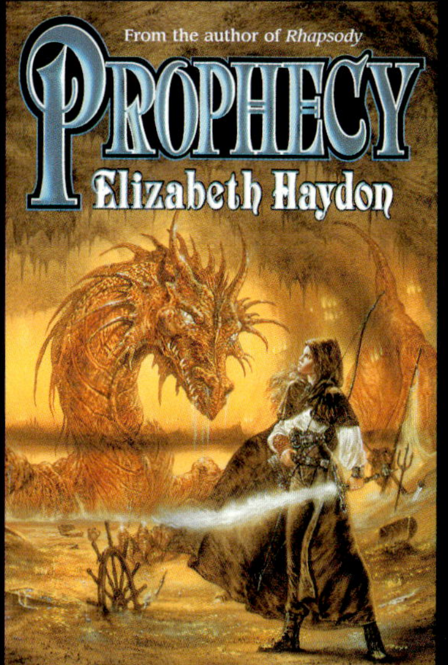

Prophecy - Tor Books - *Elizabeth Hayden*

In the center of the cave was a lagoon of salt water, complete with waves that rolled gently to the muddy edges. Rhapsody walked down to the water's edge and bent to touch the sand. When she looked at her fingers she saw that it was laced with traces of gold.

She looked into the lagoon at the rocks that held more treasures: a golden statue of a mermaid with eyes fashioned from emeralds and a tail that was made from individually carved scales of polished jade, intricately woven caps of merrow pearls, a tall bronze trident with a broken point. A secluded spot in the sand held scores of globes, the orb-shaped maps Llauron had shown her, charts and nautical renderings, as well as sea instruments- compasses, spyglasses and sextants, pulleys and tillers, and chests full of ships' logs. It was a veritable maritime museum.

PROPHECY (49 x 34 cm.) - TOR BOOKS, USA - 1999

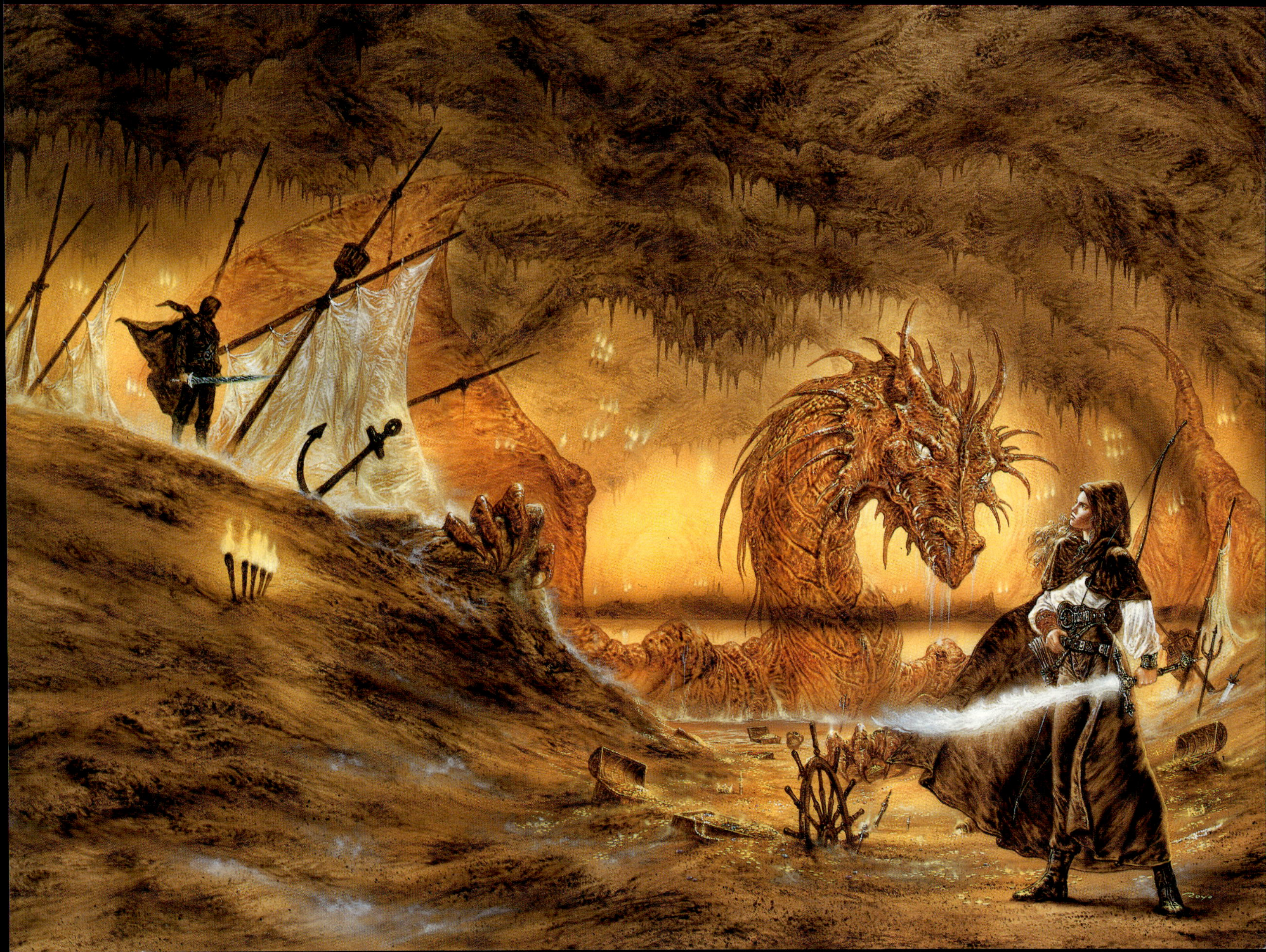

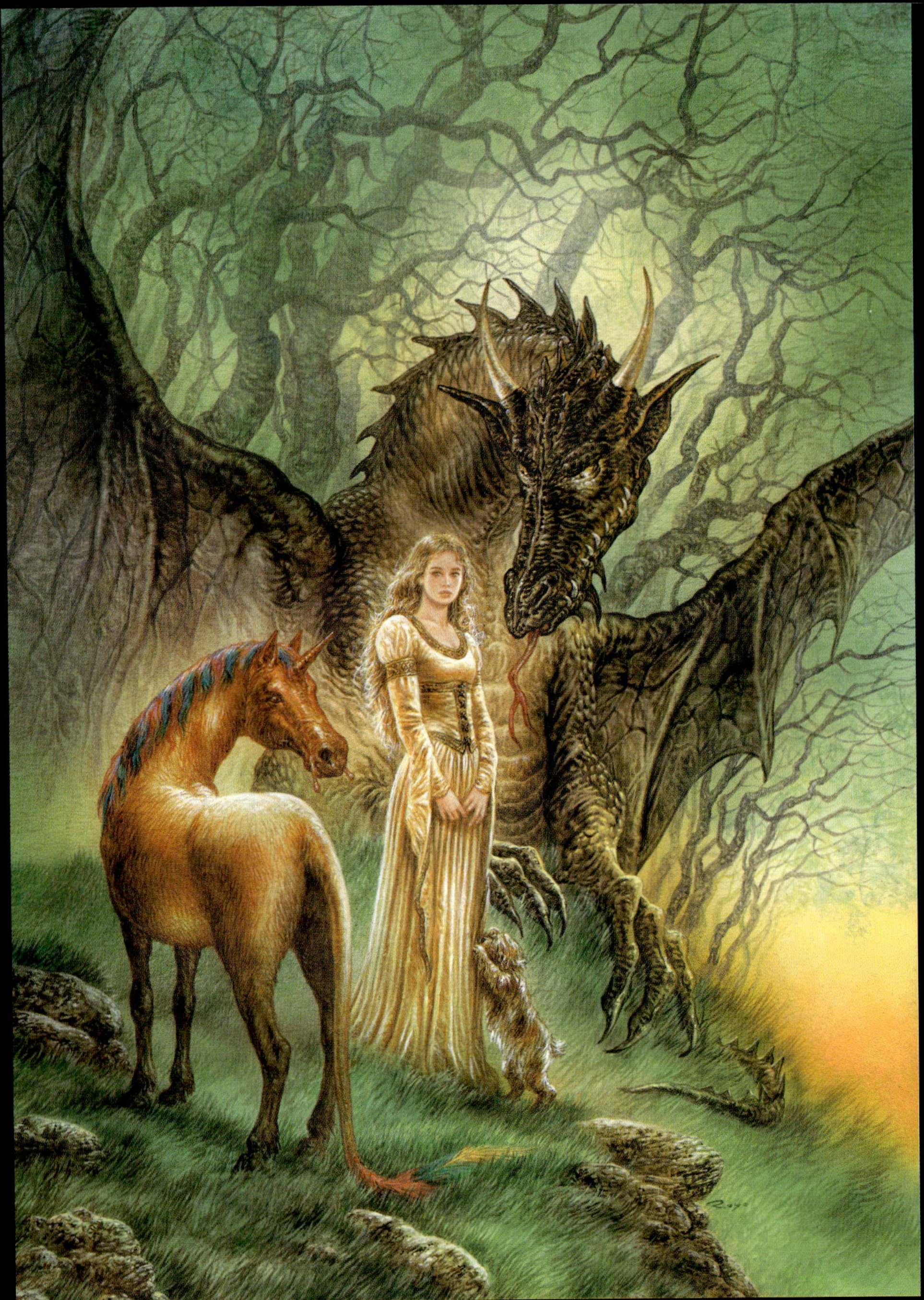

MARY BROWN'S SAGA (24 x 38 cm.) - DAW BOOKS, USA - 1999

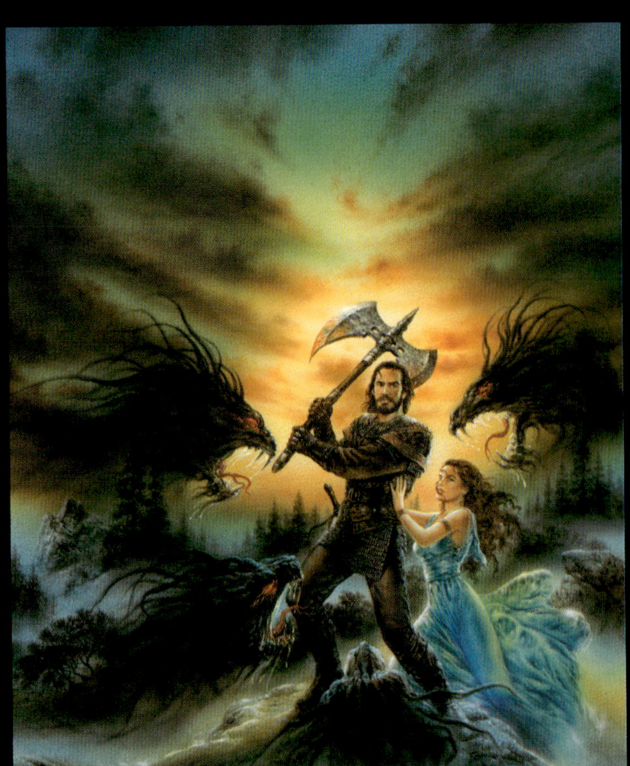

DRUSS THE LEGEND (54 x 39 cm.)
BALLANTINE BOOKS, USA - 1998

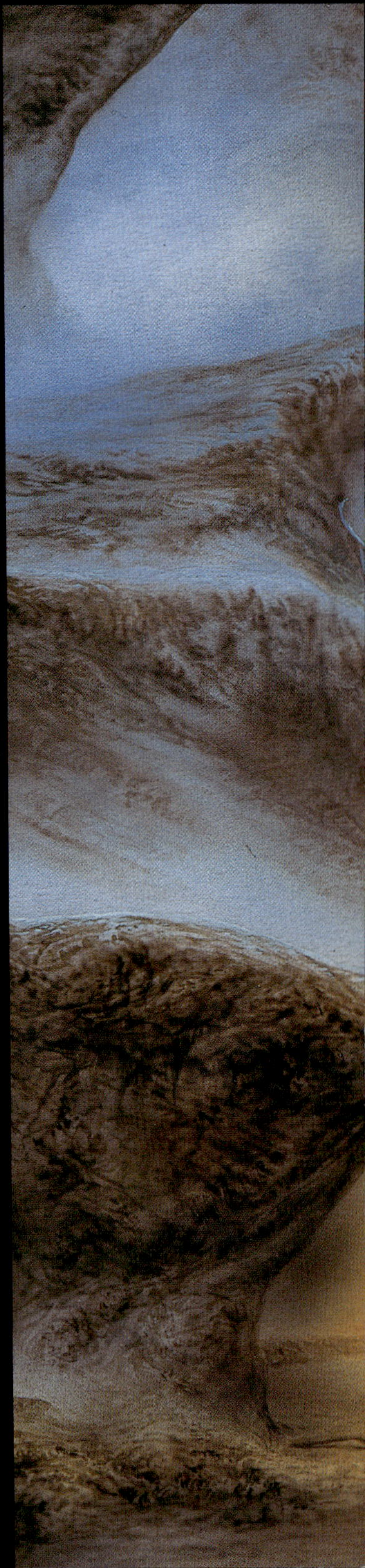

THE WIZARD'S TREASURE: DRAGON NIMBUS 4 (47,4 x 35 cm.) - DAW BOOKS, USA - 2000

The Wizard's Treasure: Dragon Nimbus 4 - Daw Books - *Irene Radford*

Snarling, with her snout and tail at floor level, Amaranta dragged herself to the center of the circle. She paused three times to look Jack in the eye, and then she crouched down next to the queen.

"Touch the baby dragon, your majesty. You will need him as a conduit for the cat to leave your body."

The queen placed her left hand on Amaranta's head, behind the horn, and softly brushed her ears. The dragon began to make a sound like a cat purring.

"Amatista, here, next to me."

The other purple dragon hid behind her mother.

"Shayla." Jack looked at the mother dragon. "If Amaranta becomes the nexus of the spell, I can't draw magic from her. I can only draw magic from a purple dragon; I'm different from my comrades. I need the additional power that a dragon's magic gives me in order to make it work. Solitary magic is not enough."

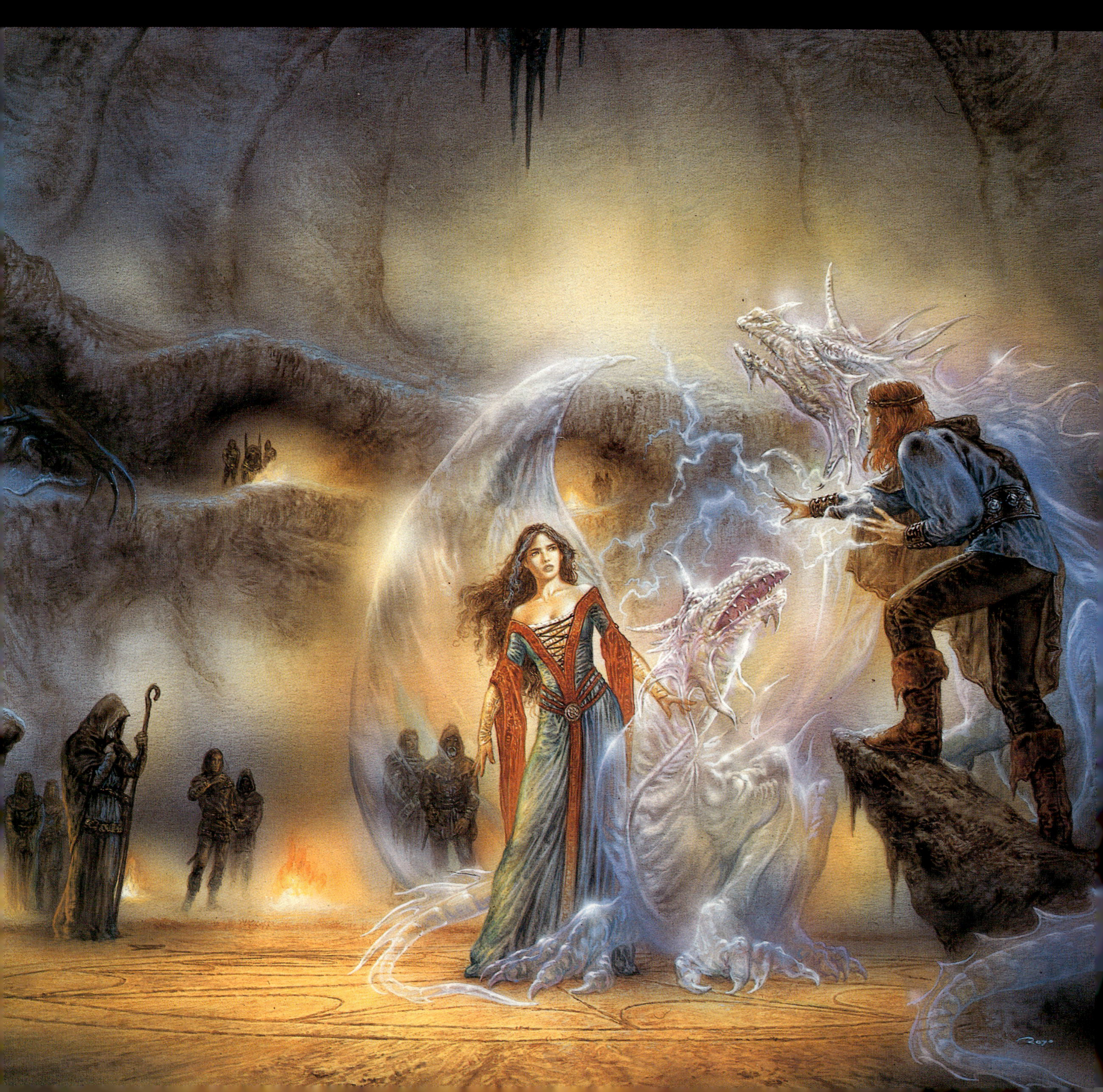

The Hallowed Isle - Doubleday Direct - ***Diana L. Paxson***

This collects a series of four novels in one volume.

They follow the career of King Arthur through the sacred places of England. They take place around the year 425 A.D., when England was plunged into chaos. The Romans had abandoned their colony, and Irish bands were making numerous raids all along the coast.

Book One, *The Book of the Sword*
Book Two, *The Book of the Spear*
Book Three, *The Book of the Cauldron*
Book Four, *The Book of the Stone*

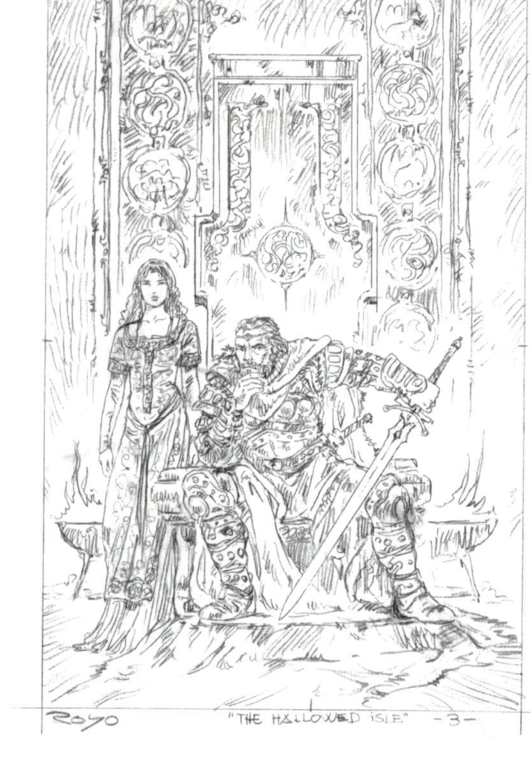

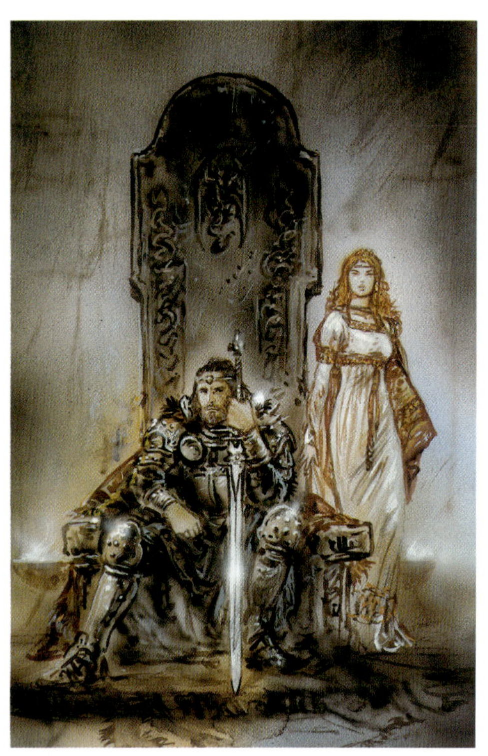

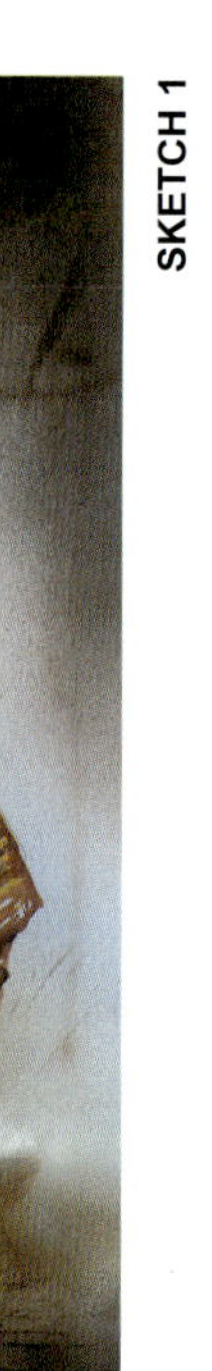

SKETCH 1

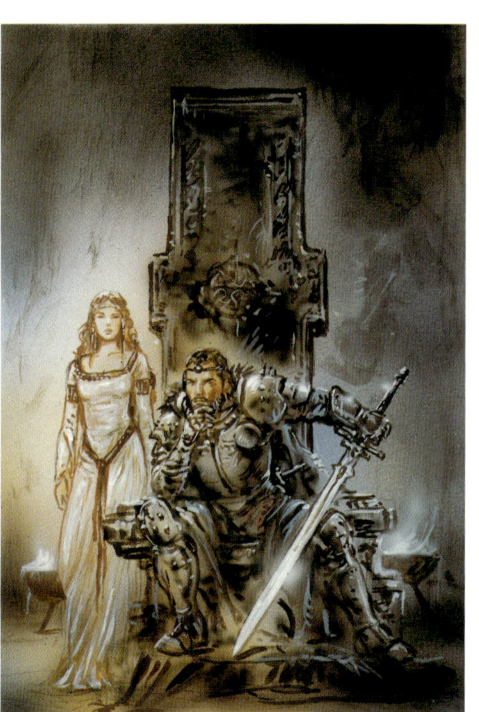

SKETCH 2

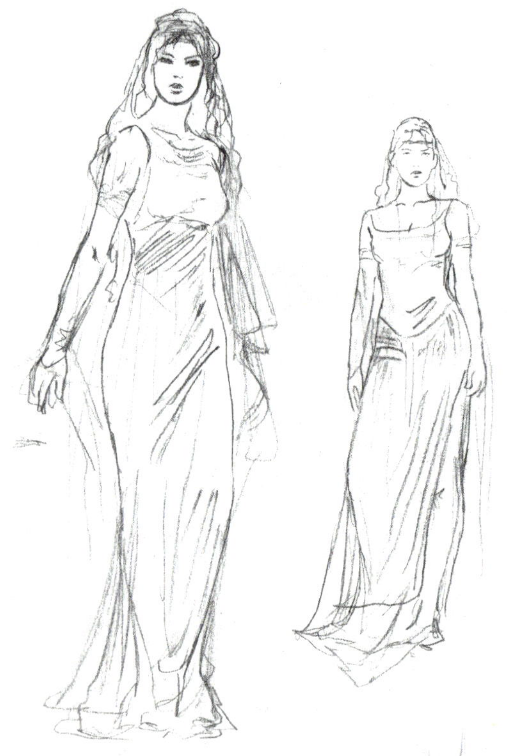

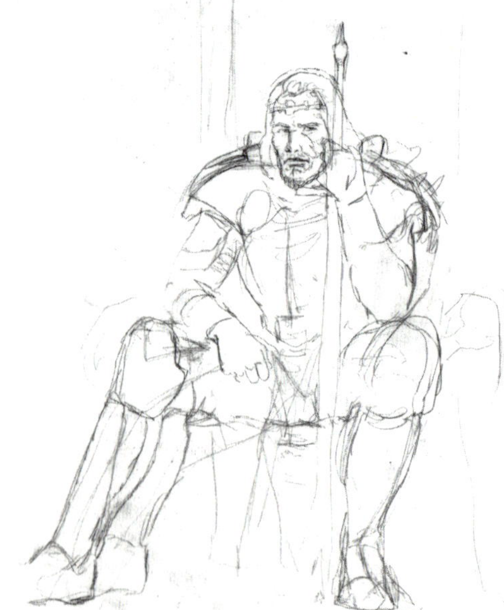

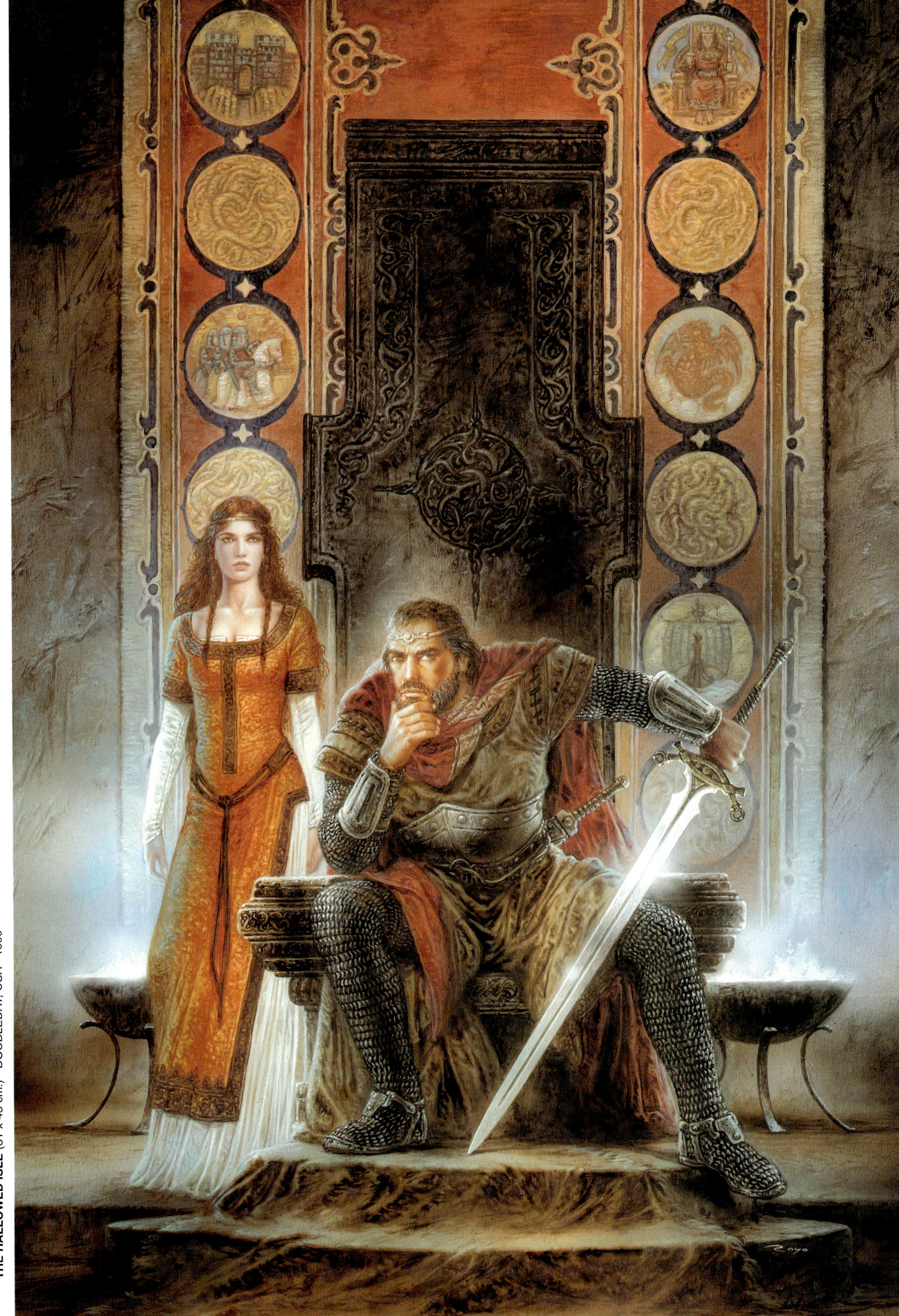

THE HALLOWED ISLE (31 x 45 cm.) - DOUBLEDAY, USA - 1999

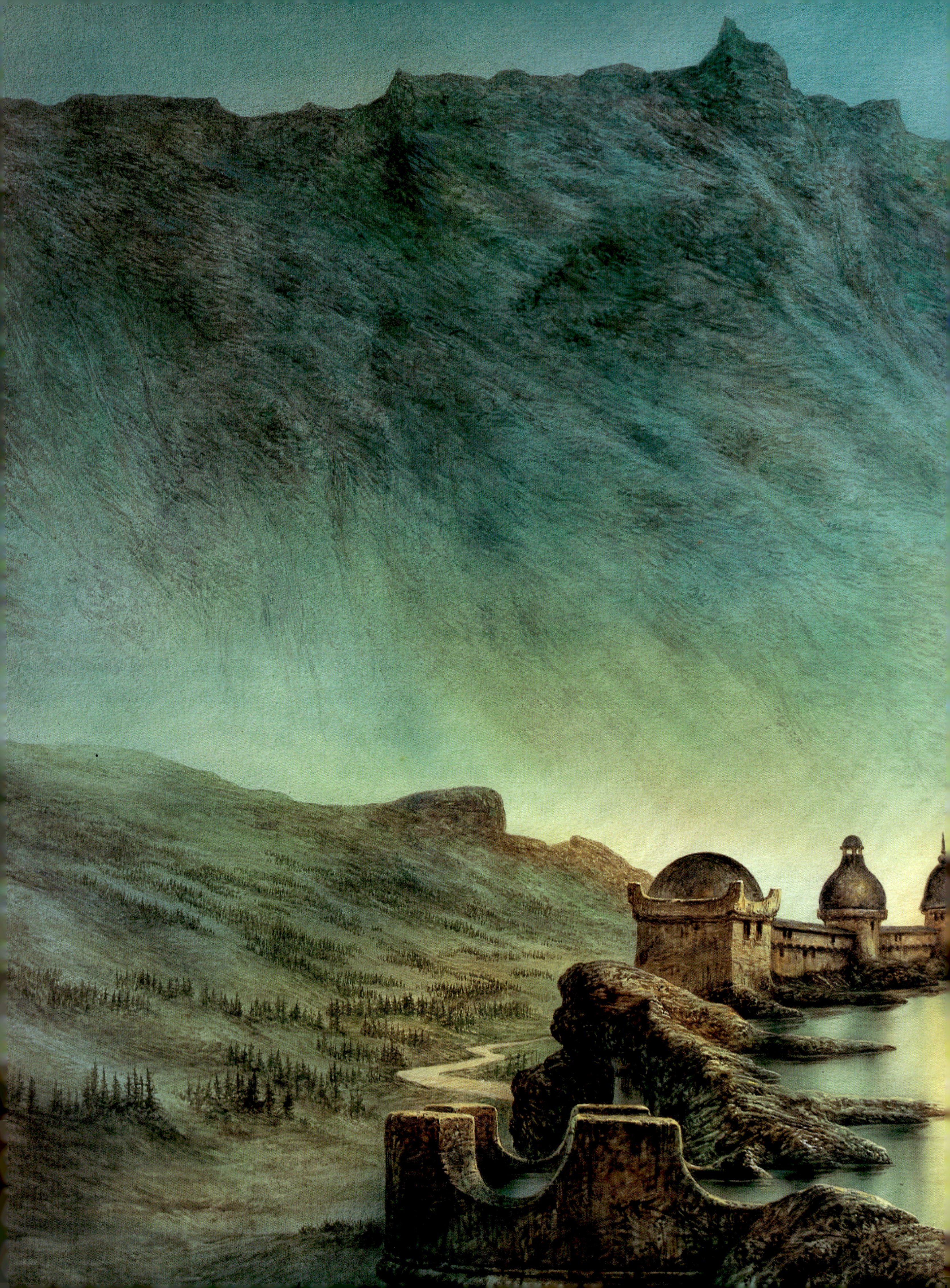

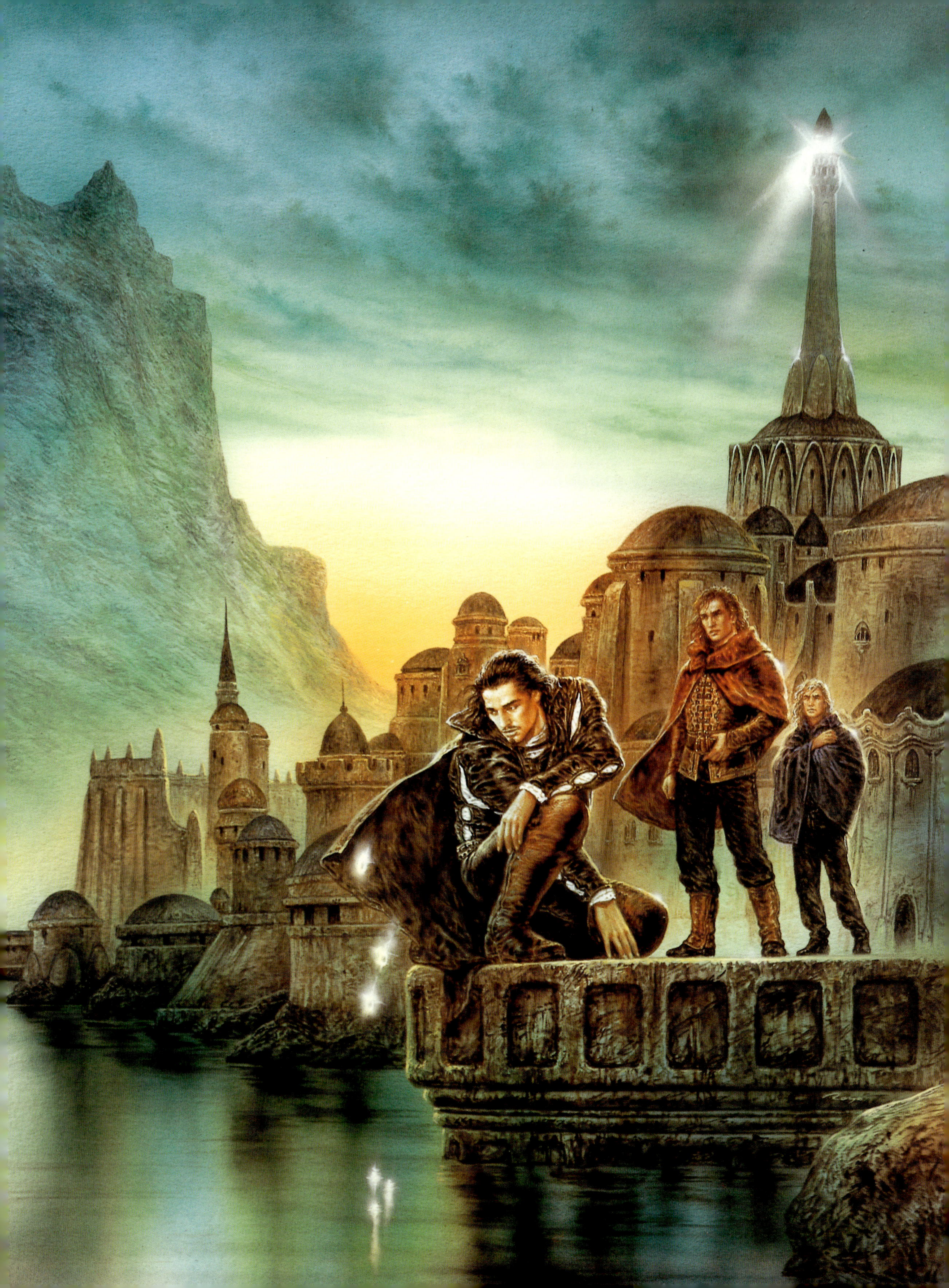

◀ **RING OF DESTINY** (51,5 x 34 cm.) - DAW BOOKS, USA - 1999

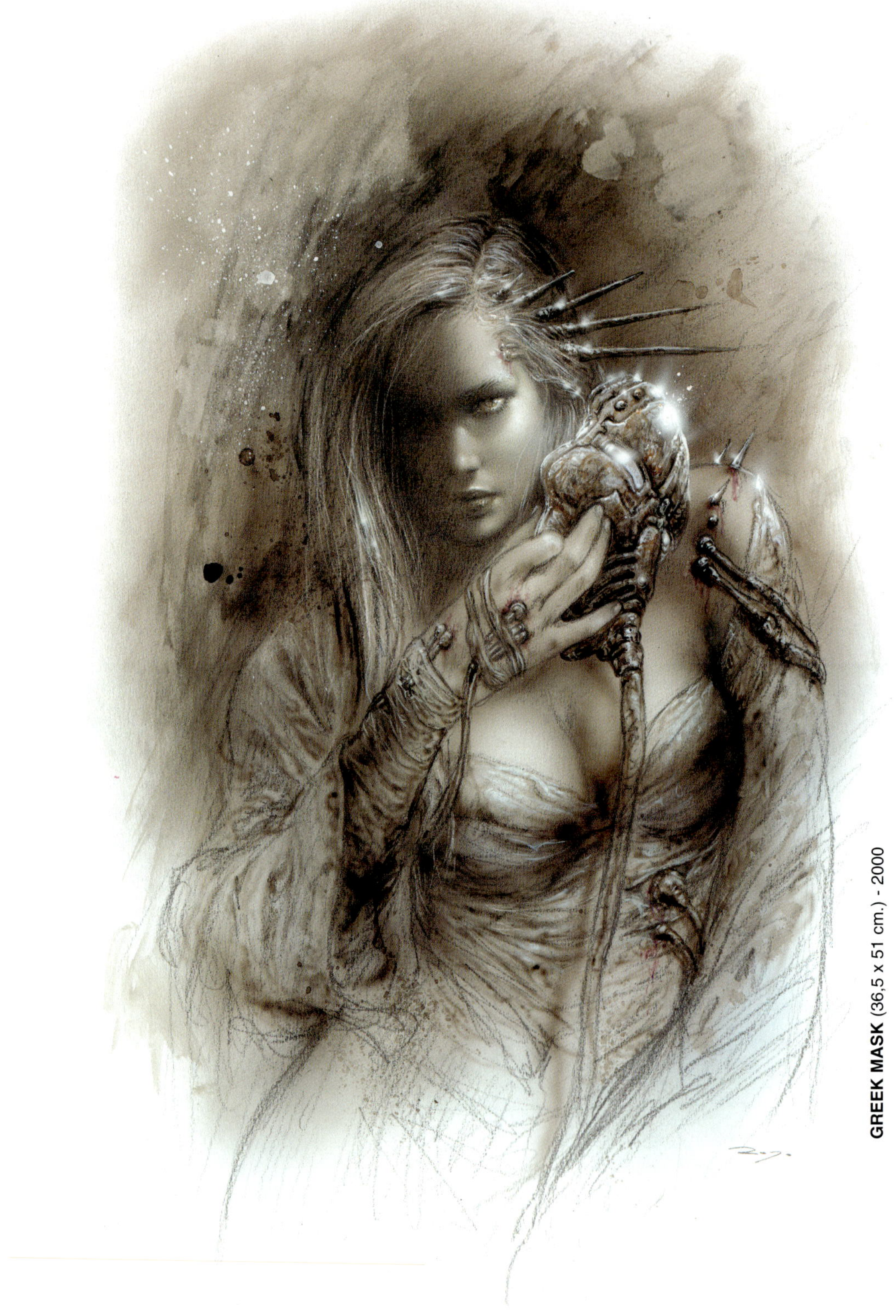

GREEK MASK (36,5 x 51 cm.) - 2000

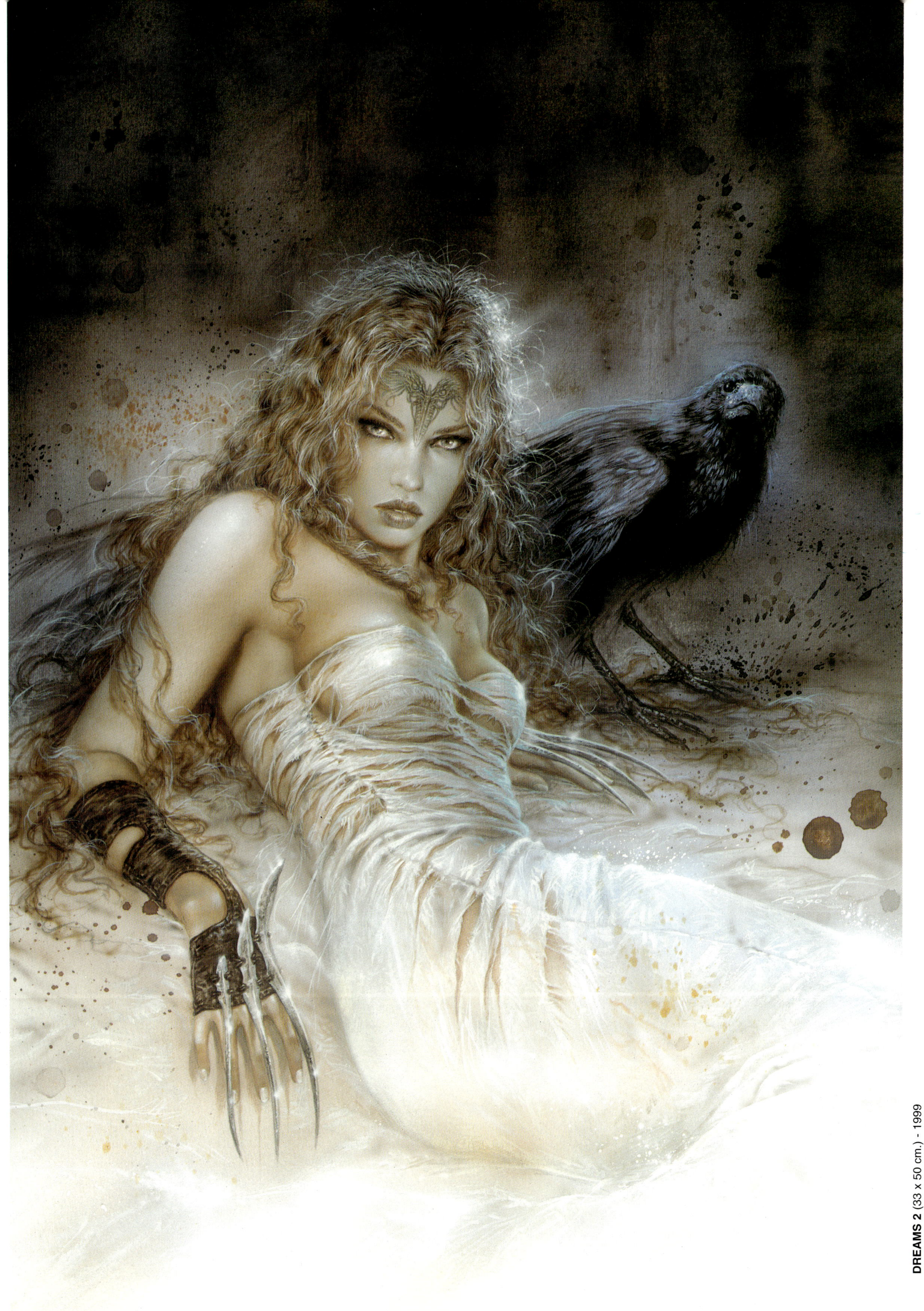

DREAMS 2 (33 x 50 cm.) - 1999

NORMA 2000 (28 x 36 cm.) - 1999

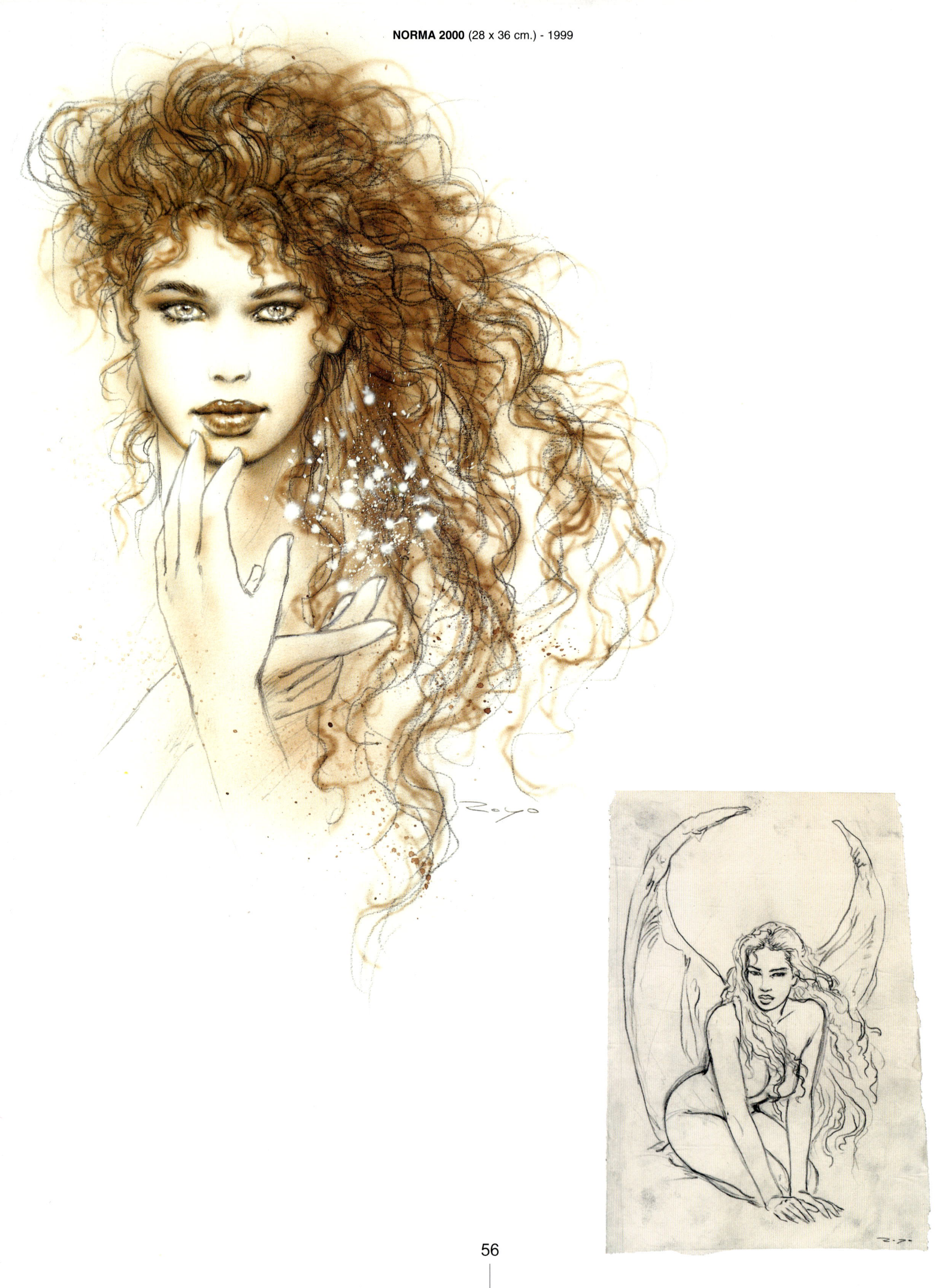

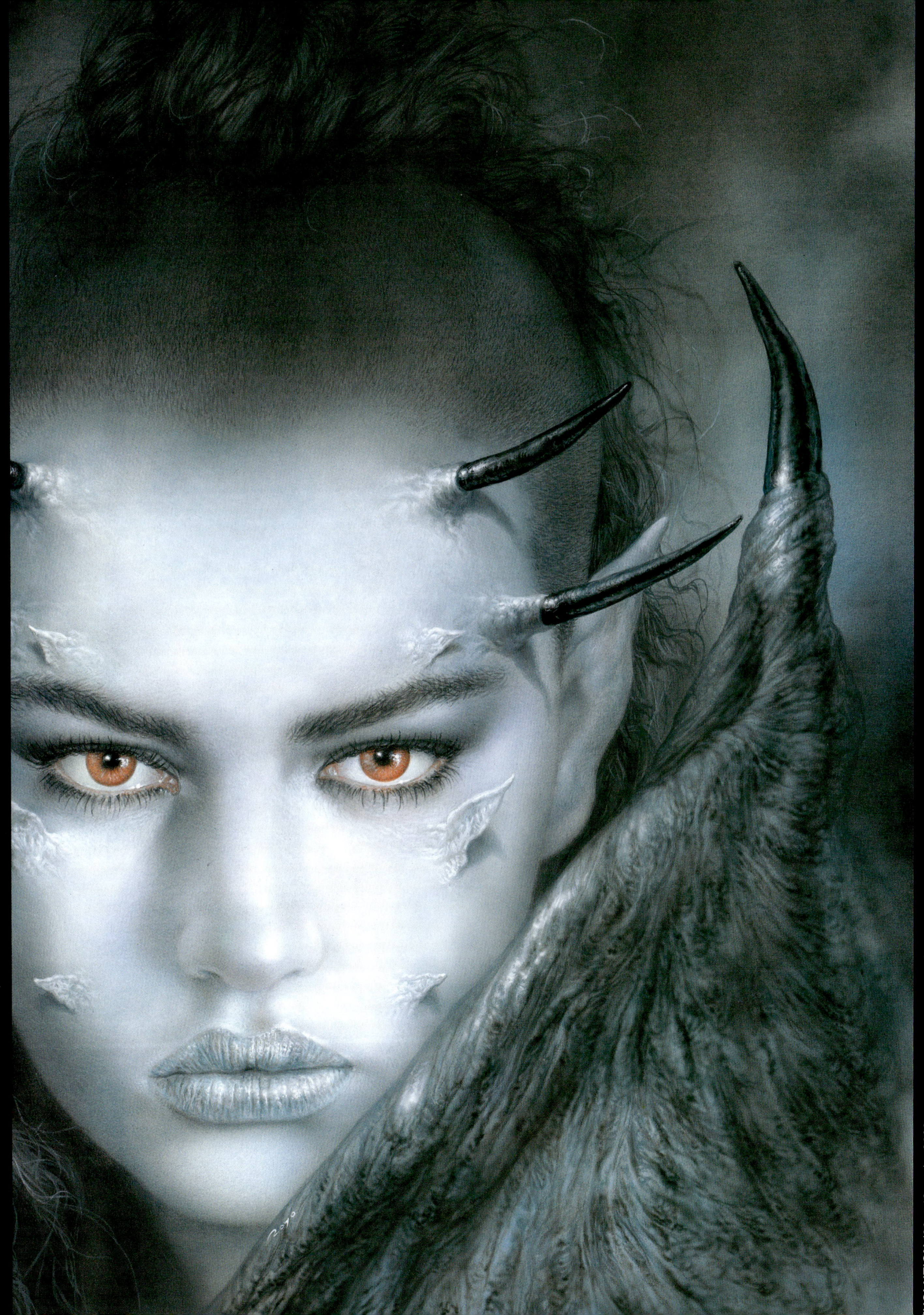

EVOLUTION (29 x 42 cm.) - 2000

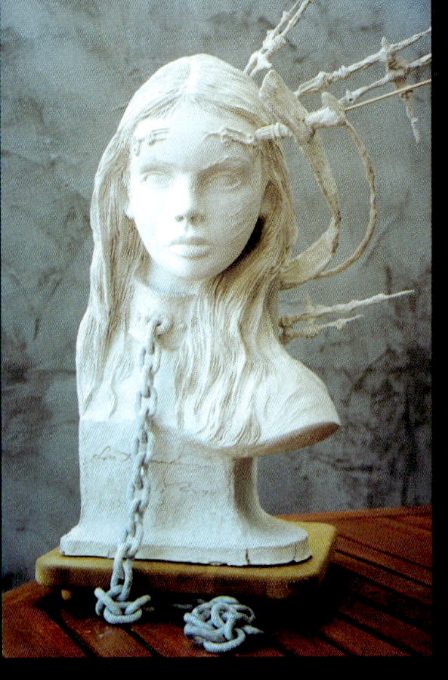

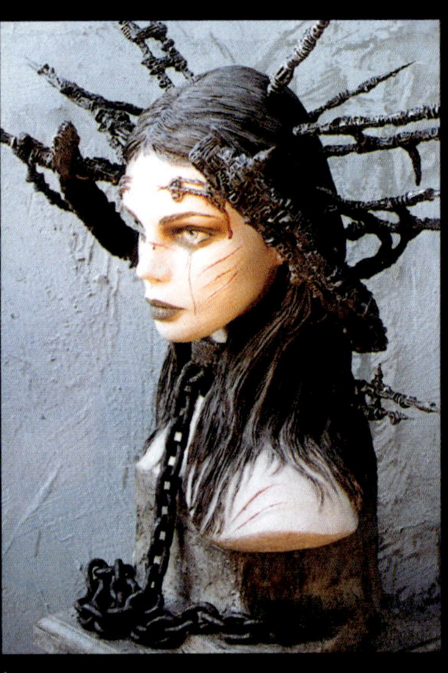

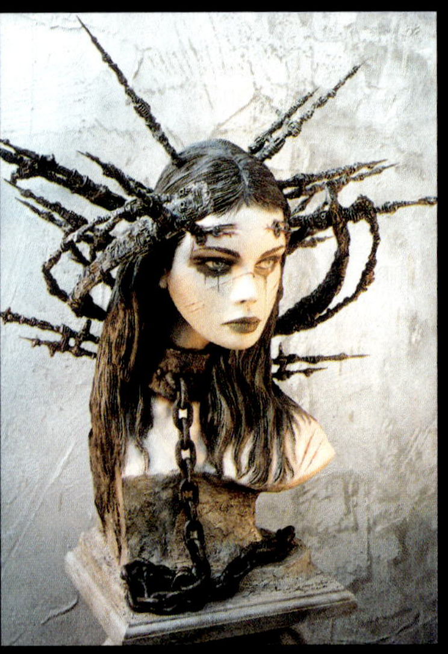

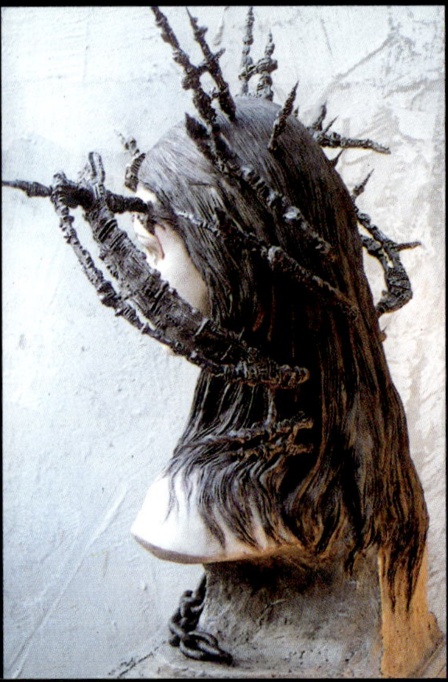

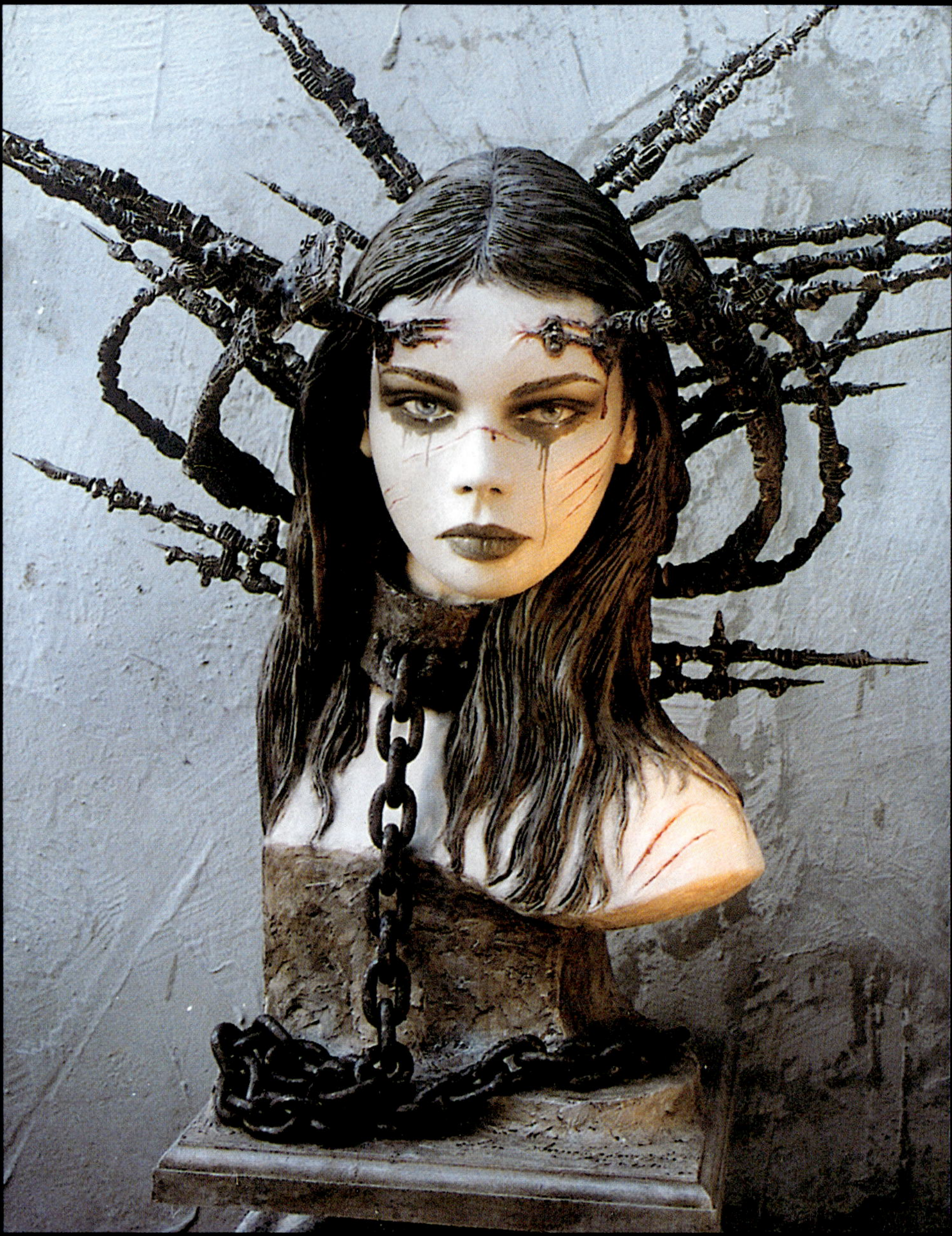

Work in three dimensions of *The Annunciation*, an image from the book *III Millennium*.

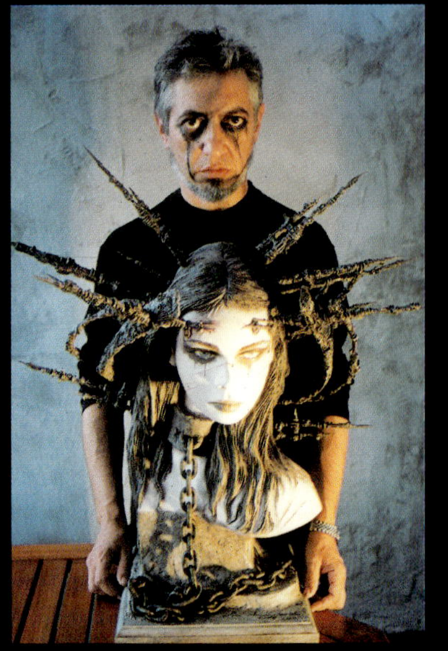

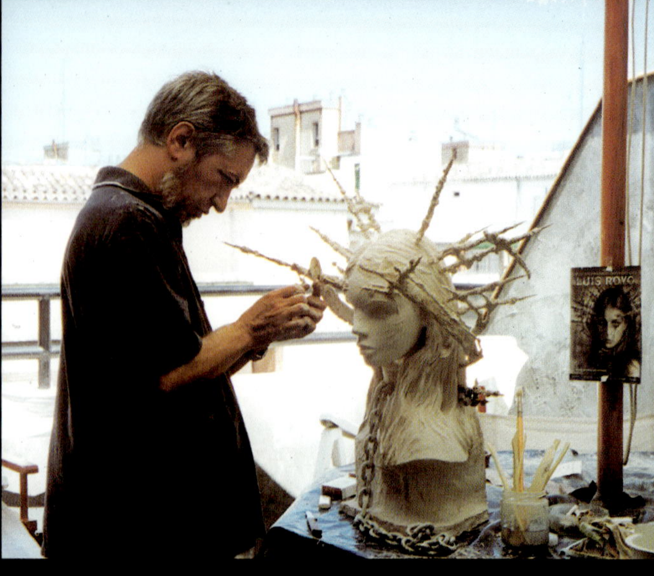

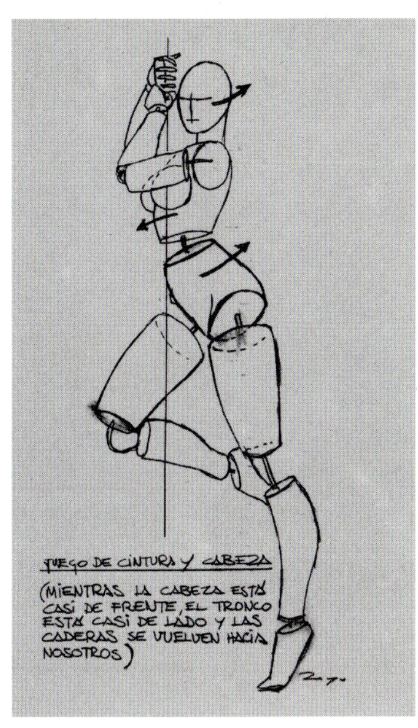

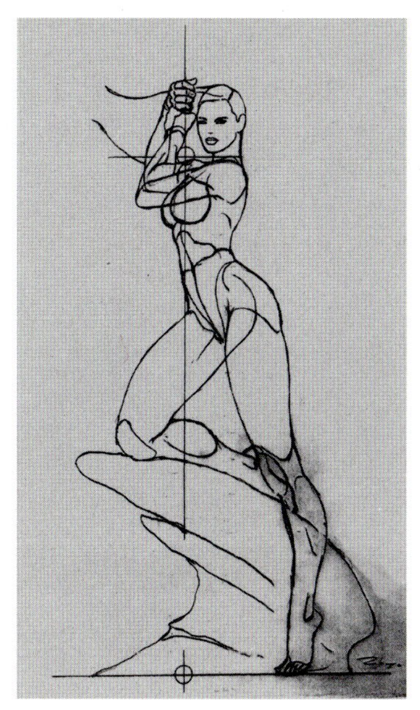

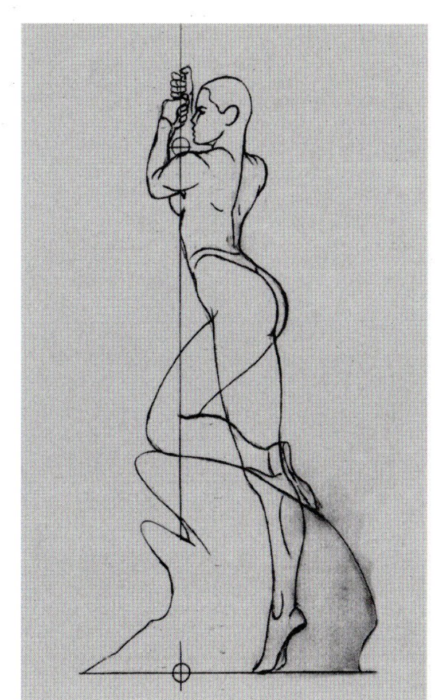

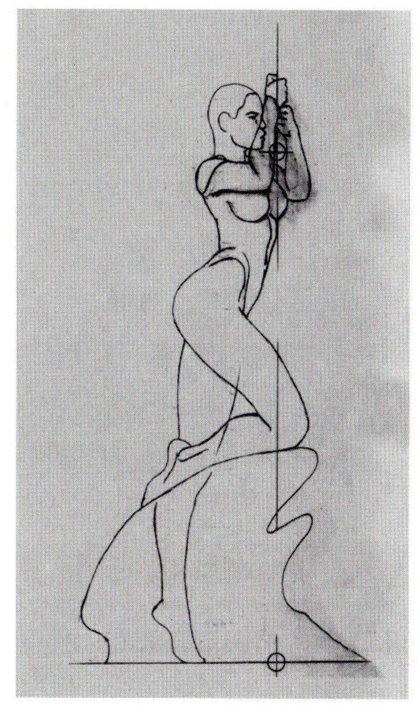

Development of the Malefic figure.

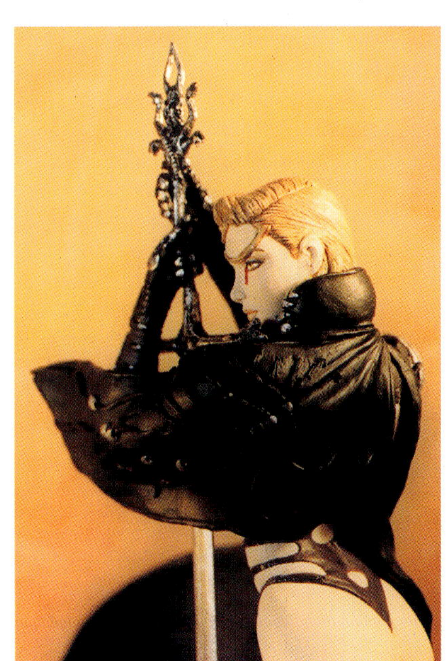

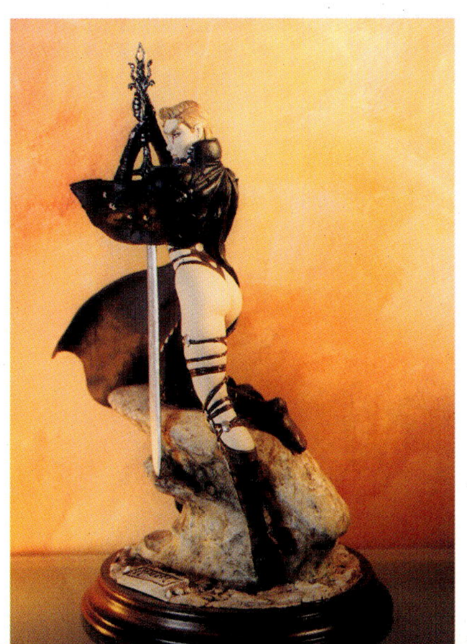

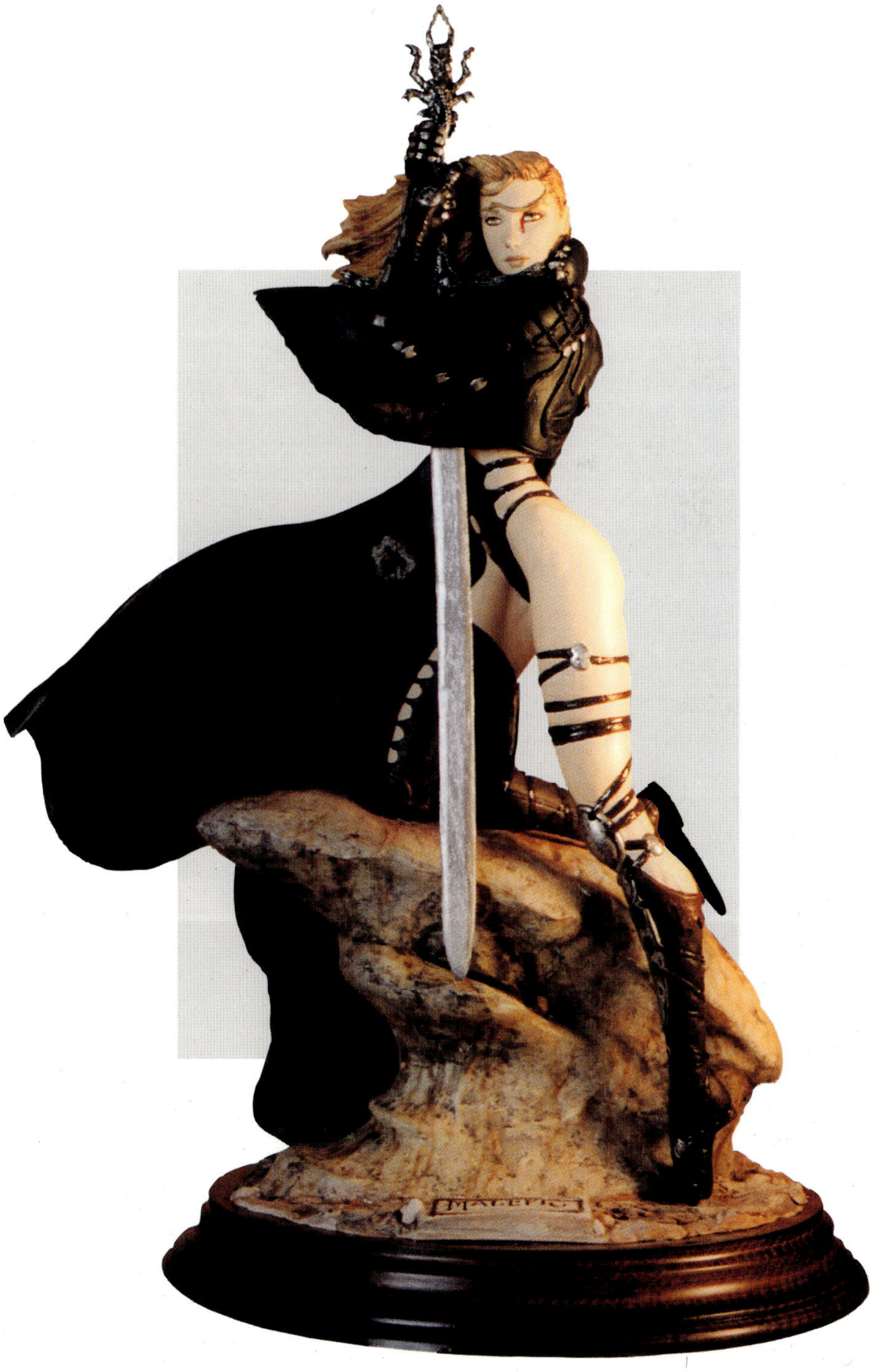

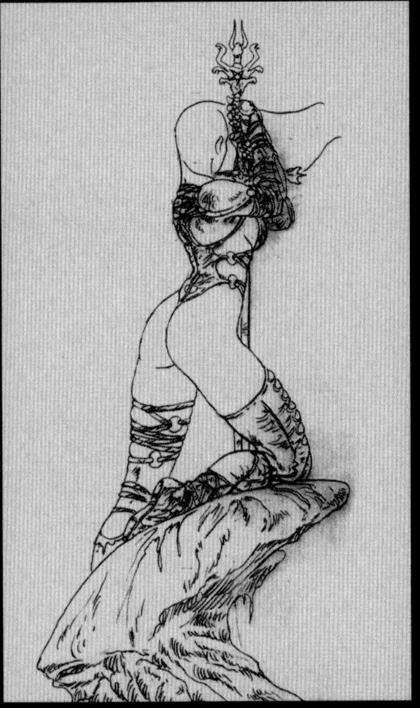
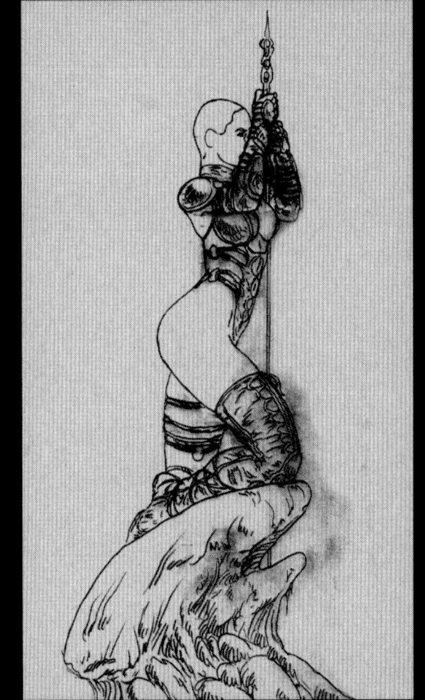
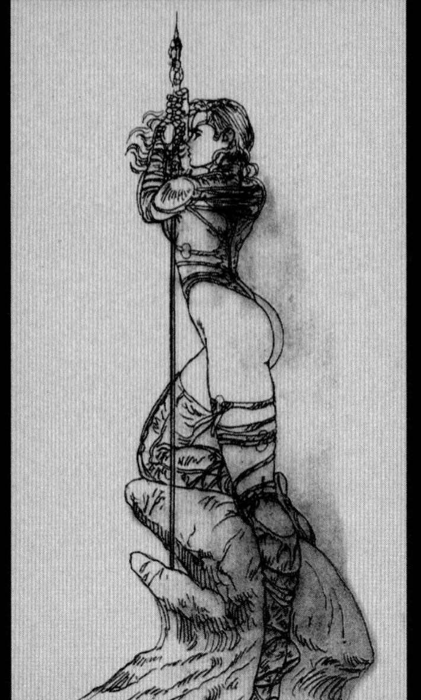
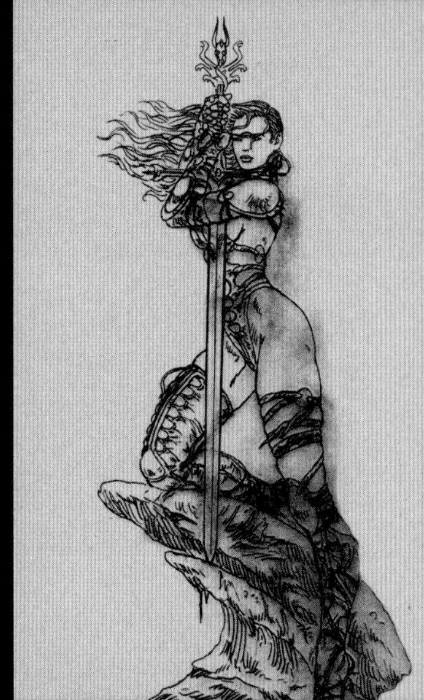

STUDY OF THE CHARACTER MALEFIC
BY TEÓFILO GARCÉS

1992 seems to be the year this character was born.

In 1993, she appeared for the first time in a book of illustrations that bore her name: Malefic.

A year earlier, NORMA Publishers (who originate the Royo books) received a number of letters from a psychiatric hospital in Barcelona. One of them contained some drawings that motivated the manager, Rafael Martínez, to pay the patient who had sent them a visit. Nothing is known about this and other visits that took place at the hospital, but the next year the book *Malefic* appeared. It is a book of science fiction and fantasy in which the character Malefic appears in only four illustrations, but her aura pervades a great part of the book.

In 1995, NORMA published *Secrets*, but Malefic only appeared in one illustration. During these years, the editor-in-chief visited the same mental hospital regularly, and revealed that the illustrator of these books was a patient there.

The publisher began to receive letters that were signed "the painter's roommate," but there were certain rumors going around to the effect that there was no roommate—that it was the same person who had made the illustrations. Nevertheless, NORMA's editor would neither confirm nor deny them.

In 1997, another book by the same author was published: *III Millennium*, where, instead of the character appearing, her world appears, reflected in the images. It seems that the idea of establishing connections had been intentionally avoided. During these years, the supposed author, a person named Royo, had been observed autographing copies of the books in various places. Some people say that it isn't really him; others claim that he's been permitted to leave the hospital and that he isn't really dangerously disturbed; still others say that a number of times in the middle of one of his signings he has lashed out against someone who, according to him, was an angel or a demon. It's also rumored that after one of these occurrences he spends long periods in seclusion.

In 1999, a new book appeared: *Dreams*, signed by the same author (who had already published *Women* in 1991); and toward the end of that year there appeared another: *Prohibited Book*. In none of these could Malefic be seen, and the only thing it was posible to say for certain was that the drawings had a style that made it possible to believe they had all been done by the same hand.

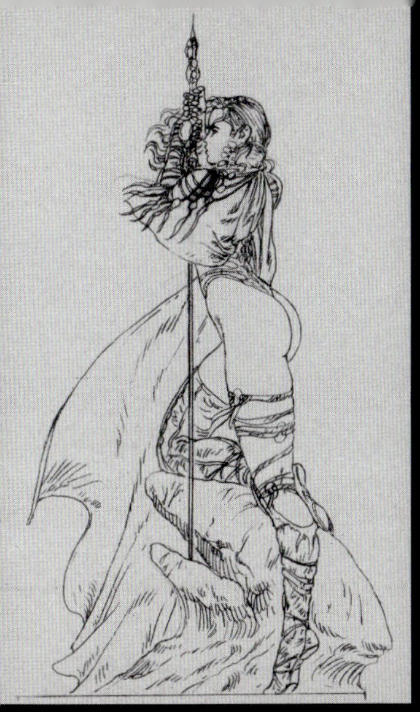
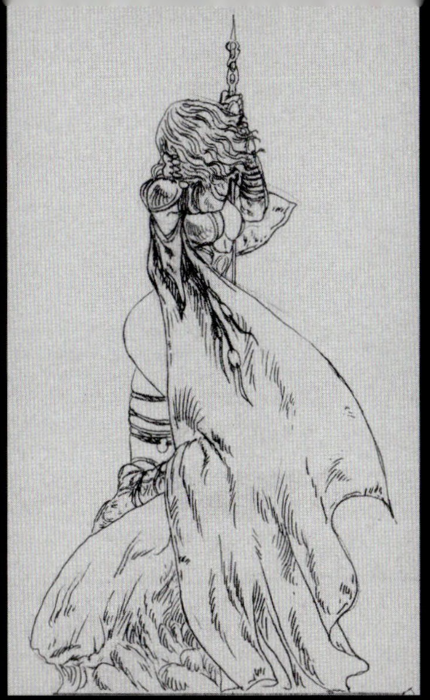
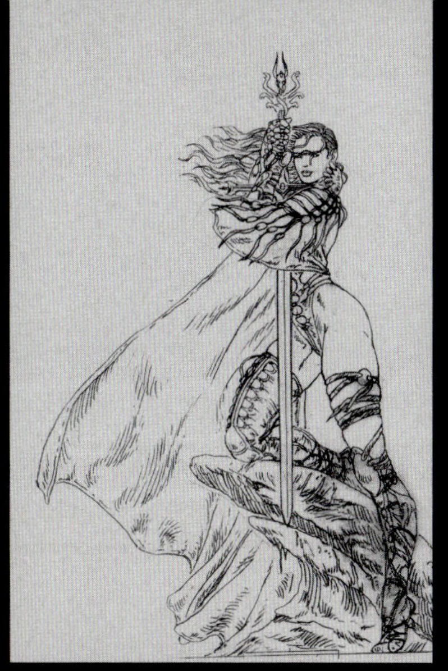
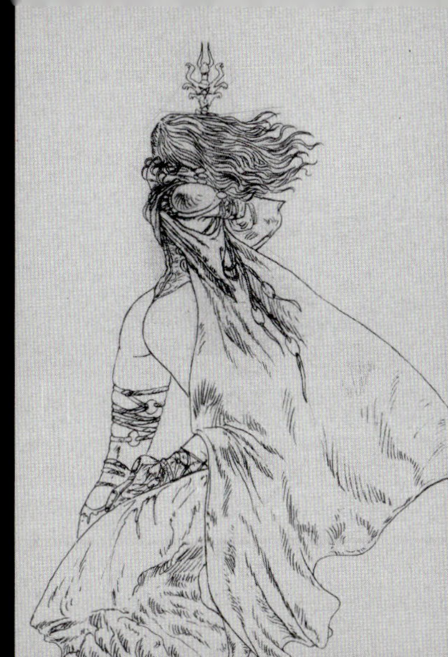

Nonetheless, the assignment the publisher gave me, to write a brief history and chronology of the character, should not influence me. The rumors are persistent enough that all the work related to Malefic up until now has come out of the same hospital. I know that there are hundreds of stories of this character in the offices of NORMA Publishers, and that all sorts of works related to her are in the works.

It is very difficult to get a word out of Rafael Martínez, the manager we mentioned before. The hospital's director, Óscar Valiente, is equally close-mouthed. All we can learn from the publisher is that they spend long periods of time in some remote little town in the area, finishing the stories and drawings that we will soon see published.

MALEFIC IN DEVELOPMENT

At NORMA Publishers, lots of things related to Malefic are taking place behind the scenes. They are preparing comics that will soon be released. There are also connections with the movie world. A group of film executives are launching a series of related products, and writers, editors, and artists are busy with the process of creation.

But the origins of this character are still unknown.

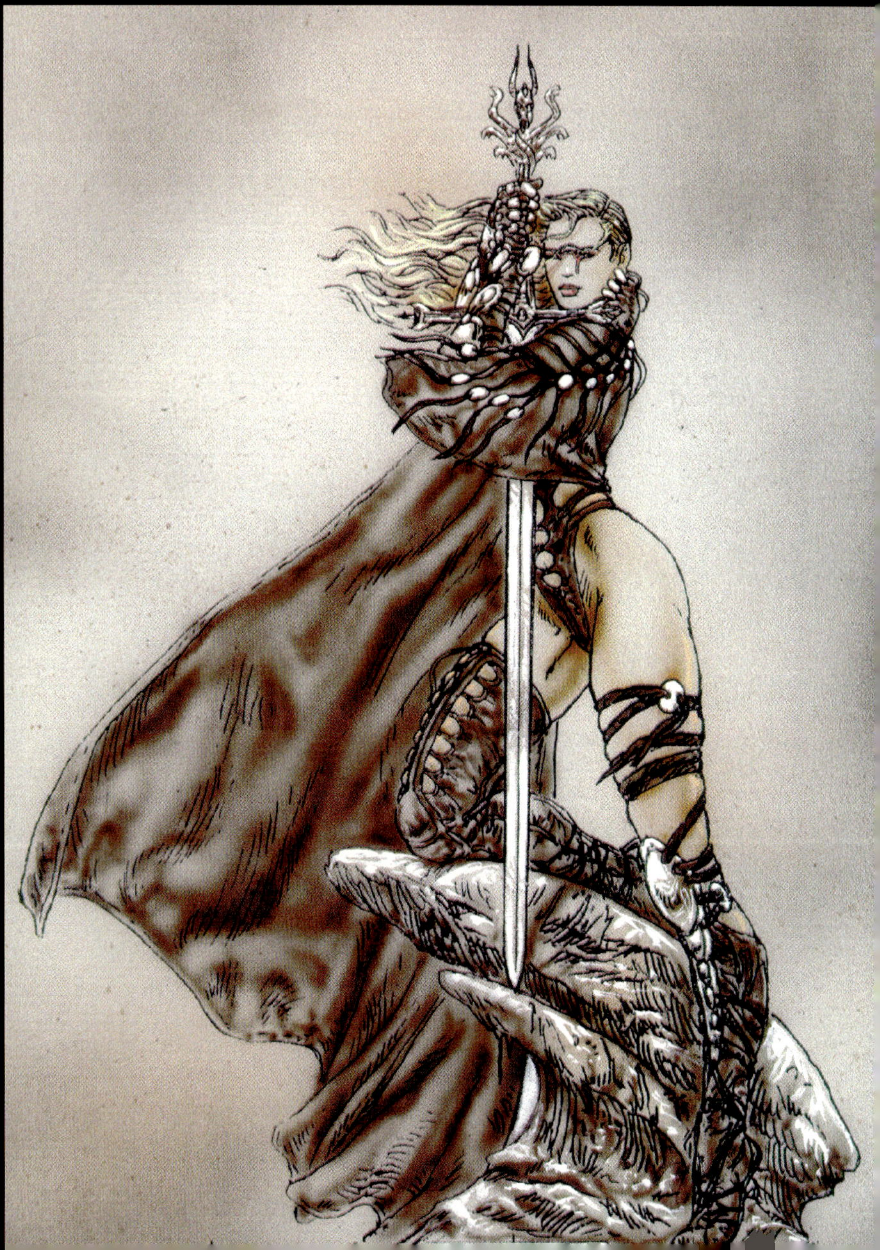

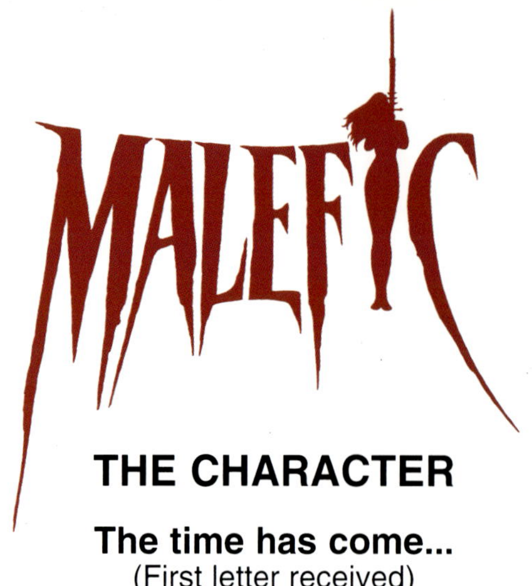

THE CHARACTER

The time has come...

(First letter received)

I spent such a long time glued to the window that I thought nothing else existed. In effect, the glass told me everything that was important. But that day, the only thing it communicated to me was the hopeless anxiety of the young woman who lived in the run down factory across the street. In fact, I only spent all my time in front of the window just to see her.
The long hours I spent there freed me from this incomprehensible present. I was a practical person, a total agnostic, one of the few who still used a computer; I couldn't make myself believe that that senselessness out there was the End of the World. It couldn't be...had the time really come?
For sure, there can't be more than two or three neighbors left in the building I live in. Ever since a few months ago, the electricity is only on a couple of hours a day, and businesses are quickly disappearing; there isn't a single one left on my street. I've seen some very strange beings around: wrinkled, impossibly tall. I saw one of them lift himself up off the ground; he seemed to have some sort of wings. It surely must be due to some sort of invention or drug. They can't fool me with all that superstitious nonsense and alarming news, even though the theory that our earthly existence is really a hellish prison seems to have come true. The words of Paracelsus seem to echo over New York: "the place where the devil was cast down, in other words, hell itself."
New York will return to its former self; they'll reconstruct those skyscrapers that are now just a panorama of metal skeletons on the horizon. At times, I spend hours looking at old photographs of the city. It was beautiful; I would have loved to look out over the world from one of the windows of the Chrysler Building.

From my window, I have also witnessed some startling events in the great expanse of the factory in front, with its walls full of cracks and dirt. I remember one of the first times I saw the girl with long blond hair. It was a hot, steamy night, with a red sky. Like every night these past few years, she was in the middle of the room, wearing only white panties, and around her on the floor were dozens of candles, giving off an unnatural blue light. Another girl, also with a long blond mane, moved around her in a strange dance, at the same time shamelessly caressing her from the tips of her fingers to between her legs, from her navel to behind her ears. My neighbor trembled, she seemed to be in ecstasy; then, suddenly she dropped to the floor and stretched out her hand and grabbed a sword. It had a strange hilt, like some enigmatic figure, with various points sticking out; the blade whisked through the air with a dry sound. My young neighbor raised the sword off the floor, and with a sudden motion sliced her companion in two from bottom to top. I had never witnessed such a brutal scene. Then she got up, divided the corpse up into more pieces, and extinguished the candles one by one. I stood there with a million questions going through my mind. Ever since then, I've spent a good part of my life by the window.

I maintained my post by the window, and it was the third time I saw her in that situation. What's more, I had never seen her in such bad shape; all morning she'd been getting up and vomiting, moving from one corner of the room to another, and she'd bathed at least five times. She seemed not all there.
I decided, in a sudden, uncharacteristic fit of bravery, to enter her room, even to help her. More than once I had gone there when she was out and browsed through her strange, esoteric, and apocalyptic books. We lived in a really strange world, but I think she surpassed it all.
I pulled myself up on the windowsill, just as I had a number of times before, then hesitated before her dilapidated door. I felt unable to show myself to her—but she saw my shadow and launched herself toward me with a shout that froze me on the spot. She grabbed the sword on her way, the same one I'd seen hundreds of times, and before I knew what hit me I found myself on the floor with her on top of me and the edge of the sword against my neck.
She looked into my eyes, and I saw the fury in hers die down. She gave a grunt like one of the owls that lived there with her in the factory, got up, and turned her back on me.
I don't remember all the words I used to try and explain that I meant to help her; I must have used thousands of them. She didn't even look at me; she got back into the bathtub. She was covered with sweat, burning up with fever.
I had muttered a thousand apologies when I felt a cold wind brush my face. Between her and me appeared a tall, thin being. It was skeletal. Its hair reached to its ankles, and it wore almost no clothes. Its skin was full of wrinkles, and it had veins that looked like electric wiring.
Lucía got out of the bath and leaped toward her sword, but before she could reach it, the unknown being grabbed her by the neck with one hand, and with the other did the same to me. In a second we were up against the wall with our feet in the air, hanging by our necks like a couple of overcoats on a hook. Lucía gave me a look, stretched out her hand to me, closed her eyes, and said, "Think of me."

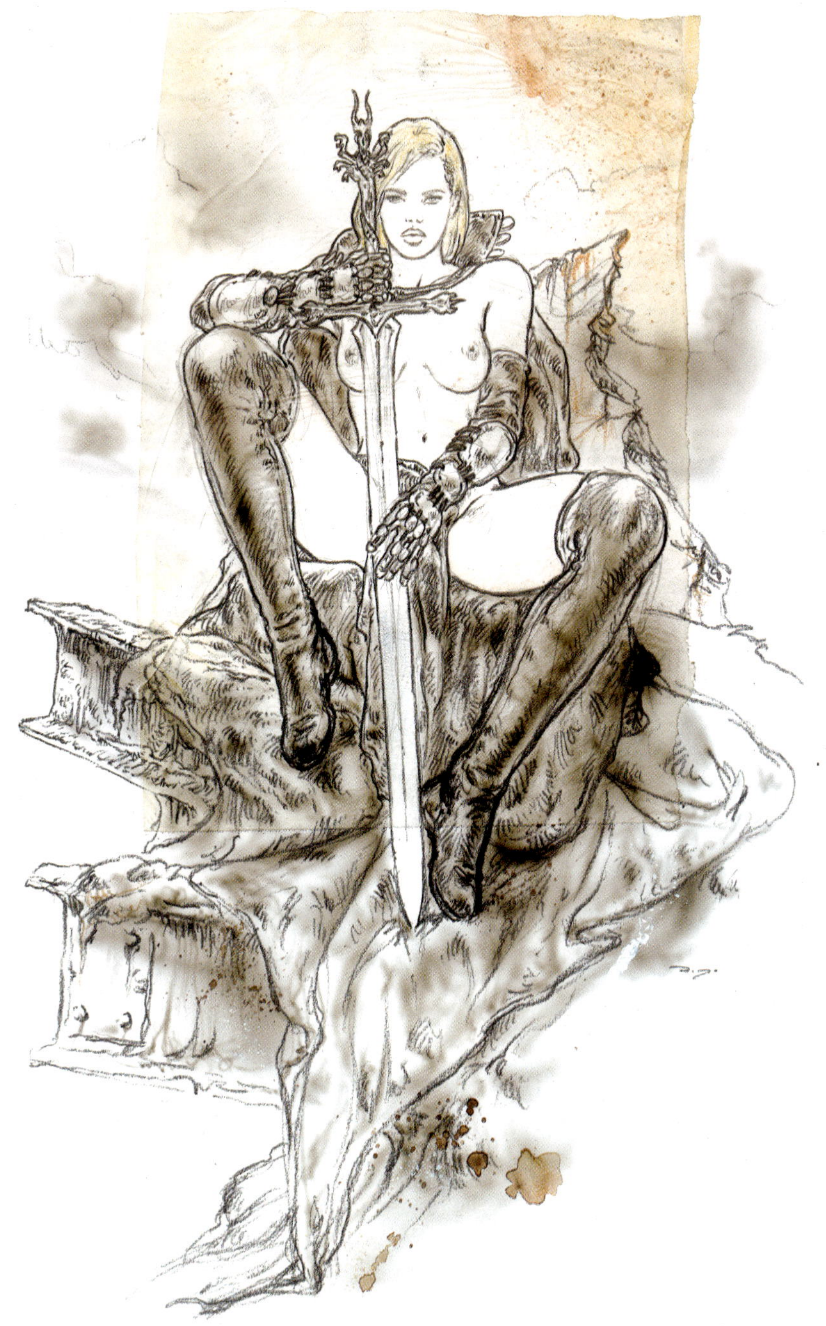

That was easy, because it was what I did all day long. Then I felt as if death had arrived. I saw white, then a long tunnel...
Down from the mountain she came with her long blond hair strewn messily across her face. She came over to me and gave me a shove. "Hey, do you remember that just a moment ago we were in New York in 2030?"
It was as though she'd suddenly tossed my brain into a cocktail shaker. She was right—a second ago I'd been in New York. Nevertheless, now I was in the year 999, in the kingdom of Navarre: I was a farmer, I'd always been one, I was married to the plump young woman over there by the cabin serving that old man a glass of wine. He was my father-in-law and he was making my life impossible. Not in vain, I had to try to forget that he let me live there and enjoy the fruits of that poor land the seigneur had granted him to farm (even though I was the one, of course, who did all the work). Somehow my wife fit into the whole scheme, too.
"You remember? Remember New York?"
"Yes..." I said almost in a whisper.
"Well, if you want to get out of here, follow me."
I didn't ponder it for even a moment. I looked down, marveling at my callused hands, and threw down the sickle I was holding. Meanwhile, out of the corner of my eye I watched my two exploiters, who didn't even seem to notice the whole scene.
We walked all day and night. When I tried to give voice to all the doubts that swirled around in my head, she made that hoot like an owl and forced me to be silent.

Suddenly I found myself in a spectacular gathering, in the middle of the mountains, in some gigantic caverns. At once I knew they were the caves of Zugarramurdi. The people of that region said that all the witches and wizards met there, that the evil ones came down to earth—even Satan himself—that they held huge bacchanals and sacrifices... they told hundreds of stories. I also recalled that I knew of the existence of this place in 2030, from a short story by Pío Baroja I'd read. There were a lot of strange beings there, many of them in the series of small caves that formed a sort of balcony around the central chamber, which was enormous and held

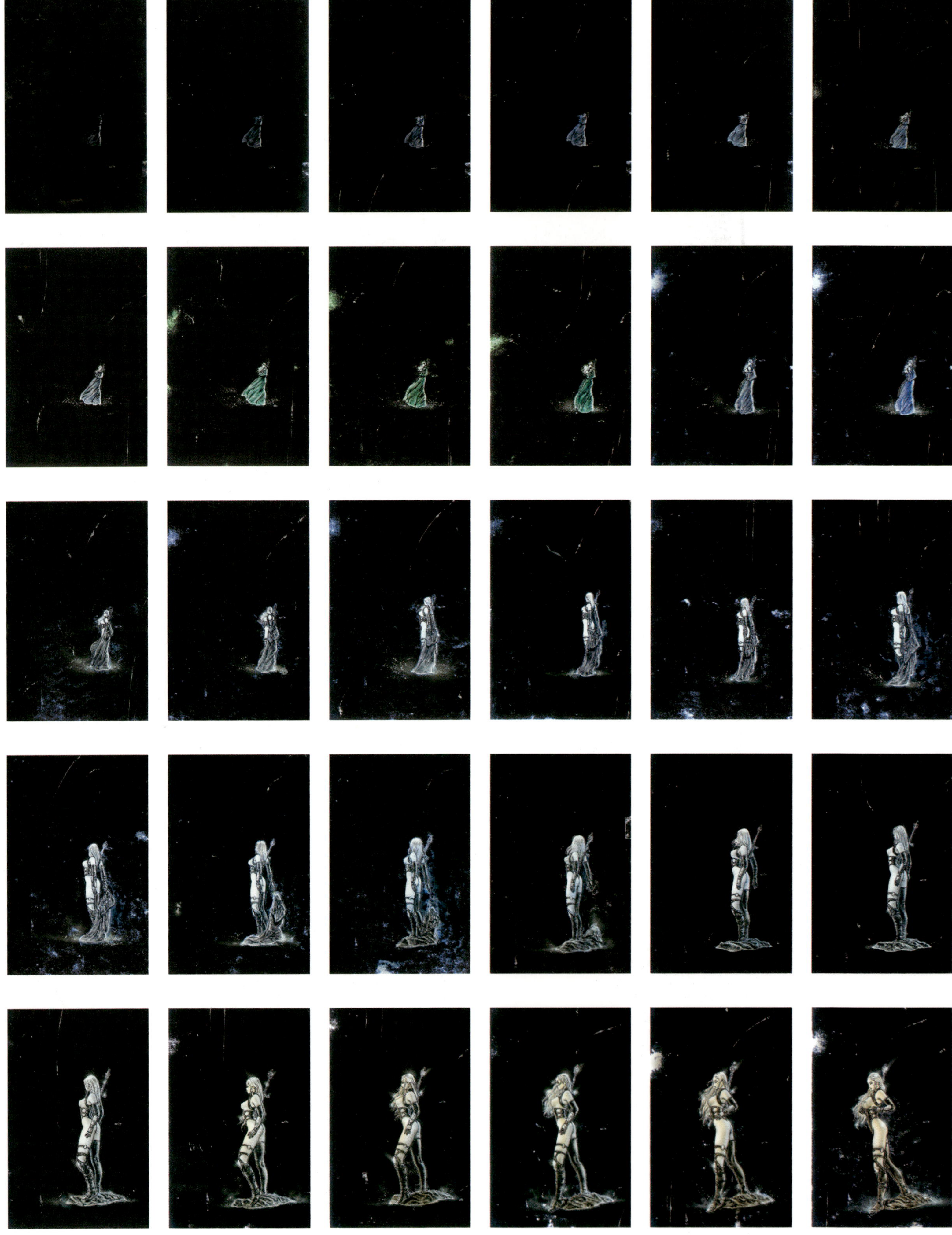

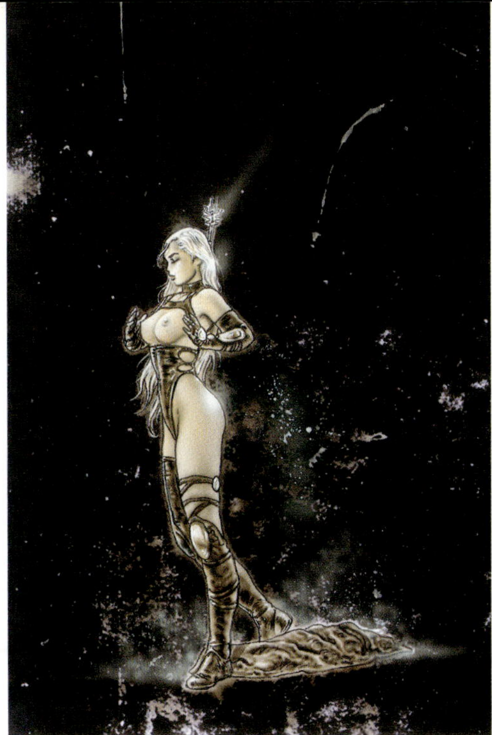

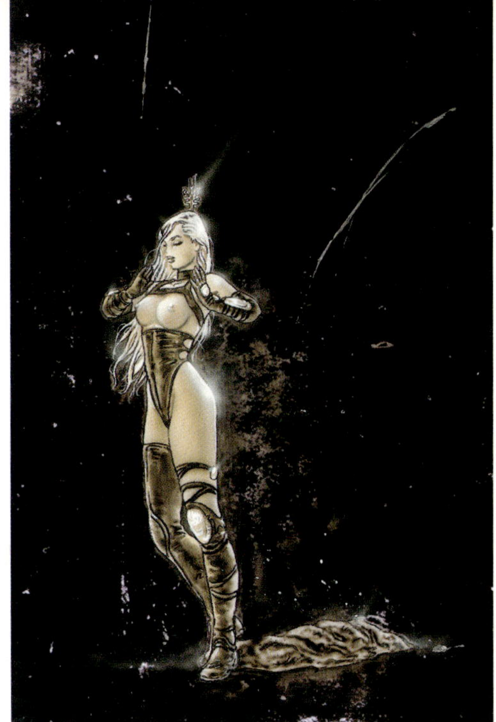

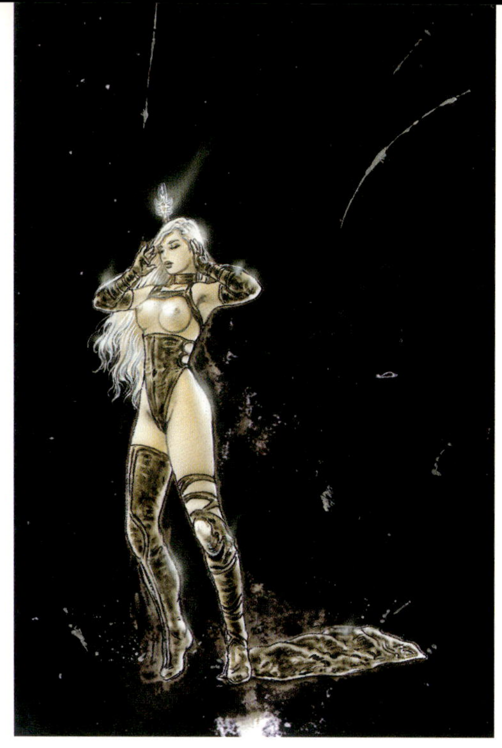

a kind of stage or altar. On it were three indescribable creatures, covered with large capes. All I could see was their wide eyes splashed with blood. In the center of the cave was an enormous circle formed by 28 naked young men and women. On the floor were drawings of the phases of the moon, crowned by a lunar dragon in the form of a serpent with the head of a hawk, inside one circle of air and another of fire, in the style of the capital of the Greek letter zeta. (Later I learned that they drew this when

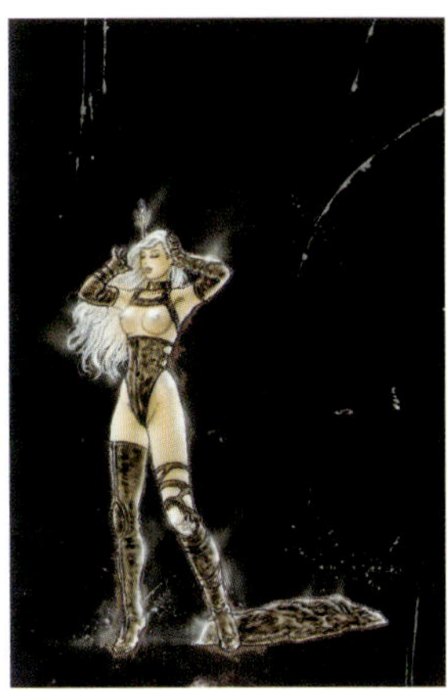

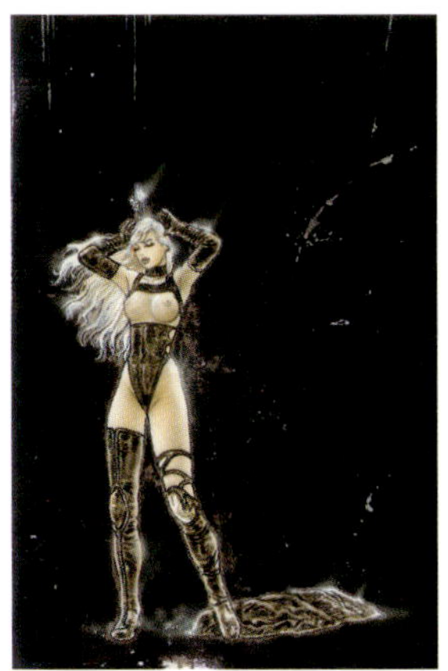

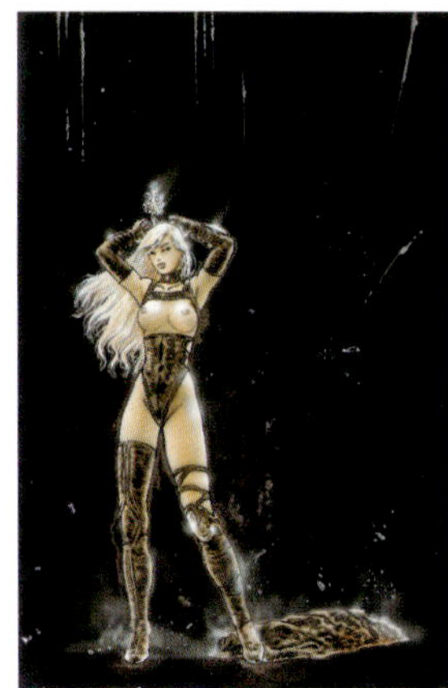

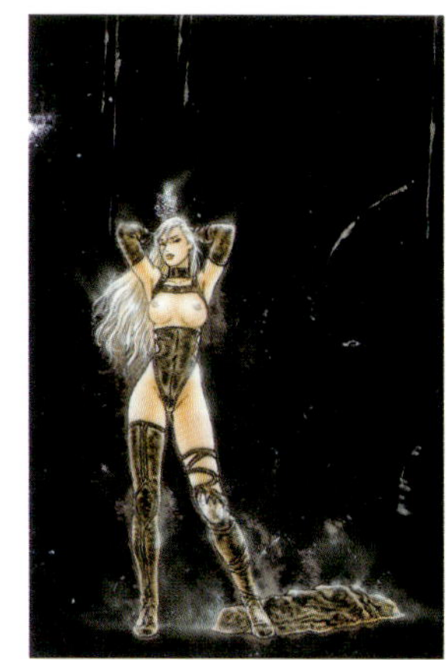

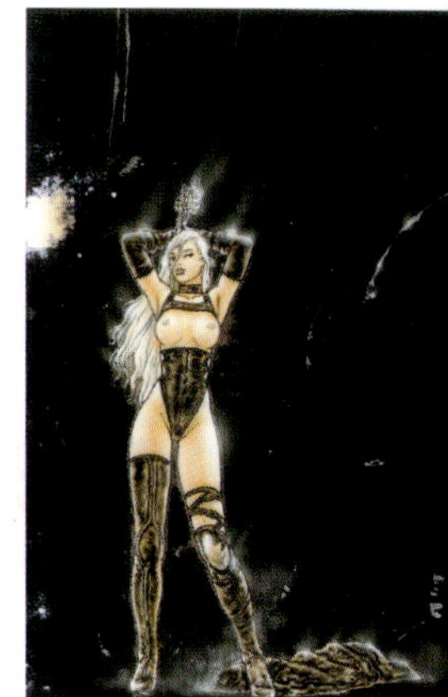

the head of Jupiter was at the center of the heavens, and that they attributed favorable powers to him when they asked for a wish to be granted. It was also the form they gave to the benevolent domestic spirit, which they represented by a serpent. The Phoenicians and Egyptians said that this animal came before all others, since they considered it to have a divine nature, due to its cleverness and its fire more intense than any other's. They inferred this from the rapidity of its movements despite its lack

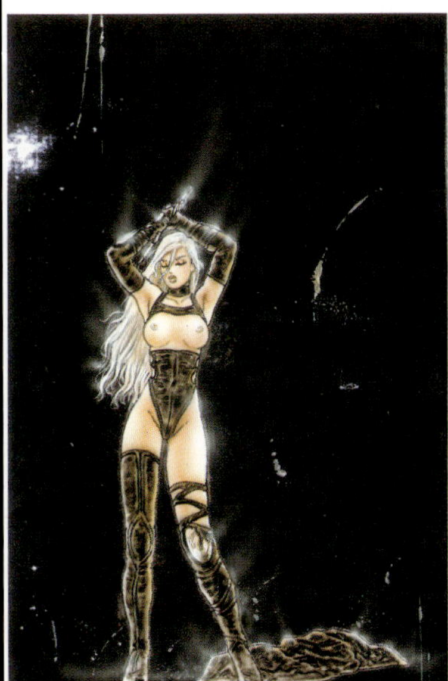

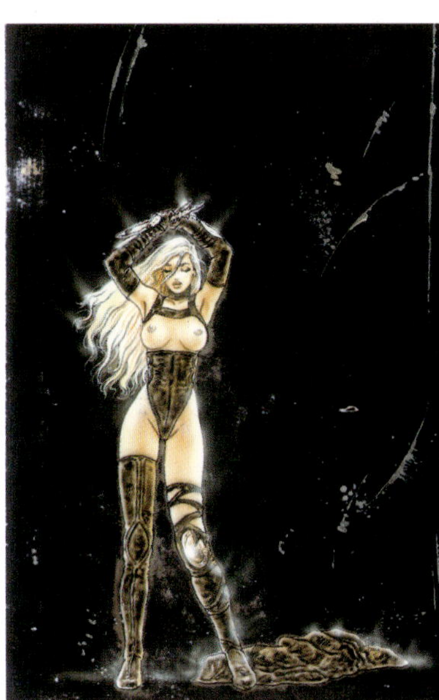

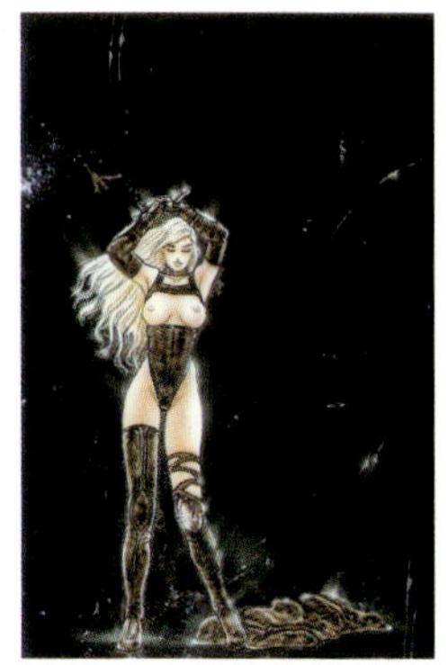

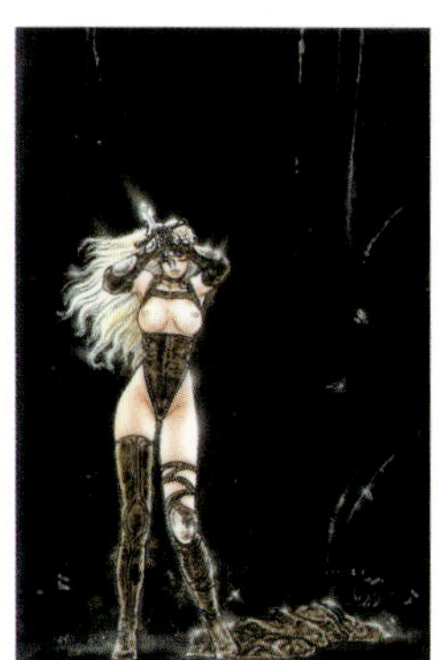

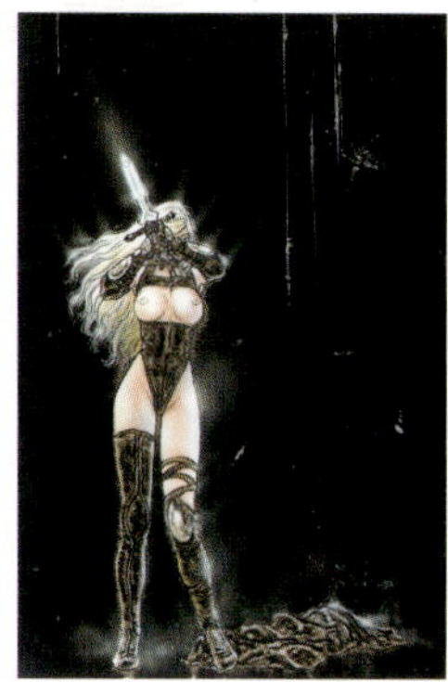

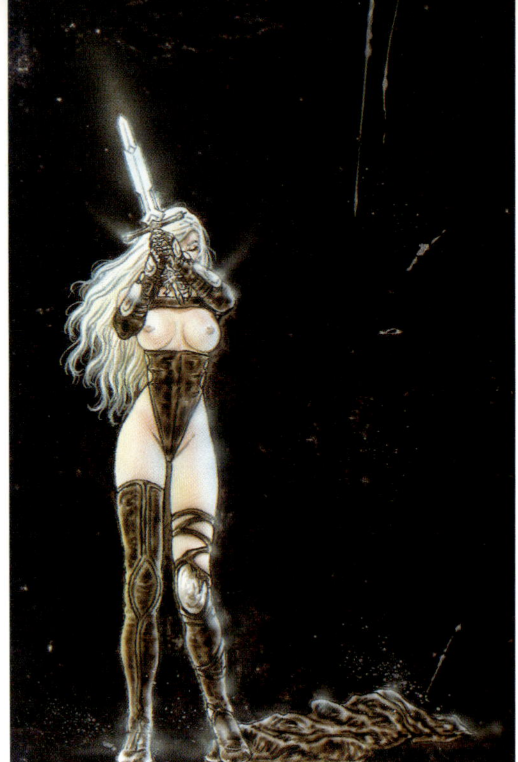
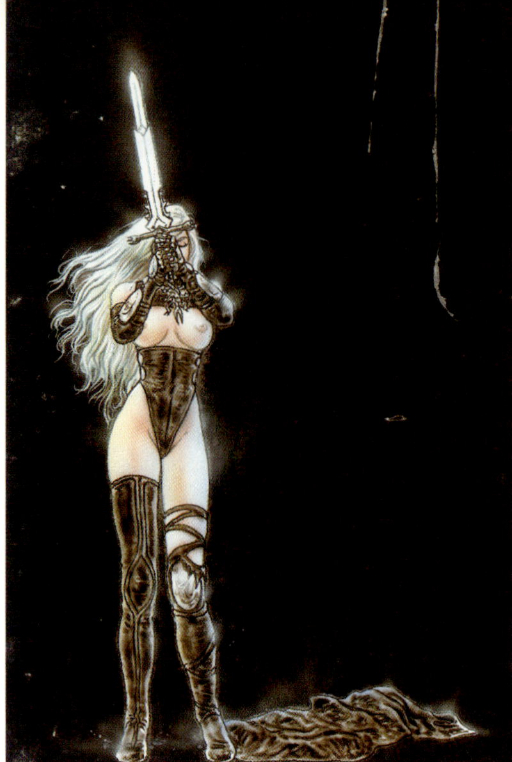

of hands and feet, and from its power to rejuvenate itself by shedding its skin. They represented the tail of the lunar dragon in various ways depending on when it disappeared or when it had an unfavorable aspect in relation to Mars or Saturn). All around us, and farther away, groups of strange people were coming together, like shadows against the walls.
Lucía approached an old woman near the wall, whispered with her, then told me to sit down where I was and stay put. She took off her clothes and approached the circle of youths, who had all crouched down and were pairing off on their hands and knees. Lucía joined up with a tall, strong-looking man. They licked each other's necks, then she took his hand and led him over and presented him to the old woman. In exchange, the old woman handed her a bag full of little bottles, roots and pebbles I'd seen her preparing while I waited. The old woman and the youth disappeared into the crowd in the depths of the cave, and I felt myself shudder. Lucía quickly got dressed, tapped me on the shoulder, and gave me a look that said to follow her. We left, and I breathed a sigh of relief.
We spent five more days walking through the mountains, barely eating or sleeping, but at last there was time for Lucía to pull me out of the maelstrom of doubts that had had been surrounding me.

She explained that she had the power to travel in time, but only to this year, 999, and only to these mountains. Apparently, Mammon, a demon she knew, had told her one day in her home in New York that she had existed once before, in the year 999, and that if someone knew for certain where and when they had previously existed and concentrated on their other life at the moment of their death, they would reappear back there and then. She also knew that I had been a farmer in the kingdom of

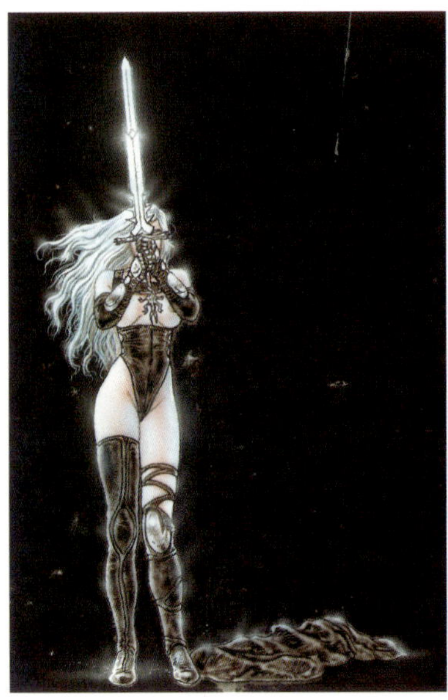
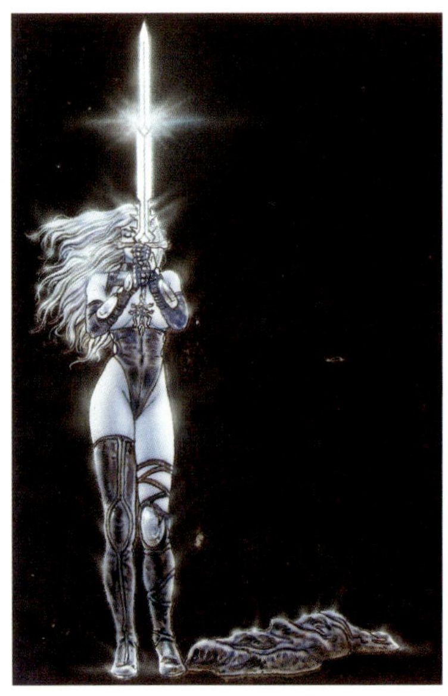
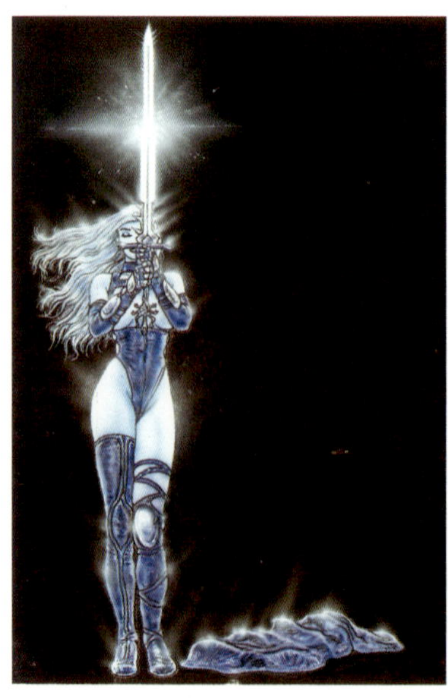
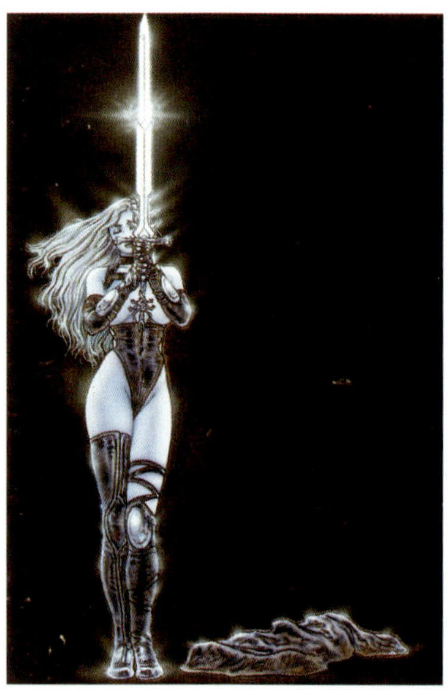

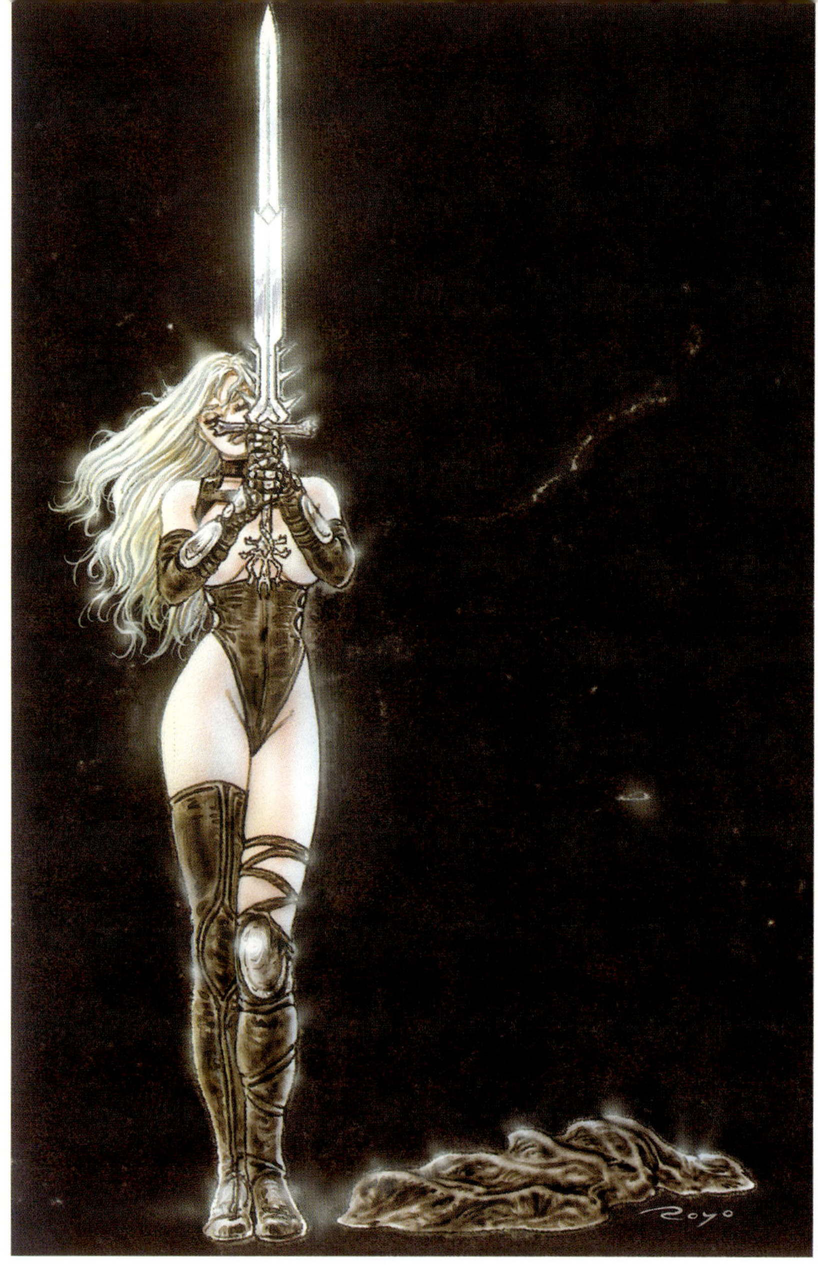

Navarre at that time; she had seen me there more than once, and when I appeared in her run-down room in New York and she threw me down on the floor, she saw my face and realized... that it must be fate. Then, in Navarre, she came looking for me. She knew where I'd be, and when she spoke to me it was as though I'd awoken from a dream: a humble farmer from the first millennium had memories of New York, a huge city that wouldn't exist for centuries. She also told me that I had to return to New York quickly after I'd left it (it was that space known as clinical death, which I'd heard so much about), and that once I returned I could never come back. She told me how, at birth, the soul of light goes down the ladder of the seven spheres and along its descent is held in turn by each planet, considered as interior creators or demons (archons). There, the soul is made flesh and folded into the clay of its mortal existence. Each planet imprints itself on the soul during its transit with a property that can sometimes become negative: Venus can tempt one into lust, Mercury into greed, Mars into wrath, Jupiter into pride, and so on. After death, the fleshly wrapper tarries in Tartarus like a larva, and the soul rises into the ethereal regions to the archons who try to impede its progress. That is why exact knowledge is necessary, to know the right path. Crossing the last sphere is the most dangerous. It is the kingdom of Saturn, who, according to the esoteric teachings, is the "forbidden" god, creator of space and time. He is the serpent who guards paradise.

We arrived at a monastery in the mountains of Huesca, in the Pyrenees: the abbey of Ainsa. It had a tall tower of rough stones, which didn't even manage to look romantic, and around it were various structures of wood and stone that encircled a few wooden shacks and a very crude house. There was a bigger, nicer-looking house in which a few soldiers were visible. I'd seen the abbey of Ainsa on my computer, but it didn't look anything like this; this must have been some primitive forerunner, perhaps dating from the Visigoths. Maybe they built the one I'd seen in photos on top of this one.

Lucía went up to the monk who guarded the gate, and leaving me in the distance, bargained with him and gave him a couple of little bottles from the bag the old woman had given her. She turned toward me and then we headed into the abbey. A monk handed down a rope ladder from a little window in the tower, and then led us up a stairway so narrow we had to crawl on all fours, until we arrived in a large room. On one wall were hundreds of old books on ancient shelves; there were desks, too; it was the library. The monk left and locked the door behind him. I looked at "Malefic" (that was what the monk had called her) with amazement; but without a word she began to peruse the books. We spent two days there, without eating, with only drinks of water from a jug in the corner, and sleeping on the floor. I heard all the monks' activities—chanting matins, working in the orchard—but I couldn't see them. The four windows that opened on the left side were high above the door, and on the right side was only the tiny window we'd come through, which faced the woods. It was autumn, and during the day I lost myself in the endless colors: yellows, browns, reds, greens—the trees seemed to be having a big festival, dressed in their most colorful apparel of the year. But at night all was wrapped in deep darkness, and not even the stars were visible. Malefic edited, selected, and made marks in the books. Once I mumbled some comment, but she just gave me a look that said that this was no time to chat. A little while later we were huddled together on the floor, drowsing in silence.

On the third day, at the crack of dawn, the door flew open and at least twenty monks and six or seven soldiers rushed in. Malefic quickly unsheathed the sword, and, with a dry sound, the blade lengthened and sharp points emerged from the sides of the hilt. A second later two of the soldiers had already lost their heads, which went rolling across the floor; the others took one look and fell back, while the monks massed together like a heap of shit—except for one who took a couple steps forward. A cold wind rose suddenly, and soon he was transformed into a tall thin being, with very wrinkled skin and hair down to his ankles. It was that same being who had choked us back in that rundown factory in twenty-first-century New York. My teeth started chattering. Malefic opened the old woman's bag, which was hanging from her belt, threw a few pebbles on the floor, then pulled out a dry twig and walked toward him. She poked it at his face and it slid into

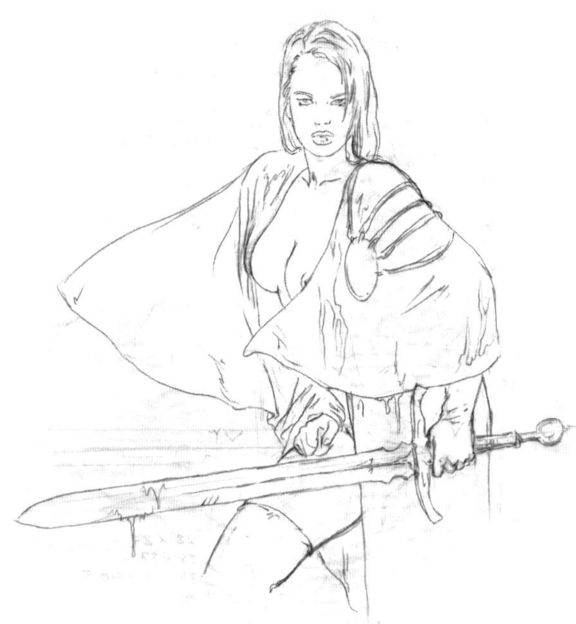

him like a fork into a piece of cake. (Later I learned that this twig had emerged unscathed from a master alchemist's oven). Then she took her sword and sliced him in two. When he'd fallen to the floor in a pool of yellowish-red blood, she hacked away at him some more until he was nothing but chunks. No one said a word; a profound stupor seemed to hover over the room. She took my hand and led me out the same way we'd come in a few days before.

For hours, we plunged through branches and underbrush, occasionally hearing voices of soldiers in the distance behind us.

Then we were crossing the icy waters of a mountain stream. She neared the shore, and the water ran down her thighs. She called to me softly, held me, and made love to me. I was speechless. Only as time passes have I been able to assimilate that moment, those wet thighs cold as ice, her wet hair caressing my shoulders. There were no words spoken, no kisses; never have I had a feeling like that. I was lost in a dream of paradise, and at the same time I could barely believe my eyes. I've never known what made Malefic take me—for take me she did. Maybe in a moment of weakness she took pity on me and decided to calm me down before we undertook a long journey. Afterwards, she took my hand and told me that at the moment the creature had been choking us in New York, she had felt as if we were drowning in the deepest part of the river.

I returned to consciousness still feeling that creature's hand pressing down on my throat in that dirty old room across from my window. Malefic was the same, but she drew back and kicked that bag of wrinkles in the stomach. Clearly, the being had lost power. Malefic once again opened the old woman's sack, which, miraculously, she still wore on her belt, and while the being was on his knees, she poured the blackish contents of one of the little bottles all over him. At once the cold breeze arose again and the being blew away, turned into dust.

Lucía told me later that the old witch knew how to gain power over Azazel, one of the chief fallen angels. Azazel had been a cherub charged with not allowing the jealous schemes of Satan to come to pass. The old woman knew where the original version of Revelations from the Apocrypha, known as the Book of Enoch, was hidden; in it, and in the Book of the Twenty-two Houses of Light, was described how the twenty-two letters of the Hebrew alphabet had been used by God to create the world. They are also believed to be related to the origins of the Tarot, though that is not certain. But more often than not, the book relates not to the interior world but to the exterior-and there lay the method of overpowering Azazel. Lucía also had two drawings on parchment from the works of Isidore of Seville, with complex symbols of

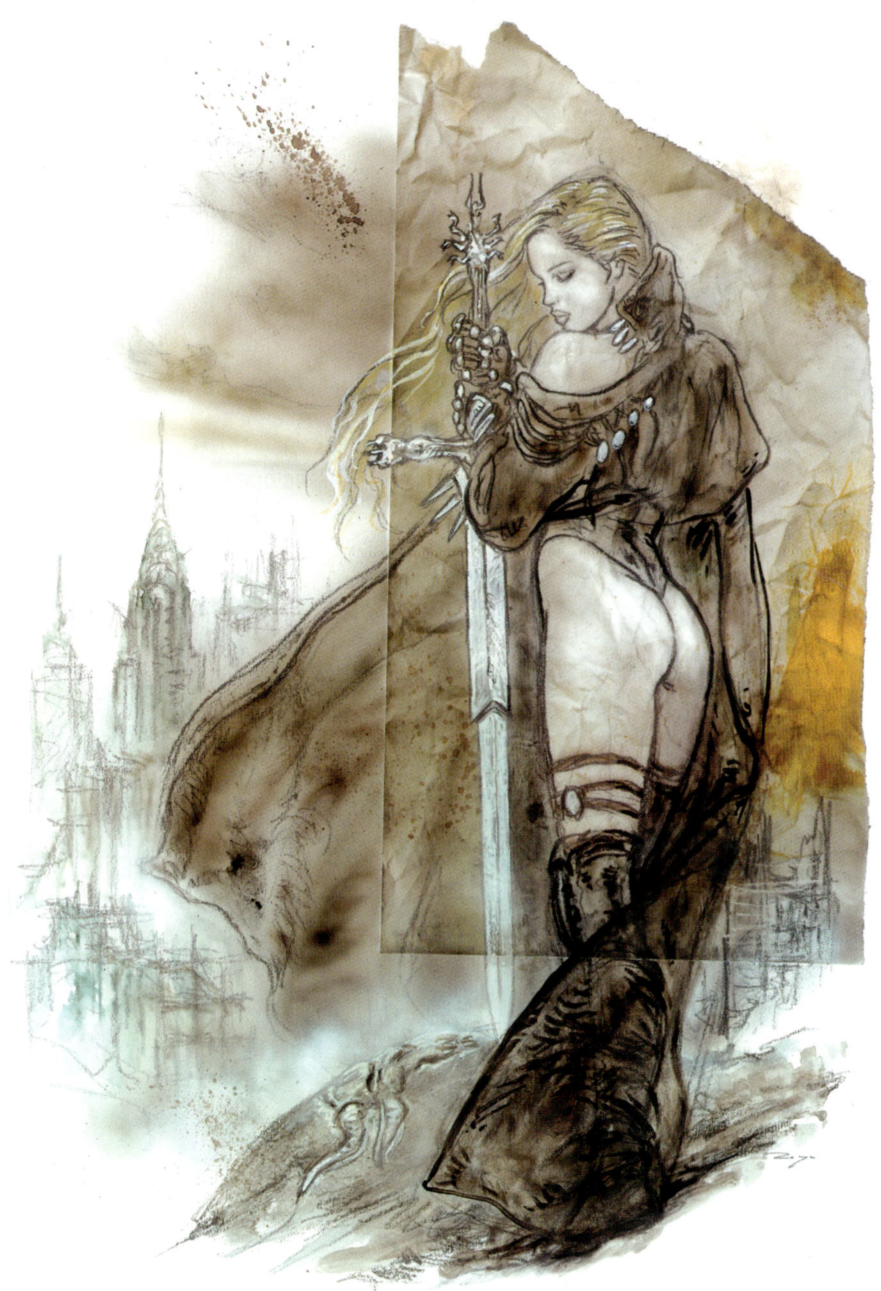

the letters of the Cabala. They were drawn over symbols of the macrocosm and the microcosm. These were what we had gone to the abbey of Ainsa for, and Malefic had brought them back in her bag. She threw the books down on the floor, made that owl sound, and buried herself in her papers. I realized what she needed. I went back to my place, grabbed what I could carry from the refrigerator, and brought it back to her. Between bites, I told her the whole story of how I'd come to know her, and how I'd seen her slice up the other girl. She explained that the other girl had been an angel, just a poor messenger, but that if she hadn't been alert she would have overpowered her spirit.

Back at my place, as I ate some more, I decided that this life definitely wasn't for me. I remembered something strange I'd seen browsing on my computer. I'd seen myself in a database from the year 1990; I was in a mental hospital in Europe- Barcelona, to be exact- I was one of the patients. I thought about it all night; I knew all about another existence of mine, not just the one Lucía knew in 999. I knew I had been a farmer back in the last years of the first millennium, but I knew I'd also been that mental patient in Barcelona in the year 2000, as well as Malefic's shy young neighbor in 2030.
It was all too much for me. I filled up my own bathtub, got in, pulled my head underwater, and drowned myself again, thinking about that hospital in Barcelona.

I know no one will pay any attention to my story and the words I write here, in this hospital; they'll think it's just a story-but I know it's all real. I have lived in 2030, and when that year rolls around, you'll all tremble in fear, because the hour of the Final Judgment will have come around at last, because you'll see angels and demons in the streets, and you'll remember my stories. You'll also remember my roommate's drawings-I've told him everything. Right now you think it's just pure fantasy out of comic books- but time is on my side.

Luis Royo

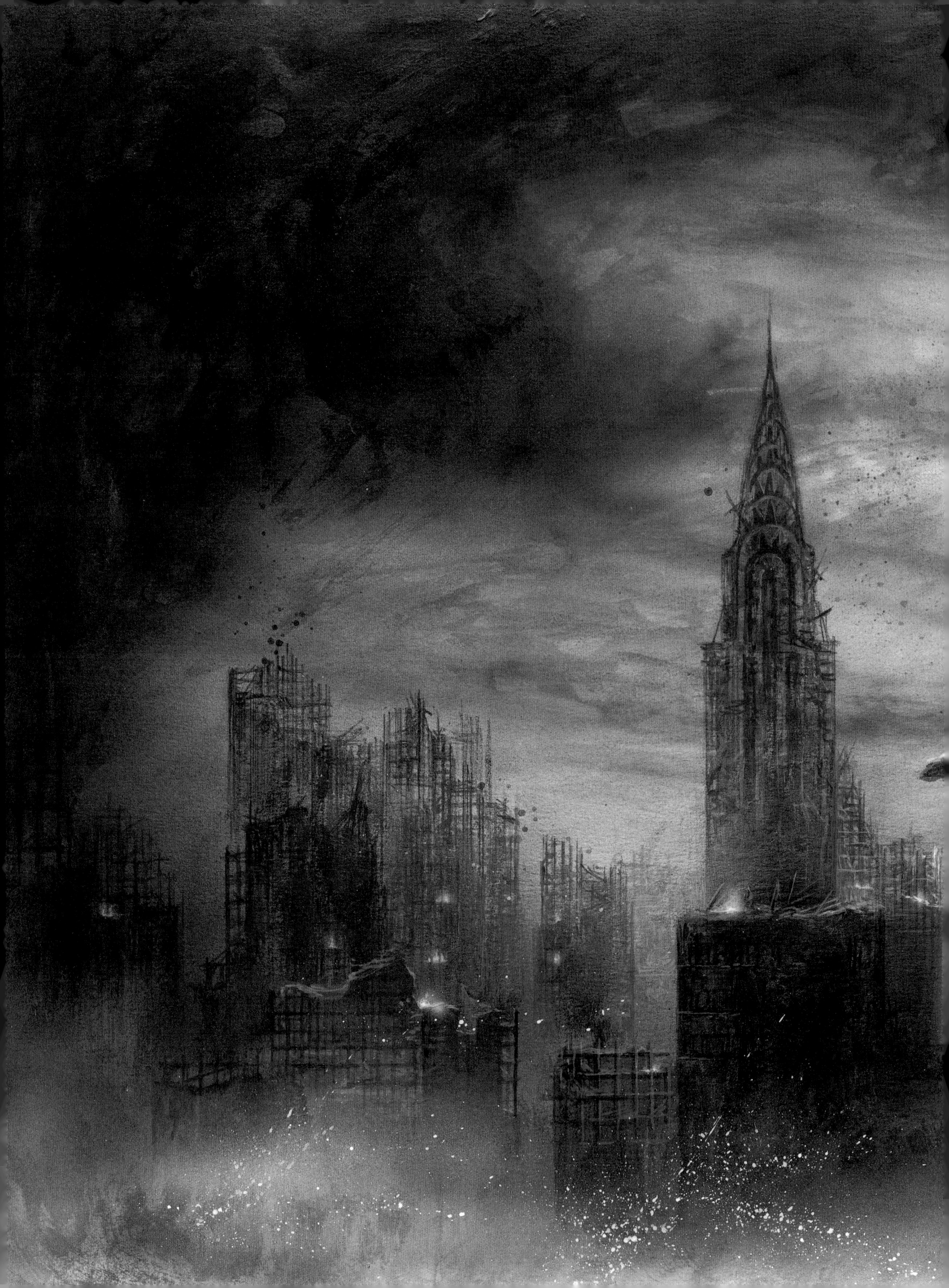

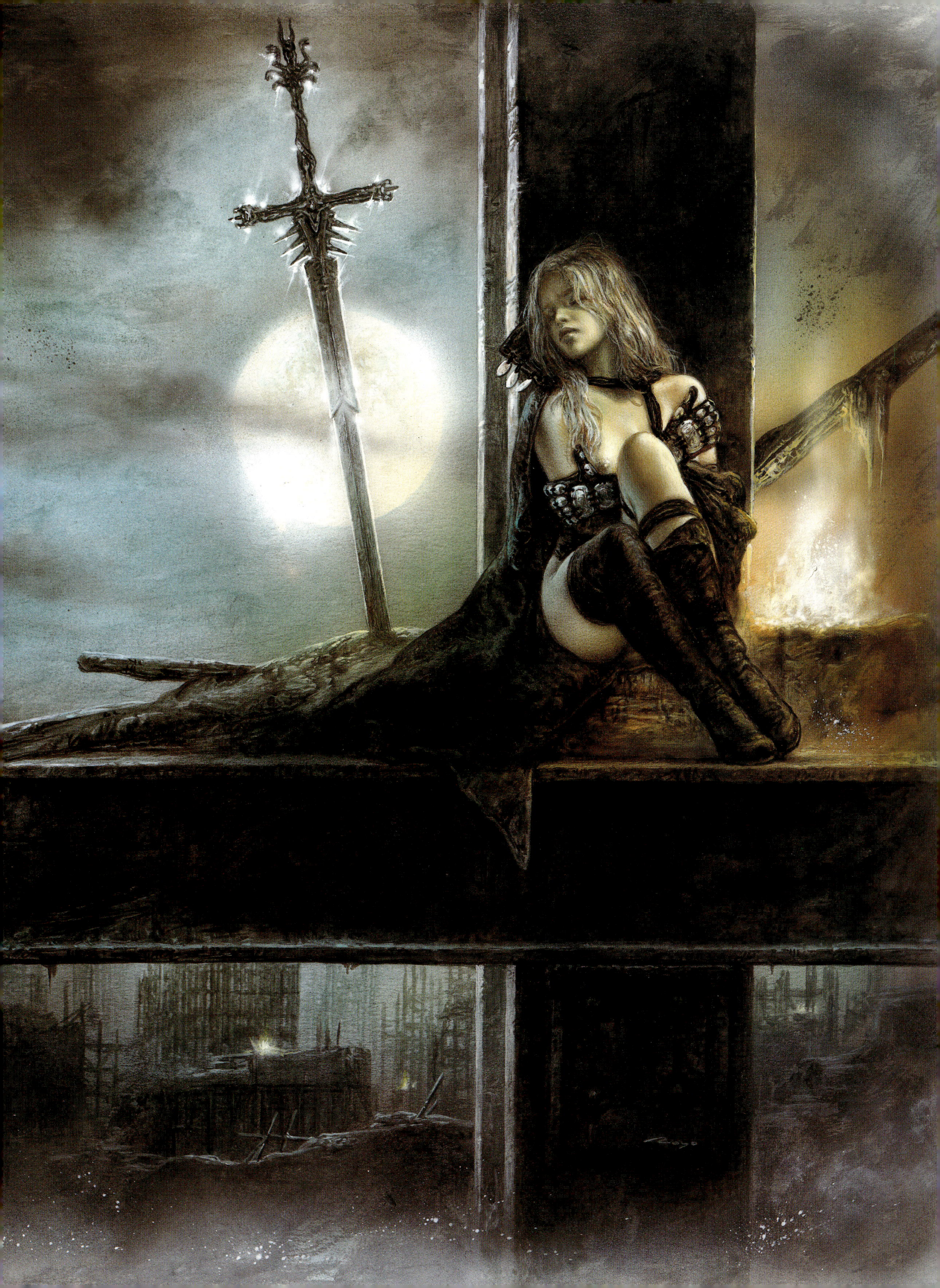

◀ **FULL MOON** (56 x 35 cm.) - 2000

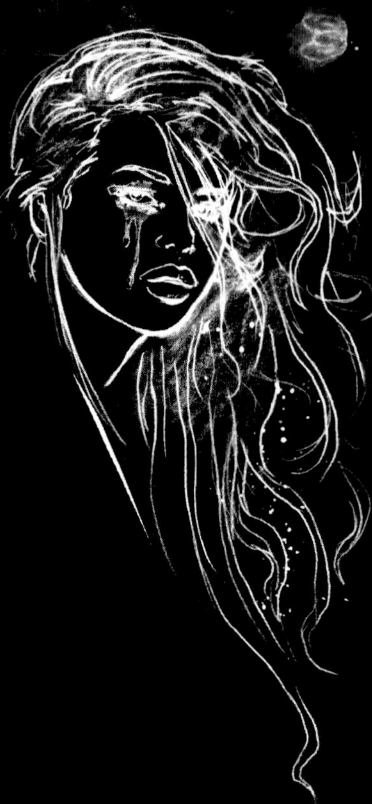

ROUGH NOTES
By Asunción Navarro

MALEFIC: AN ANALYSIS OF THE STORY

Everything takes place in 2030, in the first years of the third millennium. As all the prophecies had predicted (there's a gap of years from 2000 to 2030, owing to the monks' inexact calculations in their crude calendars in the first years of Christianity; the same thing is not true for the prophecies of the Great Pyramid, erroneously attributed to Cheops), from Nostradamus to St. John and Malachi, the hour of the end of the world had arrived. We are speaking, of course, of the end of the technological world, of the end of the second millennium. The Earth continues to exist, as well as the people on it, even though they've been decimated by the millions in the last few years. As John said in Revelations: "By these three was the third part of men killed."

The story proceeds switching through time: the present; the future of 2030, when things are in chaos; and the final years of the first millennium, with its plagues, monasteries, witchcraft, etc.

The people of 2030 don't want to recognize that they're living in the end of time, but the streets are full of strange beings, and New York is nothing like the way it's been: many of the buildings are half-ruined, or exist only as steel skeletons; the streets are practically empty, and electric light has disappeared almost completely. But it's not just New York; the whole world is different. Thunderstorms, earthquakes, and hurricanes are more frequent, and fires have consumed whole cities and forests.

Man of this epoch is changed; his survival instinct has left the morality and Puritanism of the twentieth century behind in the dust. Those obsessions with information and technology have made a 180-degree turn; people don't want to know about anything except their immediate needs. Computers, telephones, and the Internet have almost disappeared. Almost no one is interested in them; all they care about are detectors, of energy, of heat. Detectors that can mean the difference between being alive or being the living dead or an angel. Endless detectors, none of them entirely reliable. It's a society built on fear.

New York is especially full of conflicts; the city where so many people want to disappear. Too often, one sees angels and demons, souls of the dead, or ghosts. Malefic, whose real name is Lucía, has a special ability to find them; she knows, too, that they're looking for her.

There are people who go around with firearms and bullets, but they're of little use against the new inhabitants of the Earth, and Lucía knows that. (I really don't know who's crueler, because even though angels have been portrayed to us as marvelous beings, perhaps they are the most subtle in their cruelty. It's not for nothing that they conquered all the demons in the heavens according to Genesis. Then there are all those zombies, who range all the way from a rotting corpse, practically a skeleton, that you can dispatch with a simple kick, all the way to a seemingly healthy body, hard to tell from the living except by touch-they're ice cold, thank God. Then there are ethereal beings, pure energy- what used to be known as ghosts). What

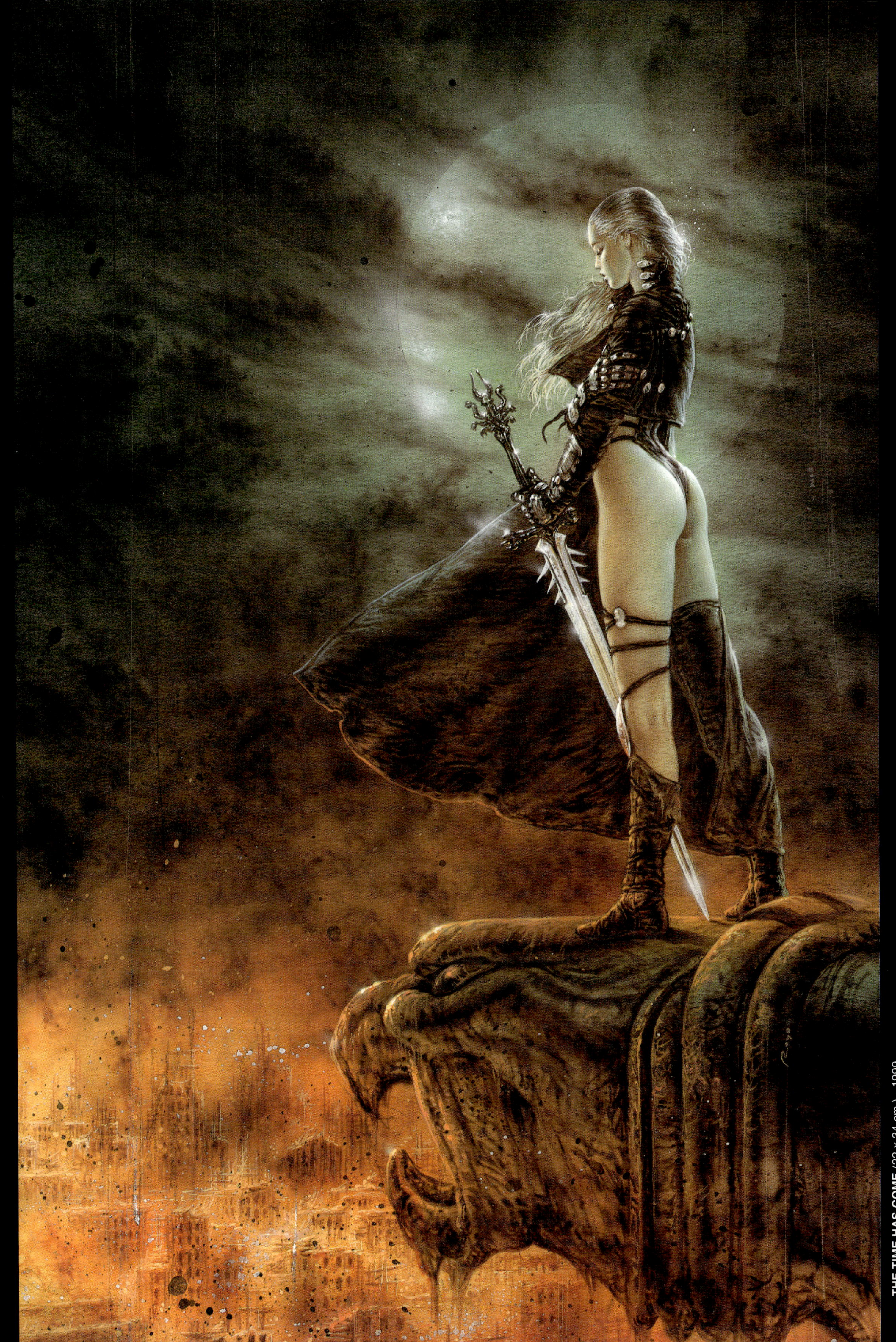

THE TIME HAS COME (22 x 34 cm.) - 1999

really works best against all the newcomers is fire- or cold steel if you can manage to chop up your enemy. Some of them carry swords of fire, and that's why Malefic always keeps her sword handy on her walks around New York in search of libraries. She knows that there, in the old books and reproductions of old paintings, is where all the clues to understanding this new world can be found, as well as to understanding her own identity-because searching for her identity is her life.

At Lucía's house are hundreds of books and papers she's found on her travels through the ruined libraries of the city, including some that are hundreds of years old: books on apocalyptic themes, books of Roman miniatures, books on Freemasonry, witchcraft, alchemy, prophets and seers, Asian wisdom, Aztec and African art, reproductions of paintings from the dawn of time, studies of Greek mythology and Egyptian hieroglyphics. It's all a complex puzzle that somehow relates to the Last Judgment.

Lucía is 19, and she knows she was raped at 13, not with physical violence but with mental torture, by a demon who turned out to be her father. One could say that the behavior of those "up above" was accepted in a certain odd way. (There are many such stories in Greek myth). All this isn't really much on her mind, except that all the strange beings who cross her path always call her "Malefic" instead of Lucía. Besides, in the course of her investigations she's discovered that her mother, too, was raped by a demon. The books indicate that the Antichrist now walks among men, and sometimes, alone in her bath, the idea that she might be the Antichrist torments her. In her studies, she has learned that the idea of God as good and Lucifer as bad is not only just a Christian idea, but a distorted one. And besides, she's always dug stories of losers-and the Fallen Angel's is a good one.
Slowly she is discovering that Lucifer is just another concept, another piece of wisdom to understand the world, more to do with instinct than with faith, and that the Antichrist is perhaps no more than the incarnation of the being who must return to begin the world again on another level. The previous one hasn't been so great, either.
But its agony to her not to know her own identity, and that's what causes her to suffer those fevers and sweats, that emptiness inside that comes when she least expects it and makes her feel like she's about to die.

After his experiences traveling through time described in his first letter, the author seems both infatuated with and intimidated by the life and personality of Malefic, unable to confront that harsh world of 2030, so he plans to travel to the decade of the 90's. He thinks it is a comfortable time, harmonious, with no surprises, but I foresee he'll soon change his opinion and come to see it as a boring, monotonous era, slavish and alienating, empty years in which anxiety travels automatically by computer. In his attempt to warn mankind with his story of what he's been through, he plays the role of John the Baptist in a way, but-and I think this is natural- I don't think anyone in their right mind will pay him much attention, and he will only be laughed at. In the 1990's, he's just a mental patient in Barcelona. I think he can write his stories there in peace, as well as draw, or whatever else anyone asks him to do. Malefic always appears in an outfit that's half medieval, half sadomasochistic (apparently, in 2030 such combinations aren't so unusual, since this combination is already catching on). She also carries a sword with a mythic hilt and a mechanism that elongates the blade and causes points to stick out from the sides. All this appears in the paintings. They try to make us believe that all this concerning Malefic, everything published in comics and books, even though it all seems like fantastic stories and images, is actually about a person who isn't born just yet, but will be soon.

There are hundreds of stories our putative narrator tells us while he cowers in his hospital room. He would have us believe that he sometimes travels to his house in New York in 2030, where he observes Malefic's confrontations and adventures, and even travels back to the end of the first millennium with her to witness other events. He says, too, that he was almost burned at the stake. (The fire would have prevented him from being reborn, and because of this he describes time travel as very dangerous. Most mortals are unconscious of their other lives and get lost on the journey; they don't know their previous identities. Even Malefic is terrified on these voyages). But he says he's become an expert due to the necessity of seeing Malefic. He says he does it with the help of a painter friend, who smothers him at night with a pillow; their hands remain clasped for ten interminable minutes. When he returns, his face looks a little older and his body thinner; sometimes he's wounded. According to him, those minutes could be several years and many experiences in his other time. He returns to our time on the same day he left, but he brings back something from the trip, something that's rapidly aging him.

He brings back tales of Malefic from these trips, her adventures and her search and with them a million questions, beginning with God or the gods: Is God yin and Lucifer yang? Is everything cyclical as it says in the I Ching, and is the Antichrist thus the incarnation of a new era?

This information and more, all of it contradictory, is taken from different notes and letters signed by different persons.

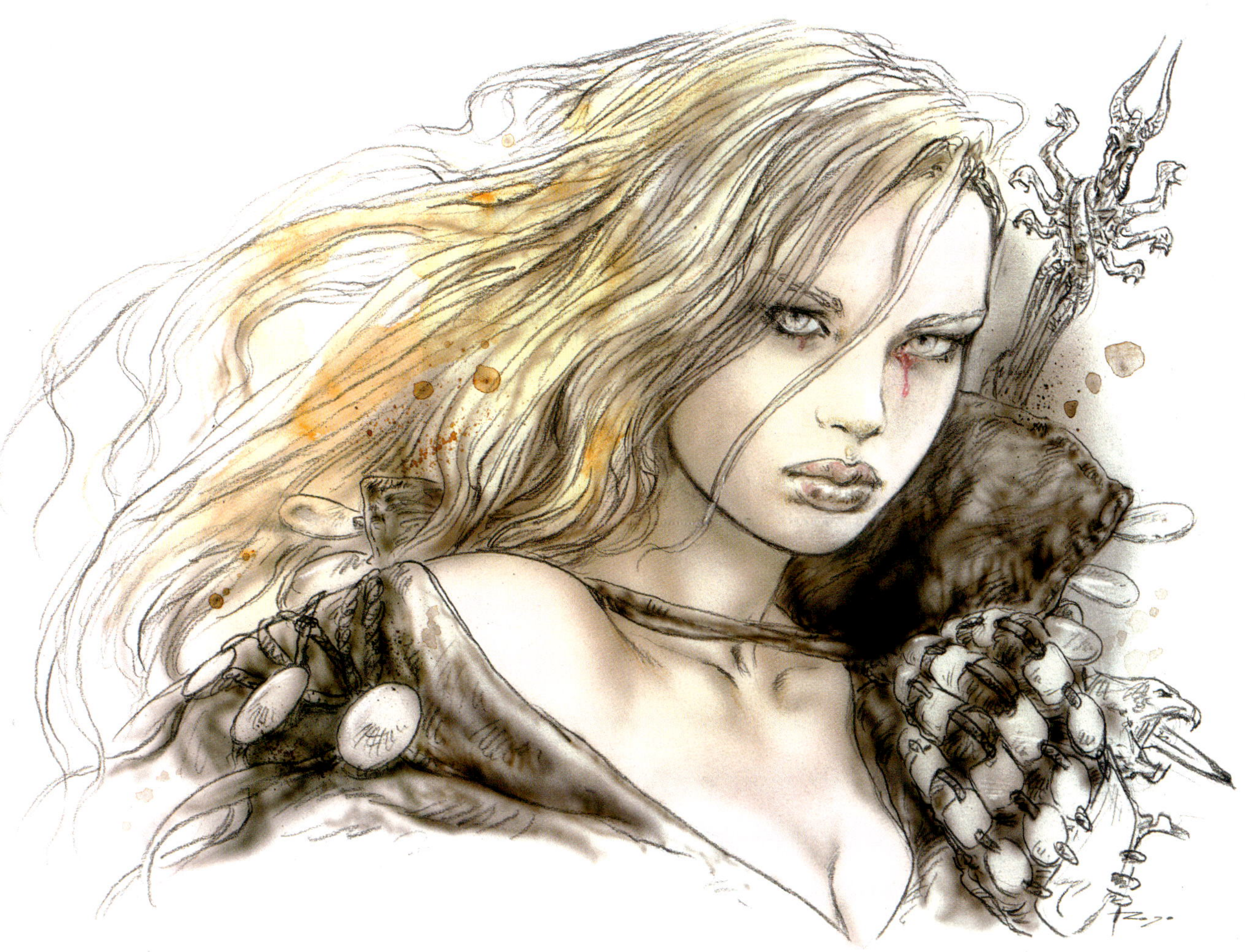

THE NINE HEADS OF THE SERPENT

(second letter received)

For a while now, I had neglected everything: my house was in disorder, the cupboard was nearly bare, my computer spent more time alone than ever, and it was hard even to maintain my personal hygiene.
It wasn't a unique situation, not even a very unusual one. I think the whole city was in the same boat, even though my motives were different.
New York spent some days submerged in a blackish cloud, others torturously baked by the sun; the skyline was like an enormous blackboard with chalk sketches of trees. I've spent more than a year sleeping badly at night and depressed during the day by all these recent developments. Nobody has an answer that makes any sense to me. The TV only broadcasts a couple of hours a week and appears to be controlled by some sort of paramilitary outfit, street guerrillas with the swagger of the Ku Klux Klan. I don't know who is governing us at the moment, or who maintains what little infrastructure there is left.
Nevertheless, in the last week everything has moved to another level.

It all began the day I saw from my window how a girl drew strange signs and symbols on the wall of a big room in the factory across the street. She was beautiful. There she was, scrubbing her naked body beneath those flaking walls covered with cobwebs, when she fell down in a faint. I thought I saw a bloody teardrop fall from her eye. After that, I spent almost the whole day standing at my window, staring at the big panes of plate glass in the factory. Every detail of her young body, of her blonde tresses, was engraved on my retinas. She couldn't be more than 20, but she moved like an empress with the wisdom of thousands of years. When she was home, in that run-down industrial space, she walked around in just a pair of white panties, or once in a while a T-shirt, also white—actually, not so white anymore, they were so raggedy. When she got ready to go out, she put on a corset and shorts with a lot of straps, pulled on a pair of tall boots with chaps and also with a lot of straps, and then wrapped herself in a long cape, all made of dirty, worn-out leather. Then I saw how she lost herself on the streets of New York. Sometimes it was a few days until she returned, always bearing a pile of dirty books and papers which she immediately spread out on the floor. The days that followed one of these outings she spent reading and pacing around the room, always restless, taking frequent baths in the claw-foot tub in the corner of the room.

Some weeks before being petrified by the incredible sight of my lovely neighbor slashing another startlingly beautiful woman to ribbons (something I have described elsewhere in my notes), I witnessed another incredible event. It was mid-afternoon; as usual, I had been at the window most of the day, a day that was darker than usual. There was no light in the factory across the street. One by one there appeared tiny points of light on the floor. Lucía was crawling around on her knees lighting the candles she always had spread all over her floor. As the light gradually brightened the room, I could see that she wasn't alone. With her was a dirty, grotesque-looking old man, covered in rags, lying on the floor. The two were face to face for a long time. He rambled on without stopping, while she listened attentively on her knees in front of him. His harangue seemed to go on forever. Then he was silent for an equally long time. Then the young woman got up, approached him, and began pulling off his rags one by one, as if in some sort of ceremony—a dance of the seven veils. Finally, the old man was naked. He got up and embraced my neighbor. It turned my stomach to see such a perfect body, young and full of life, in the arms of that old fossil with such yellowish, clammy, wrinkled skin. But it got worse—the old bag of bones grabbed her from behind and they began to move together rhythmically. He was sodomizing her. After a while, the old man pulled away; she kissed his chest and returned to her knees. Then the old man began to grow into a tall, strong creature. He rose up off the floor, and a pair of enormous, leathery wings sprouted from his shoulder blades. I could see she was shuddering, but she stayed by his side. A bluish light sparkled around him; he extended his hands in a way that reminded me of Velázquez's painting of Christ. Between his hands appeared a great sword floating in space; it had an elaborate hilt engraved with symbols that I couldn't see well from my window. She stepped toward him—I could see her trembling in terror—took the sword, which was suspended horizontally in midair, and brought it toward her body until she was smoothly stroking herself with it. Till that moment, I'd never seen such an expression on Lucía's face; all the time they had been having sex, her face had been calm, what you might call excruciating bliss. But the moment the blade of the sword stroked her thighs, I could tell without a doubt that she was having an orgasm.
The strange monster that the old man had turned into disappeared, and in his place once again was the twisted old man. Lucía gathered up the filthy clothing that was spread around the room and dressed him tenderly. Then the old man went out and lost himself on the dark streets of that winter night in an unrecognizable New York.
I learned later that the visitor that night was a demon named Mammon, the same demon who took care of Malefic's mother until she died in childbirth, who also took care of my young neighbor in her infancy, and who I would see again on more than one occasion.

After a while, I was spending more time in the factory Malefic lived in than I was in my own house. I even found something to do: I put the books and papers in order, I grouped them by subject matter, I browsed through them, and I piled them in stacks, since there were no shelves. The room began to look like a model of the city; all those stacks of books were like a miniature skyline.
Even though Malefic wasn't very talkative, little by little I managed to become her confidant. I found her weak spots. I made cups of tea when I noticed her getting absorbed in her reading, and with a few discreet questions I managed to open up her heart.
In one of our conversations I learned that her mother had been born in Chernobyl, that she had been educated in a special Russian school for children with paranormal powers. She was small and thin, an albino girl, blonde with gray eyes, almost without eyelashes. Lucía told me that on one occasion, on a walk in Moscow, her mother saw a group of Russian gangsters being arrested. There was a shot, one of them started bleeding, and suddenly the girl's eyes turned red and the whole street was covered in blood. They held her for a while in observation, they made endless tests, she appeared in the press all over the world, and then they forgot all about her. In 2010 she became pregnant, the demon Mammon told her she would bear a girl and took her to New York. They say it was Lucifer himself who took her, and then left his sword in her bed as proof of his visit. Mammon showed Malefic the sword many times during her childhood; he left it with her and taught her to use it. Her mother had died giving birth to her, and he educated her and molded her till she was thirteen. Then he disappeared with the sword. She had to begin taking care of herself. The day after she was abandoned by Mammon, she was raped by another demon. Malefic always wondered whether this, too, had been Lucifer. It had been a kind of dream where there was no violence; a lone, proud being, full of energy, appeared at her side. At first she had been terrified, but then those eyes full of blood had pierced her to the depths of her innards. She remembered nothing more. She awoke with scratches all over her body and a vast feeling of emptiness.

I had diligently studied everything I could find in Malefic's books about that sword, and it all seemed to indicate was that it was the opposite of the Holy Grail, the other side of the coin. In the hilt, you could see the head of the Great Ram; the inverted pentagram; the Hanging Man, also inverted; the Nine Heads of the Serpent (all a symbol of the palace of Pandemonium); and emblems of the Grand Dragon. There are studies that tell us that it is implicit in the nature of infinity that every object must have its own vortex behind which it exists in the form of a sun, a moon, a universe. Thus was the sword the receptacle of the wisdom of the philosophers—or perhaps she herself was the recipient of what the books and parables spoke of, without anyone understanding. (To those who wish to fry, boil, or poach the egg of the ancients, I advise you to do it without cracking the shell, because then the poison will leak out and kill every living thing, since it's the strongest poison in the universe). That sword was the alchemists' symbol of excellence, including its strange mechanism; I was convinced of it. But Malefic never spoke of it.

She consulted the Black Tarot before her trips to New York's libraries, but the security she felt carrying her sword meant

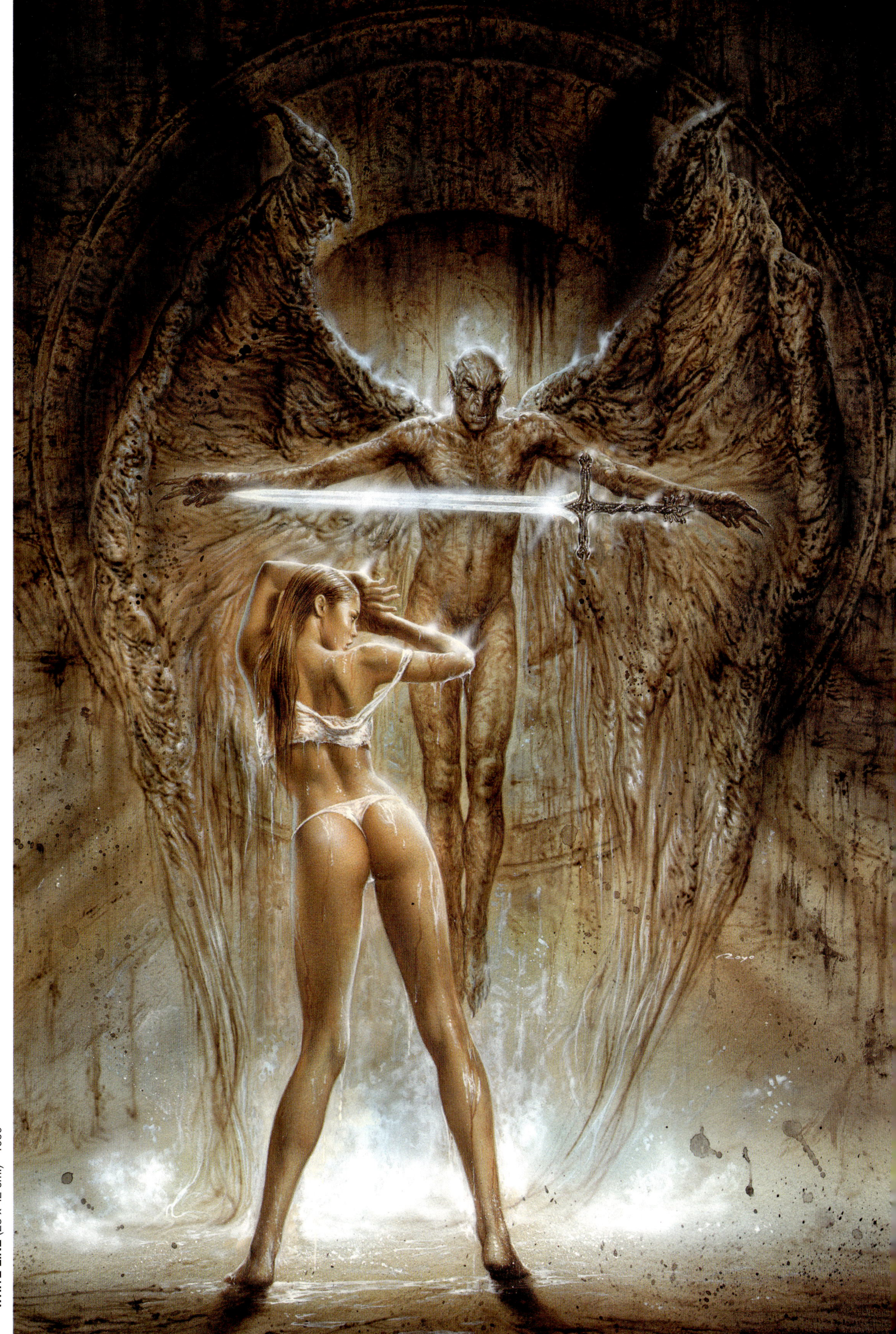

WHITE LINE (28 x 42 cm.) - 1999

that even if the omens weren't favorable, it wouldn't stop her from pursuing her researches.
I remember a trip to Butler Library, north of Central Park, near Harlem. It was the main library of the old Columbia University, across the quadrangle from Low Memorial Library, at the south end of the campus. It still held millions of volumes, one of the most important libraries in the United States, in a building clearly inspired by the Bibliothèque Sainte-Geneviève in Paris.
She could tell from the tarot that this trip wasn't going to be uneventful, but she was obsessed with finding information about the saturnalia. I don't know why, but I went with her. All I saw was a few notes on a paper of hers that said: The gold is hidden in Saturn. Thus also man, since the Fall, hides in an effigy of himself, coarse, amorphous, bestial, like something dead. He is like the rough stone of Saturn, his body a stinking corpse. He lives poisoned. On another paper it said: Look in Isaac Hollandus, Hand of the Philosophers, and in Jacob Boehme. But before we could enter, when we stood before the huge columns of the facade, totally black, as if covered in soot, three young men in long black coats—blond, offensively handsome—appeared before us. They guided us respectfully inside, into the huge central hall with a ceiling lost in the dust that seemed to float everywhere, and then stopped us there. The one in the center, who had long, curly hair down to his waist, approached us and said: "You should give it to us, we'll take it back to where it belongs"—pointing to the sword Malefic was carrying.
She drew it slowly out of the hilt, and when she held it out, it made that dry swishing as the blade extended and the points flicked out at its sides. She put herself en garde in a classic fencing posture, watching warily. The man who'd spoken let his coat fall and stood before her naked, with the beauty of a Greek god, while his companions remained stiffly at attention on either side. Then the central figure burst into flames and rose off the floor. A sword, also flaming, appeared in his hand, and then he suddenly flew toward her. She ducked to the side. Quickly he turned and was at her again. This time Malefic threw herself to the floor and managed to dodge him again. Then she leaped up and pointed the sword at him. A ray of immaculate white crossed the room and shattered the flaming sword in his hands; it disintegrated and the flames disappeared. He fell to the floor. Malefic took stock of the situation—then with one swift blow she sliced off his head. On the floor was a jagged scar that the ray had made. The other two men, each with blond short hair, turned around and left. Malefic murmured with contempt, "They're nothing but dumb messengers."

We spent over four hours searching, filling up a backpack full of books. One of them spoke of the serpent. On the cover was a cross with a serpent nailed to it, and on the first page it said: "The serpent of bronze that Moses nailed on the cross so that all the people could see it and be freed from the plagues they suffered. It is a symbol of the curative force of Mercury's elixir. The powerful king of nature cures the world with his saline ointment, but, in order for it to take effect, the poisonous physical body must be cut in pieces and the volatile spirit pinned with a nail of gold." My glance strayed for a moment to the point of the sword, which was now back in its sheath, I looked at the nine heads of the serpent and the inverted cross on the hilt, and I felt a chill run down my spine. I looked away, and we left. I knew that for the moment I should keep my mouth shut, and not even say one word. But when we got back home I made a pot of good, hot tea.

Luis Royo

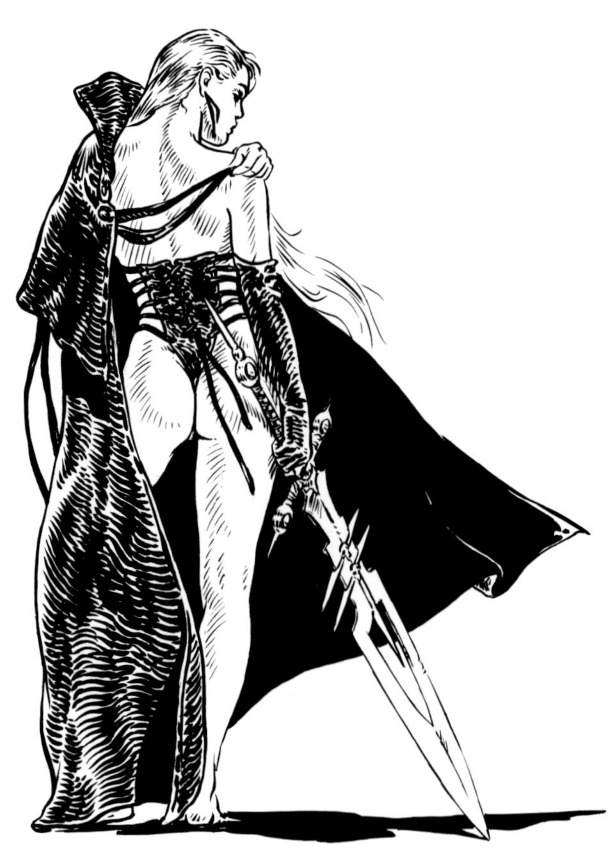

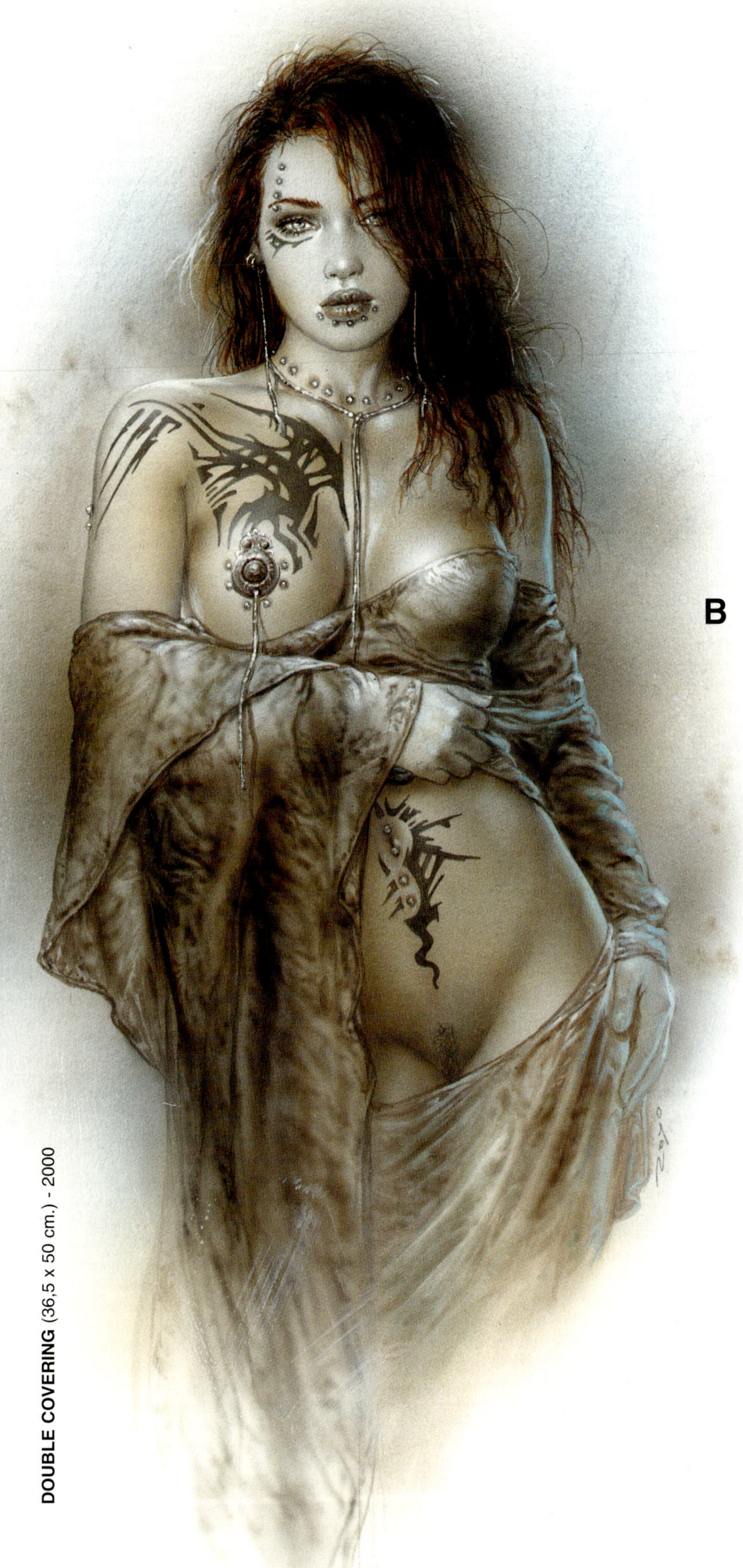

DOUBLE COVERING (36,5 x 50 cm.) - 2000

BIBLIOGRAPHY

-Books of Illustration
WOMEN
MALEFIC
SECRETS
III MILLENNIUM
DREAMS
PROHIBITED BOOK I
EVOLUTION
PROHIBITED BOOK 2
CONCEPTIONS

-Collections of Trading Cards
FROM FANTASY TO REALITY
FORBIDDEN UNIVERSE
THE BEST OF ROYO
SECRETS
MILLENNIUM

-Portfolios
WARM WINDS
III MILLENNIUM
TATTOOS

-Others
STRIPTEASE (postcards)
POSTERS

EVOLUTION